Praise for

VERTIGO

"Lauren Baratz-Logsted has tapped the Victorian fascination
with the social monster, and in *Vertigo* she concocts an ingenious
chamber opera of a novel. But whether the monster is to be
found behind bars or deep within the protagonist herself is
ultimately a question for the reader to decide."
—Dave King, author of *The Ha-Ha*

VERTIGO

Lauren Baratz-Logsted

Delta Trade Paperbacks

VERTIGO
A Delta Trade Paperback / October 2006

Published by Bantam Dell
A Division of Random House, Inc.
New York, New York

Book design by Glen Edelstein

Delta is a registered trademark of Random House, Inc.,
and the colophon is a trademark of Random House, Inc.

Library of Congress Cataloging in Publication Data
Baratz-Logsted, Lauren.
Vertigo / Lauren Baratz-Logsted.
    p.   cm.
ISBN-13: 978-0-385-34031-1
ISBN-10: 0-385-34031-1
1. Married women—Fiction. 2. London (England)—Fiction. I. Title.
PS3602.A754V47 2006
813'.6—dc22
2006040290

Printed in the United States of America
Published simultaneously in Canada

www.bantamdell.com

BVG   10   9   8   7   6   5   4   3   2   1

*For Pamela Harty, without whom I would not be seeing
this day—with love and friendship*

Can the plans of things that live and die ever
overstep the orchestrated universe of Zeus?

— AESCHYLUS, *PROMETHEUS BOUND*

Know thyself.

— PLUTARCH, *MORALS*

PROLOGUE

For nearly seventeen years, I was a good, some might say exemplary, wife.

As I put pen to paper for the first time to record my tale, it is important you know this about me from the start.

ONE

10 January 1899

Dear Mr. Wood,

I write to you having received your name and address from my husband, John Smith, who has been doing some research at the prison where you currently reside for a novel he is completing. I have never corresponded with a prisoner before. I do not know if, or why, you might have committed the criminal act for which you are serving time. My husband says he believes many of the criminals at Hollowgate to be innocent victims of injustice. I, having never been in any prison, have no way of knowing the truth behind his assertions. I do know, were I in prison and deprived of the companionship of family and friends, I should find it a consolation to have another person with whom to share the occasional thought. I hope I can be that person for you.

Wishing you well,
Mrs. John Smith

One week later, I had my first reply. Though the writing was crude, the paper it was written on still worse, the words themselves were put together in an educated enough fashion:

Dear Mrs. John Smith,

    I do not know why you have taken it upon yourself to do this, but I do so wish you would stop.

Chance Wood

TWO

31 December 1898

Mr. and Mrs. John Smith," announced the Collinses' butler as we made our way into their crowded salon at the top of the cascade of stairs, the house yet festooned with the remnants of Christmas, the scents of pine, myrtle, oranges, cinnamon, and cloves in the air, the applewood burning in the fireplace as if the season might never end.

We were twenty-four at dinner.

Beneath one of three chandeliers adorned with glass globes and crystal prisms, I sat near the head of the table, the legs of which were carved to look like a bear's claws, on one of the leather-upholstered chairs in the long scarlet dining room. To the right of me was Joshua Collins, the head of the household. Captain Brimley, portly as ever, was on my other side.

Captain Brimley was thought to be an overly feminine man, but he was a delightful conversationalist, frequently called into service as escort to Lady Collins, Joshua's widowed mother. Lady Collins herself, still a sparkling woman at nearly seventy, had adorned her perpetual mourner's black clothes with jet bead for the occasion and was seated to one side of John at the other end of the table, opposite to me; on John's other side was Joshua's wife, Maeve, a lilac gown softening a natural severity of feature brought about by bearing far too many children.

"Tell me," said the captain, mustache bristling mischievously, "what is your good husband working on now?"

Taking advantage of a lull in the talk as diners bent heads to the soup à la reine, I half shouted down the table, repeating the captain's question.

John set his sterling soup spoon down carefully, planted elbows firmly on the table, rubbed one palm against the other. "Well, Captain," he spoke studiedly into the relative silence that had fallen over the table hard upon my half shout, "I can tell you that if you want to know about my next novel," he paused dramatically, the candelabra before him reflecting as a pleased glint in his eye, "all questions you have will surely be revealed when you purchase a copy upon its publication sometime next year."

The table roared at the captain's expense. All assembled were familiar with John's reluctance to discuss works in progress. The men all rested on family fortunes large enough they needn't work, so in essence John was the only one with a career to speak of. Well, except for Captain Brimley.

"You're a heartless man, John," spoke the captain, mockingly clutching at his chest as though wounded.

"I can tell you this," said John. "It has to do with a prison."

"Which prison?" pressed the captain.

But John had already taken up spoon again, turning his attention away.

Not long afterward, I found myself sitting before the fire at Lady Collins's feet, garnet skirts spread about me, knees tucked under chin. The floor beneath me was solid wood, in keeping with the current practice of using as little carpeting as possible for sanitary reasons; Joshua Collins was nothing if not modern. Listening to the fading murmur of men's voices in the dining room on the other side of the draped portiere, where the men lingered over port and cigars, I recalled being at home earlier in the evening, preparing to go out.

"You look beautiful this evening, Emma," John had said.

John's words came as he stood behind me, while I was seated before the vanity. I suppose I might have taken his words as being the rote delivery of a well-versed husband, were it not that he had spoken similar words, along with declarations of love, every day of our married life.

"I am indeed a lucky man."

I turned my brown eyes upward to meet his blue ones in the mirror. Even were I standing, he would still tower over me, his fair hair and fine features—aquiline nose, affectionate lips, sturdy enough jaw—a full head and a half taller than I.

Behind us in the mirror, I could see the woven coverlet, dust ruffles, and pillow shams of our large four-poster bed, made of solid rosewood, intricately carved, the aubergine sheets rumpled from a fortifying nap.

"Why do you say that?" I asked, twinkling.

After sixteen years of marriage, I knew a number of the reasons he might respond with, but it was still a source of amusement. Would he tell me I was more intelligent than other women? Admire my ankles? Praise the job I was doing raising our six-year-old son, Weston?

He held my gaze as he bent down so his reflection was even with my own, his fair features side by side with the dark ringlets I was fashioning into an elaborate design upon my head even as we spoke. I was aware the darkness of my hair created a strong picture combined with the garnet-colored gown I had selected for the occasion. I knew it was not John's favorite color on me, but it was a color I loved nonetheless. The ringlets framed pale skin, my cheekbones still high and firm despite my thirty-four years. In fact, the only part of me that showed my age was a less than girlish fullness to my figure, a fullness John claimed to adore.

"Because you are not in the slightest like the other ladies," he replied.

Then he delicately traced the outline of my mouth with one long finger, and kissed me. It was the kind of kiss any woman who has been married for sixteen years can identify; it said, "I love you, I even still want you, but we are already going to be late for the party, and I have no intention of getting dressed a second time."

Now, seated at Lady Collins's feet, I heard in my mind's ear the words of John playing the "You know what I love about you, Emma?" game. In this instance, I was sure he would say of my solitary and unladylike position on the floor, as all around me the ladies sat properly, opened fans, and preened, "It is that you refuse to put on airs."

"You know what I dislike most about my husband?" asked Sara Jamison, adjusting her seasonally jade skirts on the sofa. The abundance of jade needed to cover her overfull figure did nothing for the perpetual florid condition of her moon face, framed as it was by yellow hair.

Sara was frequently the one to set flame to what I thought of as these exercises in futility and, as was also customary, she did not wait for an answer to her rhetorical question before supplying one herself.

"It is that he is possessed of the belief that only I am capable of straightening his handkerchief. Certainly not his valet. Never himself."

It took so little, really.

"Well, *I* always say," said Hettie Larwood, who always said much and, with a wasp-thin waist and thinning auburn hair, looked like she should eat more, "George would not even know which fork to use if I did not repeatedly remind him."

Constance Biltmore said Charles was a poor sport at cards.

If they were going to dislike something most in their husbands, could they not at least find something more substantial to pick at?

And, yet, everyone played, save Maeve, whose husband had just provided an ample meal for all; and Lady Collins, a widow, although I had long suspected when Lord Collins was alive she never skewered him.

"What about you, Emma?" Hettie asked with some degree of asperity. "You never say."

But I just shook my head and smiled shyly, hoping all the while they would read my reluctance to speak out against my husband not as a defiant act of cool superiority but as testimony that John perhaps had so many fatal flaws, I didn't know where to begin!

Why was I even interested in perpetuating such a deception, particularly when to speak out was more in keeping with my nature?

Because, despite my personal inclination, these women—more properly, the men these women were married to—mattered to John's world, mattered a great deal. If, occasionally, I had to be a slightly fictitious woman to help my husband out, what matter that?

I looked at the others, on tête-à-têtes and sofas, their dressed heads close in gossip. In their own way they resembled the putti: the cherubs and cupids cavorting on the curved backs and arms of Joshua's furniture.

The only one I felt a real fondness for was Constance. Timid, even among those who had known her long and presumably well, I recognized the cost to her of publicly criticizing her husband. Of the wives' complaints, hers had been the only one of substance. As I watched her trying to keep up with the gossip of the others, and failing miserably, her guileless blue eyes wide under blond feather brows a shade darker than her white-gold hair, it occurred to me that of all the women, whom I had known for years, I should like to know her better.

"You're not like any of the others, are you?" Lady Collins's words to me were more a conspiratorial observation than a query.

I had always liked Lady Collins.

John was the first of the men to enter. Immediately, before I could move my skirts to make a place for him, he lowered his lanky form to the floor, leaning back on one elbow as he stretched out beside me.

"Know what I love about you, Emma?" He whispered the words, not waiting for my answer. "It is that you refuse to put on airs."

I smiled back at him, the warm glow of the gas fireplace almost like another presence, uniting us in a way that made me feel as though we were momentarily alone. But I said nothing, a brief coldness stealing into me as I reflected how, just occasionally, I felt as though *he* were an air I had put on—something that suited me best when I wore it out into the world.

Joshua Collins entered, consulting his pocket watch, as though he did not know exactly what time it was right down to the minute.

"The New Year hour draws near," he announced. He struck a pose, elbow casually resting near the marble mantel clock on the fireplace, as the butler distributed champagne glasses. "There is much that has passed into the history books in the last year. Gladstone has died, Bismarck—"

"Not to mention Lewis Carroll, Stéphane Mallarmé, and Theodor Fontane," interjected John.

"Yes, John," Joshua acknowledged indulgently, "you writers have had a very busy year…in terms of dying. Still, in less than an hour, we will be entering the last year of the century. Shall we play the resolution game?"

No one objected. Joshua was known for his propensity for seeking out the appropriate game for any occasion, and what better one that night?

"I will go first," Joshua said. "Let's see…" He paused long enough to make it appear he had just formulated his resolution on the spot. He raised his glass. "I resolve to host an even better New Year's party next year."

"Hear, hear!" The assembled all toasted his resolve in return.

"Darling?" He turned to Maeve on his right.

"And I resolve to do everything in my power to help," she said.

More "hear, hears" all around.

Next week, I was certain, when we dined at the Larwoods', Maeve would be back to telling us her usual complaint of how infuriating it was when Joshua trimmed his nose hairs within her sight. If she were really daring, she might say she sincerely hoped he never visited any more children upon her—she already had more than her friends could reliably count—but I doubted such honesty would ever be forthcoming.

Paul Jamison resolved to learn how to position his own handkerchief.

George Larwood added his desire to master the individual uses of silverware; not that any of us believed Hettie would ever let him eat much.

Charles Biltmore could not, in all honesty, resolve to be a better sport in the New Year, and so, he resolved to forsake cards altogether. Not that any of us could picture Charles, such a natural at a baize gaming table or at York racing week, his brown hair never cut quite enough, his collar never exactly straight, ever walking away from his passion.

Still, I almost laughed. Had they somehow heard us even

through the din of their own loud chatter as they lingered over their port? Or did they know the hearts and minds of those they were married to, in spite of what their wives might think? But to a man, their faces gave away nothing.

Lady Collins declined to make any resolution, concluding, "I am quite sure my words would only come back to haunt me in the following year."

People "hear, heared" her right to dissent, although some looked put out at her refusal to play.

When it came to his turn, John did not hesitate. "I would like to finish the novel I am working on to my satisfaction and I would like to make my wife the happiest woman in the world."

"Unfair," chuckled Joshua Collins. "The rest of us had to content ourselves with one resolution. You cannot now claim for yourself two. You must choose."

"Very well, then." Again John did not hesitate, looking straight into my eyes. "I choose Emma. I will always choose Emma."

At last, it was my turn. Watching the others, it had seemed easy. Now it came to it, however, it felt somehow as though there really would be some profound import attached to my selection, as opposed to the relative unimportance in the greater scheme of things behind Sara Jamison's firmly stated resolve to consume fewer fairy cakes in the coming year.

The room awaited my resolution, some with more patience than others.

I thought of my life so far.

It is perhaps strange to say, but up until this point, I had only thought of my life in a very unthinking sort of way. I knew I was adept at the many roles I was called upon to play. I was a good enough daughter; at least my father thought so. I was good at parties, even if I could not be depended upon to be drawn into every game the other women seemed intent on playing. I would even go so far as to say I *liked* our social world; for, after all, is there not great human satisfaction to be found in doing a thing well? In being able to retain one's own sense of individuality when in a group and yet somehow manage not to give any serious offense?

Still, outside of being the best mother I could be to Weston, what had I really achieved, save the attachment of myself to John's star?

I had always been preoccupied with being good. It was my strength. It was my weakness. Now I wanted something more.

"I would like very much to be a better person." I spoke the words more fiercely than I had intended.

It was almost the New Year.

John met my gaze steadily, with an approvingly prideful one of his own. "Then you shall be," he said, as if it were as simple as that.

THREE

John always said writing was a way to cheat the rules of the living. "Without it," he would say, "I would only get to live one life. Not that it is a bad life, mind you; God knows, I am eternally grateful to have you and Weston. But one can only ever travel on one road at a time. When I am writing, at minimum, I get to live in at least two worlds at once."

―――――――

As I sat at the small table in the nursery, finishing up a second breakfast with my son, I thought about John's words the night before, how matter-of-factly he assumed I could make this leap from my present being to a better one. When I had come up here an hour ago, to this cheery room with its tall windows, charming pale-blue-and-white wallpaper illustrated with pictures from nursery tales and rhymes, the amusements of childhood littering the floor, I had left him to work in his library on his novel. An hour ago, we had both yet been too tired, what with the late night and the excess of wine, to broach any subjects of greater magnitude than whether the eggs were firm enough or no. Now I wondered if he might not be ready for an early break.

"Hannah?" I called.

A form emerged from a seat at the corner by the window. My age, but dressed in gray up to her neck, she was all angles and bony ridges, making even the bun beneath her bonnet look more geometrical than rounded. For six years now, I had been trying to convince her no one in the household would mind it should she ever choose to wear a more vibrant color. But she demurred all such suggestions and Weston set such great store by her—for she could be a great companion to him when they were alone together, belying the indications set by the sharp angles and the omnipresent gray—I hesitated to press her, not wanting to give offense.

I dabbed at the corner of my mouth with a napkin. I could never eat breakfast with my son without being the one who wound up with an unseemly quantity of jam on her face.

"Hannah," I said, "I know I was going to take Weston to the park myself this morning, but something has come up."

"Of course, madam. I will take him, although I know he will miss you."

Hannah was always careful to make a point of the fact I was the absolute sun in Weston's universe, rendering my husband the moon and anyone else, such as herself, a lesser star. Still, she need not have worried. I was secure as to my position and yet I also knew, while Weston loved having me there, Hannah, bun and all, was capable of coming up with games to entertain his fancy that were as imaginative as any I could.

"I don't think he'll mind quite so much for one day," I said. "And, anyway, if it is as bright and beautiful outside again tomorrow, we shall get another chance. Is not this glorious weather for January?"

———————

I had always liked my husband's library: the floor-to-ceiling books with their wooden ladder, the forest-green walls, the sturdy dark furniture, the fire that always roared, and the fact that the door was never entirely closed to me.

What I did not like so much was the aquarium he kept: the underwater garden with fish, supported by a metal frame and sitting on a magnificent stand. I did not like seeing things in cages. To me, it always seemed as though the fish would be happier in a larger body of water outside.

"John." Ignoring the armless chair on the company side of his desk, I hopped up on the desk itself, right next to where he was writing, my skirts skewing his papers a bit, thus making it impossible for him to ignore me.

It was indeed a matter of my good fortune that John was one of those rare writers who could tolerate an unexpected interruption without being driven totally mad. And not just a rare writer, but a rare husband, for it was hard to imagine Joshua Collins or Charles Biltmore tolerating a wife who hopped up on desks. It often occurred to me to think on how much more fortunate we were in our match than others in our acquaintance. I could not imagine life with a husband who had no interest in my mind or whose own mind offered me little of interest.

"Have you come up with anything for me yet?" I asked.

He removed the gold-rimmed glasses he always wore when writing, rubbed his eyes. "It might be nice, if just once you asked before disturbing my work. Still, I suppose it is too much to expect you to change now."

His smile told me he would not necessarily welcome such a change, even if I could somehow manage it.

"Now, then: What is it I am supposed to be coming up with for you? And it had better be good. After all, I just left Molly Henshaw"— he referred to his heroine—"destitute, upon the death of her father, who entailed his estate through the male line upon a distant cousin. I do believe Molly will have to become a governess." He chewed on the earpiece of his glasses before adding, "Possibly in Yorkshire somewhere."

Wasting no time, I reminded him of my resolution the night before.

"Ah, yes," he considered, "your resolution. You never said last night, Emma: *Why* do you want to be a better person?"

"Because," I burst out, feeling the frustration anew, "what have I done for the world? I take care of Weston, I take care of you—"

"And we are no longer enough?" he cut in, stingingly.

"It is not that." It was so hard to articulate what I was feeling. "It is that I feel I should be doing *more*."

"Very nicely put. You say we are *enough* but you want *more* anyway."

I could see he was hurt somehow, angry.

"It is so hard to explain," I said, desperate he should understand me despite my lack of words. "I just want to be worth more and the only word I can think of to describe that nebulous 'more' is 'better.'" I looked at him imploringly. "I do not mean to hurt you in any way," I hastened to add.

After a long moment, his look softened and he brushed my concerns away. "Well, dear, if you ask me, I don't believe you need improving upon in any sense. To my eyes, you are perfect just the way you are."

He must have seen the look that crossed my face, for he hurried on: "But I do not suppose you are asking me for my opinion of *that*. I see that now. Very well, then: If you feel called upon to *improve* yourself in some way, why do you not consider some form of good works?"

I was taken aback at, well, the lack of originality behind his scheme.

"What do you mean," I asked, "knitting socks for the poor?"

"No," he agreed, "I do not suppose that was the sort of thing I had in mind for you. Although you need not make it sound as though to do such a thing were as superfluous as, say, darning the queen's stockings."

"I'm sorry. It's just that I already do that sort of thing through the church."

"I see your point. Perhaps, somehow, doing good works and being a better person are not strictly synonymous. Hmm..." He paused for a long time. "Well," he finally said, taking up my right hand gently and placing his pen in my palm, "you could try doing what I do."

Despite the lightness of the instrument, it felt somehow heavy there, peculiarly both liberating and dangerous at the same time.

"You think it would benefit the world if I became a novelist?" I asked.

"Hardly. There are already too many of us to go around. No, I was thinking more along the lines of doing something to actually improve another human's existence. What could be more noble than endeavoring to bring a glimmer of brightness into an otherwise dull life?"

That was when he told me about the prisoners he had encountered during his research visits to Hollowgate Prison. Having tackled the war in the Crimea, he had determined to take on the ever unpopular topic of prison reform, much as Mr. Dickens had done before him. Further, he was hoping to make his polemic somehow more palatable by shackling it to the tale of the financial misfortunes of Molly Henshaw.

"In so many ways," he finished up, indicating with a flick of his hand a sheaf of what I assumed to be research notes on his desk, "they are an extraordinary group of men!"

For a writer, my husband had a most scientific mind, always analyzing the world about him. Indeed, he had a great interest in the insect kingdom going back as far as my earliest memories of him in our youth, had an affection for the works of Darwin most in our acquaintance would be reluctant to own, and seemed to wage a continual war between the Reason and Romanticism within him.

"It is fine to sit at home and safely assume not only is Justice always blind, but she is fair as well," he said. "If only such were the case. Rather, it would appear whether one can afford to pay off the right people and whether one can afford to obtain counsel that is even remotely competent dictates the order of the day. If we could just make a case for—"

"Where do I belong in all this?" I asked, stemming the flow.

It was not that I did not care about what he was saying. But rather I knew my husband well enough to know, should I let him really get going on a topic for which he felt so much passion, by the time he finished I would forget all about what I had come to him for in the first place.

"Well," he said, resuming a more amiable tone of voice, "could you not see yourself corresponding with one of these wretches? Not all of them are the basest creatures of the earth and some are even not stupid. I think, were I in jail for a crime I did not commit, or without family and friends to care any longer whether I lived or died or what my daily existence was, well, I think I might appreciate corresponding with some reasonably intelligent person from the outside world."

"Are you suggesting I write to a male prisoner?" I was shocked. "Would it not be more natural for me to write to another woman?"

To which he just shrugged.

"It is to the male part of the prison I go to do my research," he said. "It is there I am friendly with the governor."

I felt a further almost unnameable outrage at his suggestion.

"You want *me,* your *wife,* to correspond with dangerous men?"

But he refused to rise to meet my outrage.

"Did I not just *say,* Emma," he said, with a coolly patient impatience, "that some of these men have been hard done by? Besides, they are in prison; you are out here. Where is the danger to you in that? There is none. It is not, after all, as though I were suggesting you go bodily to a slum area and seek out someone to help there. This is different from that. Can you not *see* yourself, in your efforts to be this 'better person' you claim a desire to be, trying to give some sort of solace to some unfortunate person who will never again enjoy the freedoms you so daily take for granted?"

I at last conceded I could indeed see myself assuming such a task.

"Very well." He took up his glasses again and oh so gently brushed his hand against my skirts where they covered my buttocks; a hint it was time I left him to Molly Henshaw. "At the first available opportunity, I shall ask the governor if there is a suitable prisoner, one who preferably is literate enough to know what to do with pen and paper."

———

My mission successful, I moved back through the corridor quickly. The unusual corridor—all glass on one side, solid wall on the other, with black-and-white tiles underfoot—separated the family section of the house from the more public rooms and John's library. I usually moved through it quickly, trying to avoid an uneasy dual feeling of protection and exposure.

But sometimes, a few times, I courted it.

When I knew John was gone from the household, when Weston was elsewhere, I would sometimes sit on the tiles, knees tucked up under my chin, skirts spread, the black-and-white diamonds swirling outward around me, the hot glass at my front, the cool wall—so dark a blue as to almost be black—at my back, a lightness seen, a darkness glimpsed.

I had an awareness, in those moments, of being a person me but not me, or perhaps a person more myself than I was anywhere else. In those moments, I had an awareness of myself as being a far more interesting woman when alone than when in the noise of company.

But those moments alone were rare. Or felt so. It seemed nearly every moment of my days was taken up by the demands of John and Weston, the day-to-day concerns of running a household.

And perhaps, I thought as I hurried through, once this correspondence John had suggested began, perhaps I would be able to leave those moments alone in the corridor behind me forever. Perhaps, in the act of bringing peace to someone else, I would bring peace to myself as well.

FOUR

Two days later, as I sat on the tapestried love seat in the back parlor, legs tucked under me in a most unladylike fashion to keep them warm in the chill of the room, John gave me a card on which was written "Chance Wood, Prisoner, c/o Hollowgate Prison." My first impulse was to laugh.

"He sounds just like a character in one of your novels!"

"Surely not *my* novels, dear," John said, squeezing in beside me, stretching his legs out, "although I am unfortunately familiar with those of which you speak. Still, I do try to at least tell myself so long as people are reading *something*..."

I held the edge of the card to my lips, tapping it twice before speaking. "So, what is this prisoner like?"

"I have no idea, do I?"

His words startled me. "What do you mean?"

"What I mean, Emma, is that I have not met the man myself."

I was taken aback at the level of his nonchalance at setting up a correspondence between a noted criminal and myself. True, he had said there was no danger to me in this, but was he not in the least concerned?

"Well, then, do you know anything about his crime?" I pressed. "The reason he awaits Her Majesty's pleasure?"

John yawned as Timmins brought in the post.

Timmins, a gift to us from John's parents upon our wedding, had been with John's family since John was a boy. Nearly sixty, Timmins resembled a graying arachnid—being all angular sticklike limbs that somehow gave the impression of numbering more than the usual four—with icy blue eyes and a mouth that only ever genuinely smiled for John. I did not like Timmins, nor was I ever given reason to suspect, outside of John's hearing, he had ever liked me. I secretly longed for his days as a butler to come to some sort of graceful end, but no such end was in sight.

"Hardly worth the effort of going through it." John tossed the post aside. "I know it is said he murdered his wife."

"Pardon me?" I had been so busily nursing my daily preoccupation of wishing Timmins gone, I had momentarily lost the thread.

"Your prisoner," said John. "It is said he murdered his wife."

"Well, now, that's charming! I wish to do some good, and you set me up writing placating messages to a violent criminal?"

"We do not know for a fact he is violent."

There was that scientific mind again, that sometimes infuriating mind demanding precision in every utterance.

"What do you call it, then," I said, "when someone is imprisoned for murdering a wife?"

"I don't know. What do you call it—railroading? Mistaken identity? A need to restore calm to an agitated community by not letting the notion fester that a truly violent criminal might yet be at large in their midst?"

"Are you saying this prisoner was somehow framed?"

"Hardly. I do not know anything about his particular case whatsoever."

He was so cold at moments, so analytical. There were times when, despite how long I'd known him, his behavior was yet peculiar to me.

"Then why are you pleading it for him?" I wanted to know.

"Because that is the point, the point with so many of these men I *have* visited at Hollowgate. Do you have any idea how often justice is miscarried in England? And we are a civilized country! I shudder to think what is done in the name of justice in Australia or, God forbid, America."

He must have realized how weary his lack of coming to the point was making me, for he sighed. "Very well, Emma. As I told you I would, I went to Governor Croft to learn which of his prisoners he thought might best benefit from a correspondence with you. It is, of course, a highly irregular situation and he was reluctant at first. After much persuasion, however, and appeals to his vanity, he consented to provide me with a list of possible names. My reaction was not so very different from yours to that name, Chance Wood; it impressed me as a thing made up, which made it stand out. I would like to be able to claim my selection process was more scientific, but such would be a lie. As for me exclaiming to you he might be innocent, I can only say in my defense, having encountered so many prisoners within the horrible confines of Hollowgate who *might* be, well, I see no reason not to consider he might be as well."

I was satisfied: My husband would never allow me to become involved in something that might harm me.

After John left, it occurred to me to go out, to search out archives of newspapers in the hope of learning what exactly this Chance Wood had done to his wife. And why. I was curious, more curious than I would have imagined myself being about the actions of one I did not know, one who was no more than a name on the card before me.

But then I thought better of it. Had not John said many of these criminals had already been prejudged by a world all too predisposed to believe in the guilt and evilness of men? Let Mr. Wood be a blank slate to me then. Let me judge him for himself.

If there were things I needed to know, I would learn them in time.

———————

Still later that very afternoon, the world grown darker and colder on the other side of the French windows and doors of my ground-floor bedroom, I set about writing to Chance Wood for the first time.

I had never had any problems with writing a simple letter before, and yet it took me several drafts until I managed to create a thing with which I was satisfied. An introduction, an extension of sympathy, an offer of help—what more could possibly be needed? And yet it was hard, a thing I'd never done before, writing a personal letter to someone I did not know, someone who knew nothing about me.

At last, crumpled sheets all around me on the escritoire, I struck a tone that, if a little stiff, felt to me to be just right.

10 January 1899

Dear Mr. Wood,

I write to you having received your name and address from my husband, John Smith....

FIVE

The night I received the stinging letter from the prisoner, Chance Wood, I had sexual relations with my husband for the first time in a very long while.

John had come to bed with the evidence of his desire pressingly stiff between us and I had not the heart to turn him away. Unable to sleep myself, it seemed a small thing to be able to do for the man with whom I had lived for so many years, had known through all the significant memories of my life, the father of my dearest Weston.

I felt John's hand pass over my breasts now in the usual way, felt him insinuate his hips between my thighs just prior to entering me.

Did it give me pleasure? That is, peculiarly perhaps, hard to say with any degree of certainty. I cannot say it was ever, except in the very beginning, specifically *un*pleasant. And even on the very first night we had ever laid together, that first night of pain, I had sensed something just beyond what my body was experiencing. Indeed, I had come to like, for the most part, our couplings. I liked the feel of skin pressed to skin, liked the sensations, even if there was something not quite complete about them.

Had I but words for it, I might have told him that while there was something peculiarly enjoyable in the invasion of my body by his, I felt there was yet something even greater, out on the peripheries, I should like us to strive for; that I would dearly love to experience whatever it was that made his own body stiffen as he shot fluid into me.

But of course I couldn't say that.

The one thing that was certain was that the act pleased John; and if, for my part, I sometimes spent part of the time reviewing household lists of things that needed attention, John was never the wiser.

That night, I found myself using the time to compose my next letter.

After the rebuke of his letter, it was very hard to think of writing Chance Wood again. Would it not make more sense to stop? Or at least ask John for the name of a different prisoner? But no. I did not want John to think I had failed so quickly, given up so easily. I had promised myself I would do this thing and it did not seem sufficient to say after one failed attempt at contact, "Well, I have tried. Now what's for dinner?"

Dear Mr. Wood,

It appears we have gotten off on a slightly wrong foot here. I believe, in reviewing in my mind the contents of my previous letter to you, I may have presented things to you in an inaccurate fashion. I set the case down as though it were I who had all the benefit to offer you, placing you under my obligation. Nothing could be further from the truth. In fact, it is I who would benefit more by such an association.

As you may or may not be aware, there are not many in today's society with whom one can hope to conduct any sort of honest discourse. It is hard to say why this must be so, and yet I don't imagine our times are substantially different in this from previous ones, nor do I see any reason to forecast a change in the future. Maybe it is simply the way people's minds are made. Like the countries of the world, like our very bodies themselves, there are boundaries in our minds that act as the last line of defense from outward invasion.

I do not know what it is about the twenty-two words in your previous communication—words that are equally cold and direct in their delivery—that lead me to believe you wish to conduct such an honest discourse with me; but such, I find, is the case. Should you choose to do so, Mr. Wood, as alluded to above, it is not you who would fall under my obligation, but I who would find myself obliged to you.

I look forward to receiving your thoughts on this, and anything else you might care to add.

Mrs. John Smith

I felt John roll off of me.

He patted my hair, his voice still slightly out of breath as he spoke: "Good night, Emma."

I rolled in the other direction.

"Good night, John."

SIX

Well, **I had said I** wanted to be a better person, had I not? And I had also said I wanted to make more of an effort to befriend shy Constance Biltmore, had I not? Why, then, should I reserve my energies for a prisoner who had so far made no indication of having any interest in taking advantage of those energies?

With these intertwined resolutions in mind, I set off to pay a visit.

I had not given much thought to it before, the way I was with other women, but as I walked, my boots clicking against the cobblestones, my breath making its own miniature fogs within the greater fog of air, I did so. Previously, I had always been content to let others seek me out. But I never sought out others for more contact, for greater closeness. For the most part, I felt I knew the people I knew as well as I wanted to.

But I felt differently about Constance, felt

there was something more going on beneath the pretty surface of this woman I'd been seeing for years.

With this thought in mind, I raised my gloved hand to her door with its beveled-glass inset, knocked, removed my coat in the drafty entrance hall. Then I waited in her front parlor while the butler, who thought she had said she was going outside to cut flowers—who cut flowers in winter?—told her I was there.

Like fair Constance, who mostly wore clothes of sunny hues, her front parlor was decorated in a similar fashion, the sofa I was seated on a white shot with threads of silver and gold. On the marble-topped center table there was a vase with an overabundance of peacock feathers in it; a fashion Constance had perhaps taken too much to heart, as there were feather fans on the walls as well.

Constance swept into the room, the color high in her cheeks.

"What a lovely surprise!" she said, pressing her icy-cold cheek to my own cool one as I rose to take her hands in mine, sitting again only when she sat. "To what do I owe—"

"I was in the neighborhood," I supplied, unoriginally, "and realized visiting you was a thing I had long wanted to do but never done."

We spent the next few moments catching up on the doings of the people we mutually knew. But neither of us was a natural gossip and so the conversation soon fell awkwardly short.

How do you say to another woman, I wondered, *"Are you happy with your life?" How do you say to another woman, "Are you happy within your marriage?"*

Well, of course, one could not say that.

All I could do was look at Constance, look at her when I did not think she could see me looking: She did not look happy to me.

"This is such a sunny room," I remarked, proceeding carefully. "My own never look so bright. How does Charles like it?"

There was that Constance eye movement to the corner, as if something interesting might be found in vacant space.

"Oh," she tried on a laugh that didn't quite fit, "he does not like it. He says all the yellow gives him a headache and the peacock feathers cause him to sneeze." Now that false laugh really did fail her. "He says he should not have allowed me such freedoms. He says he should have had his mother select the things for our home."

How awful. And how cruel in such a small way. I could not

imagine John ever being so demanding about such petty things. True, he'd said many times before he didn't love me in garnet, but what of that? He was objecting to a single color, not that his objection ever stopped me.

"I am sorry," I said, smiling, trying to make a light thing of it for her sake. After all, to point out that things were far different in my own household would only serve to make the hurt more hurtful. "I suppose some men never do understand quite what we are about. And so, even when it comes to the interiors of our houses, our instincts are a complete headache-inducing mystery to them."

As I listened to myself prate on, I was appalled at the nonsense coming from my own mouth. Did I believe a word of it? Of course not. All that seemed important at the moment was that I help Constance pull her protection back up around herself.

In her eagerness to take me up on my mood-changing, energetic chatter, she turned to me with enthusiasm.

"Oh, I know just what you mean," she said. "Charles always says—"

"What?" And there was Charles standing in the doorway, a not quite restrained anger in his eyes. He moved into the room like a dark cloud, tossed a racing card on the center table. "What does *Charles* always say?"

Not wanting to cause any further harm, having first assured Charles that I'd merely been asking Constance what her husband's choice of main course was for Sunday dinner, adding that John preferred a nice roast, I hastily departed.

———

"I must go to the prison to ask just a few more questions," John was saying, "ones that will allow me to add some realistic touches to my book. Perhaps I will get an opportunity to visit your prisoner."

Did I imagine the emphasis he put on that "your"?

I did not look up from where I was playing on the floor with Weston.

In the late afternoon, rather than remaining in his nursery, I preferred to play with him on the floor of the back parlor, catching the last light of the day between the long shadows that fell across the comfortable furniture. Convention dictated that mother and son be together only so many moments in the day. If we were to be thus limited, I would make the most of our time. So what if we made a mess? Someone would clean it up before morning.

We had large sheets of paper out, on which I was drawing animals for Weston's amusement. For his part in the game, he was crumpling up the depictions of those animals he did not care for very much just as quickly as I could draw them.

"Please tell him I said hello," I said.

John laughed so hard I looked up.

"I was just teasing you," he said. "Of course, I do not have time to pay mercy visits. I am going there to work."

SEVEN

I was not, I am sorry to say, as fond of my own mother as I was of Lady Collins. A gentle countenance belying the steeliness within the soft and powdered exterior, I found it difficult to believe she had stopped having children after my birth simply because the doctor had cautioned that with her slender frame it might be unwise to have more. Naturally, this was not something I was able to articulate as a child, but I did sometimes get the feeling that if she could have somehow taken back the act of bringing me into this world, it would not have bothered her in the slightest and might even have proved to be to her advantage. Although I called her Mother to her face, I never failed to think of her in my own mind as Louisa.

My father was a different matter. If Louisa was someone with whom I endeavored to maintain a civil relationship because my bond dictated it, my feelings for Edward Crane had little to do with bond and everything to do with instinct.

Taller than the average man, a genial smile ever gracing his soft brown eyes and fondly wrinkled features, he had turned entirely white-haired some years before. Lacking a son, he had made me into a daughter with whom he could share his pursuit of reading. And, once I married John, my husband became the son my father had never had.

Now I sat in their front parlor.

My father stood next to one of the tall windows while my mother sat on the same sofa as I, a footstool beneath her feet, beside me but at as far a remove as the sofa would allow, stirring her tea. I heard my father clear his throat and glanced up at him, still wondering what had caused them to summon me for this rare visit alone. My father had no sooner opened his mouth, however, than my mother began to speak for him.

"It has come to your father's attention," said Louisa, "that you have taken up a rather irregular correspondence. It does not please him and he wishes you to stop."

"I do think, Louisa—" he began.

"Yes." Louisa held on to her china cup with iron hands. "He does wish you to stop."

I must confess I was a little startled at this outburst. How laughable that there should appear to her to be any threat in said "correspondence," which, as I well knew, so far numbered only two bungling attempts on my part and a terse two-line "go away" on the part of my correspondent!

I picked up one of the pillows from the sofa, upon which was the only embroidery my mother had ever made: "God Sees Everything." I idly fingered the tasseled decoration as I spoke: "Where, may I ask, did you learn of this?"

"Why," she said, "from your husband, of course."

Frankly, I was stunned. Why would John tell Louisa of all people?

"I am not sure I understand," I said, "what it is that displeases you so."

Again my father opened his mouth to speak; again Louisa cut him off.

"We might start with the appearance of impropriety, if you wish."

"Oh, yes, well, by all means, let us not ignore any of the proprieties."

She stiffened as she reached for a biscuit. "You needn't take that tone of voice with me. Your father does not like it when you do."

I turned slowly, raised one eyebrow at him, saw it was all he could do not to laugh at my expression. Somehow, seeing this tempered my own impulse to react with more heat than light.

"Yes, Emma,"—he cleared his throat, concealing a laugh—"perhaps you should listen more closely to what your mother has to say."

"Very well."

"It is simply," she went on, "that what you are doing is just not seemly for a woman in your position."

"My position?"

"Oh, yes. You do realize, don't you, that as the wife of a respected novelist—not to mention the daughter of a well-respected gentleman—it is your duty to avoid any appearance of impropriety?"

"I am not sure that is entirely correct. Should that be the case any more so than, say, if respect should accrue to me based on their merits rather than my own merely due to the accident of association?"

"Why, that is the most absurd thing you have come out with to date!"

"Be that as it may, and you must forgive me if I appear reluctant to concede to an accusation of ultimate absurdity, should not your quarrel be with John, since it was he, whose reputation you are so concerned with my besmirching, who arranged this? Obviously, he does not find it improper."

"John?" She laughed aloud. "*John?* Oh, well, dear, if you are going to base your decisions on proper behavior on *John's* ideas..."

"What does that mean?"

"Well, you do know, he *is* a novelist."

I looked at my father helplessly. What, really, was the point?

But Louisa was not done with me yet. "I do not know why," she said, "if you must have contact with criminals, you cannot do what a normal woman would do in similar circumstances."

"And what," I asked, "pray tell, would a normal woman do?"

"Why, join the Ladies Association, of course," she said, as though the answer should have been obvious to any sane person. "I have read about them in the newspapers. Haven't you? They visit the women prisoners and read to them from religious, instructional, and sometimes even entertaining books. Why cannot you do a thing like that?"

I pictured myself going into a prison with other helpful Ladies, reading to female prisoners from tracts that were meant to be morally uplifting. I pictured myself writing to Chance Wood. The former definitely lacked the attraction and challenge of the latter.

"Because," I answered, "that is not what my novelist husband has arranged for me to do."

EIGHT

Some said his wife was a woman who deserved to die and his sentence, in fact, for such a crime had been light, as though bearing this out. After all, should he not have hung for what he did?

I would ask myself, *Why do I not feel a more burning need to know the details of this?* Surely, I was curious. Surely, I did want to know; or at least a part of me did. And yet...and yet... another part of me could not help but think the deed spoke for itself. After all, he had killed her. What, ultimately, did the *why* of it matter? Unless his own life was somehow in danger, he could have walked away. He could have chosen that. It was the choice that mattered, the deed that mattered, the actions taken that mattered, not the cause. When faced with a certain set of circumstances, murder had been his choice of action.

And perhaps part of the thrill in writing to him was in knowing he had been at least at one time dangerous, knowing just the bare outline of the story of what he had done.

The section of Hollowgate he inhabited was characterized by its leniency toward the prisoners, who were seen as having been dangerous, as Hamlet had been mad, merely north by northwest. It was rumored the guards there hardly ever beat or tortured the convicts.

I learned all this from John.

"They all say he had a very good reason for killing her," said John, absently, more concerned with peeling his hard-boiled egg. "I don't know that there can ever be a good reason for committing such a crime, but that is what *they* say, at any rate."

Who were "they"? I wondered. Prison officials? The newspapers? But something about John's look did not invite questioning on the matter.

We were in the pale yellow breakfast room. The windows were long, the lace curtains letting in the best of the morning sun...whenever there was any. With John's back to the windows, sitting to his right as was my wont at this casual daily meal, sometimes the light behind him shined too bright, making me squint as though he were a thing from a greater world in which mere men might be bigger than celestial bodies.

At his last word, Lucy entered with the toast.

Lucy had been hired as a maid three years previous at Timmins's suggestion. Had I been a jealous woman, had my husband ever given me even a glimmering of cause to become one, I might have felt threatened by the voluptuous figure that no staid uniform could ever conceal. As it was, upon first marking its proportions, I barely had time to remark it in my own mind before reviewing the impressive recommendation from her vicar Timmins handed me and hiring her on the spot.

Girlish, barely out of her teens when she first arrived, Lucy never crossed my sight without my seeing in her guileless cornflower eyes and short jumble of loose blond curls the John I had known in childhood. I also never looked at her without thinking, not unkindly, she could no more prevent herself from indiscriminately parroting every word spoken in front of her than Weston could.

"Will there be anything else, madam?" Lucy asked.

"No, that's quite all right." I surveyed the breakfast spread across the table. "If we do not have it here already, I cannot imagine we need it."

I turned back to John.

"No good reason for killing a spouse?" I attempted a laugh as I reached for a piece of toast. "I am very glad to hear you say it. I should not like it much if you gave me cause to think *you* thought such extreme behavior might ever be advisable. After all, if you did, I would be forever looking over my shoulder to make sure you were not coming at me with a knife."

"Did I actually say he killed her with a knife?" The manuscript he was correcting distracted him. "No, I don't believe I did."

"That is a relief. Although you do realize I was only making sport."

"Odd, then, that." He finally looked up. "Because they say that is as near as anyone can guess to exactly what did happen. His wife provoked him into a towering rage over something and he stabbed her to death."

"How horrible!"

"I suppose," he said, "some might very well think it horrible, when viewing it on the merits of mere facts alone. At any rate, though, her brother certainly didn't."

"Whose brother?"

"The brother of the prisoner's wife. I believe her name was Felicia. At trial the brother testified the only reason his brother-in-law had the misfortune of being in a position where he might be hanged for the deed was because the brother had never got around to doing it himself! Naturally, his words were purged with prejudice from the records, but one of the prison officials who witnessed the trial told me about it. And, of course, his words did carry great weight: the victim's brother sympathizing with her killer."

I marveled John could so coolly discuss this man he had brought into our lives. It was one thing to be analytical about fish in an aquarium or exotic insects pinned down in his collection and quite another to talk objectively about a murderer who was really only a letter away from me.

"How horrible!" I could not stop myself from exclaiming again.

John gazed at me more closely. "And how odd it is for you to make the same observation twice within the same conversation. It is very unlike you, to be so unoriginal." He turned back to his pages. "At any rate, even if everyone in London believes killing Felicia was no great crime, I doubt it will have very much bearing on the fact your prisoner is himself apparently destined to spend the rest of his days in jail."

How horrible, I thought once more, but I did not dare permit myself to say it out loud. Instead, I sought to change the subject.

"John?" I put some jam on my cold toast, untouched as yet.

"Yes?"

"Why did you tell Louisa and Father about my correspondence?"

"I don't know, dear. It was not as though I planned on it. In truth, it was more a matter of that I had run into them on the street, I ran out of new things to say, and finally just inserted that into the conversation because it came to mind. Why? Has Louisa been nettling you about it?"

"I would not mind that so much. But should it not more properly have been *you* she came to about this? After all, it was *you* who came up with the idea."

"Yes." He smiled. "But we all know how much your mother prefers to come after you. Besides,"—his smile took a mischievous turn—"she may like the success of my chosen career, the public respect and money it brings, but you and I both know she still thinks novelists are no more sound of mind than the lunatics in Bedlam."

How well he knew her. His words tempted me to smile along with him. But still:

"I am so very glad I have been able to amuse you this morning. The fact remains, however, that Louisa, *my mother,* is attempting to interfere in a relationship that is...that is...that is not even any sort of relationship at all!" I had shown John neither my letters to Chance nor his one to me, but I had informed him of their benign nature. "It hardly seems as though it should be worthy of her time. And if you had not set her on my trail—"

He put a finger to my lips, grabbed my hand with his other one.

"Shh, now," he soothed, "I'll take care of it."

"When?"

He smiled, light mischief in his eyes. "The very next time I run into Louisa, and find myself at a loss as for something to say."

I felt his finger stopping my lips, felt the warmth of his hand holding mine, but I could not stop myself from wondering: Why, when he must surely have known how she would vex me about it, had my husband told Louisa about the correspondence with Chance Wood?

There were times when I suspected my husband took pleasure in keeping me on edge.

And there was another thing that was troubling me, something else Louisa had said.

"Why," I asked, "didn't you simply recommend I join the Ladies Association?"

He drew away, made a disgusted sound. "That is not for you. What—go with those useless women to read religious tracts to women prisoners, so you can then tell yourselves afterward that you have done great things in the world and now all will be well for everybody, as you scurry along to tea? No, Emma, that is not for you."

———

That afternoon, I was playing on the Turkish carpet with Weston, as the daylight drew to a close and the room's shadows grew long. A more accurate description might be to say he played while I watched, since he was in one of those children's moods in which he wanted to do it all himself but only if I was right there to be his audience of one.

I had always liked winter well enough, certainly had always appreciated living in a country where the change of seasons was marked, yet I was already beginning to long for spring. Thinking of longer hours of daylight, greater warmth, brighter flowers, I was also thinking with half a grudging mind that soon I should summon Hannah to take Weston to change for dinner, when Timmins brought in the late post.

"Mr. Smith has not returned yet," he informed me, as if I might not know.

"Thank you, Timmins. I will take that."

I watched his back for a moment as he went, wishing he might be going much farther than just to the pantry, flipped through the post. I was halfway through before I came to a letter from Chance Wood.

Normally, I hated to have Weston away from me as much as custom dictated was necessary, prized whatever moments we could steal together, but now I wanted to be alone.

I called Timmins back.

"Please send for Nanny to come fetch Weston."

"But, Mummy, we were just getting to the good part."

"I know, dear." I hugged him to me, not aware in the slightest of what "part" of his game he was referring to. "But if you go with Nanny now, there will be a great treat for you later."

"Oh, goodie!" And off he went.

How easy it was at times.

Alone at last, I could see my hand shake, for no reason I could think of, as I handled the letter. It had been so long since my last letter to him, I had all but given up waiting on a reply.

I tore it open. This time, he had managed to distill all he thought concerning what I had written him down to a single sentence:

Dear Mrs. Smith,

I think you must be an exceedingly lonely woman.

Chance Wood

After that, I could not bring myself to write to him again for a fortnight.

Was it his presumption that bothered me so much? The accuracy of his mark? I could not say.

NINE

I did not know what he looked like, of course. Not that it made any difference. It goes without saying, however, I spent more than a little time imagining what the truth of his appearance might be.

Was he an older man? A handsome man? Short? Tall? What were prisoners permitted to wear?

But it is a far greater truth that the lion's share of my attention was given over to fantasizing about what his next words might be. Even though the words of his last letter rang out harshly, repeatedly in my mind, it was like a peculiar progress of sorts. As insulting and invasive as it felt to read those words, it was yet a coming forward, far different from the veritable door-slamming of his first letter.

And then I had to stop myself. I had to remind myself we did not know each other yet at all; that whatever talking had been done had been on my part. All he had done was first tell me to go away and then invade a part of me I did not usually like to think about. Why, then, did I already feel as though there were so much more between us? In a way, it was like watching a chess game in which one of the two players is suddenly revealed to be one's self.

In a week, I had my answer to the question of what he would do next. Having written nothing myself since the last letter I had received from him, the one that had shaken me so badly, the one that had so coolly identified the sterility I at times experienced, I was frankly shocked at the heat behind his new words. After the briefest of salutations, inquiring as to the state of my health—was I unwell? was that perhaps why I had not written in two weeks?—he cut to my heart.

> *My dear Mrs. Smith, I must ask you:*
>
> *When was the last time you were touched such that your response was not a duty? When was the last time you moved to meet a hand rather than waiting for it to come for you?*
>
> *Chance Wood*

Heedless of the impropriety, of what he had written and my reaction to it, I felt the sheer shock of it cause an interior shiver to move through me.

It was as though someone had opened up a door and let air in.

TEN

It is impossible to know what other women experience under similar circumstances, since certain taboo topics are never touched upon. Suffice it to say I went to my wedding night with no knowledge gleaned of what I might expect or what might be expected of me.

It had been a prettier day than one had the right to look for in February, but such had been John's persuasion that we pledge our vows on Saint Valentine's Day, his reasoning stemming from the traditional belief that birds choose their mates on this day, I could not find it in me to resist him.

One never stops to consider, when one is making such seemingly small sacrifices, the toll their accumulation comes to when added up over time.

Scotland was a beautifully moody country, even if perhaps the month of February was not the time of year to show it off to best advantage, nor were the Highlands perhaps the best choice for a honeymoon. The damp chill was even more insidious than at home; craggy hillsides, which probably looked best when tufted with green, instead studded with patches of stiff brown grass. Where we lodged, in a small travelers' inn situated on the lake in a tiny village, it was cozy enough, with extra quilted blankets in the small rooms and fires that were constantly lit. In the mornings, it took hours for the mist over the lake to lift.

But none of that mattered really, since I quickly became aware that John's primary intent in Kinloch Rannoch had nothing to do with the atmosphere.

No sooner had we finished dinner than John was leading me back up the winding and slightly crooked stairs to the cozy room under the eaves where the innkeeper had earlier stowed our traveling bags.

John shut the door behind him, turning the key in the lock.

"I thought perhaps first I should—"

I was going to finish the thought by saying I wanted to use the bathing facilities to get myself ready for bed, but I never got the chance. His mouth was over mine before I even had time to register he had swiftly closed the space between us.

Up until that point, I had only ever been kissed by him in a chaste way, not much different really from when my father kissed my cheek; nor, might I add, had it any greater of a stirring effect upon my passions. Now what John was doing was different. He was pressing his lips hard against mine, prying my mouth open with the force of his, inserting his tongue searchingly. It all happened so quickly, I hadn't sufficient time to register whether there was any pleasure to be had in what he was doing or not.

Then my clothes were removed with surprising speed, in spite of moments of fumbling confusion, surprising when one considered how long it took me some days to get dressed with the help of my maid.

I stood naked before my husband.

Well, I suppose if I had thought about it in advance, I would have known it would inevitably come to that.

But I had not thought about it in advance, believe it or not; with the exception of the occasional frisson of anxiety—specific source unknown—I had not given it any thought in the slightest.

And yet, in spite of all of the unsettling things that had happened already, there was still worse to come.

As I stood there, naked before my husband, he hurriedly began to take off his own clothing, never once tearing his eyes from my naked body. I would have liked to hide from that devouring gaze, but for a wife to hide from her husband seemed incorrect to me somehow. Trying at first then to avert my own gaze, curiosity got the better of me as bit by bit, with the shedding of each article of my husband's clothing, his masculine body appeared before me as a revelation.

How very different it was from my own! What an amazing thing, that men and women were made so differently, one from the other, with some of the parts even complementing each other!

Once again, however, I was given no time to register if I did indeed like the differences or was simply amazed by them, because before I knew what I was about, John was pressing me down upon the quilted bed, passing his hands briefly over my breasts—so fleetingly it was not until a moment later I registered in my mind that the accompanying tingling sensation in my body had been pleasurable—and prying my legs apart with a firm knee, pushing something into me so searingly my mind felt itself blinded by the shock, pushed for just a moment beyond reason.

ELEVEN

I looked at Chance's words before me on the page, for what seemed the thousandth time.

When was the last time you were touched such that your response was not a duty? When was the last time you moved to meet a hand...?

I should have ended it right there. I know that. I should have told John I was no longer interested in being "a better person," not if to do that was to do this. I should have told him I'd grown bored with the exercise. If I had to, I should have shown him the invasive letters of Chance Wood, making John stop it for me.

But I didn't do any of those things.

I chose to go forward.

After all, as John had so persuasively pointed out to me, he was in there; I was out here.

And the letters I was receiving from Chance Wood were the most exciting things I'd ever read.

TWELVE

I don't think it is possible to overstate how much a union was expected between John and I. From the moment his father took up the deed to the estate bordering my father's when I was six, it was as though our mutual fates were sealed, the banns read, the knot irrevocably tied.

John certainly viewed it thus. I must have been eight, putting him at around eleven, the first time John asked me to marry him.

It was summer, one of those rare still and clear-skied days when it could take nearly a whole afternoon to trace a single cloud's progress across the entire bright expanse of blue. John was seated on a white-painted lawn chair, legs ranged forward, Louisa's cape draped around him, so we might play a game of my own making, entitled Twins. He was supposed to be mine. He had been looking at me for some time without speaking and I had begun to feel as unsettled by it as a bug realizing a two-legged creature possessed of far fewer eyes is staring it down none-theless.

"What are you staring at?" I asked suspiciously, accusingly.

"You," he replied.

"That is obvious. But I do wish you would stop. You are begin-ning to make me quite uncomfortable, and," I added, "I am quite cer-tain rudely staring at me is not one of the rules of Twins."

"Perhaps not," he conceded, "but I don't believe you can do any-thing to stop me."

This was a new John, a different John from the one I'd grown used to.

"Not stop you?" I barked an unsure laugh. "I'm sure I could."

His words came out in slow measures. "No, I don't think so. You could try, of course. But I am now quite a bit bigger than you, and if it pleases me to look on you, I don't imagine you can stop me anymore at all."

The nerve!

Never one to place much of a barrier between my brain and my vocal cords, no sooner had I thought the words than: "You cannot do whatever you want to, John Smith, just because now you fancy your-self bigger than me!" Studying those rangy legs, I felt even testier. "Fine. So maybe you did get awfully bigger overnight, but that still gives you no right—"

"Marry me, Emma?"

"Are you insane?!"

"Possibly. But I do know that, already it seems as though I've known you my whole life. I'll never meet anybody I'll know better."

"You *are* insane, John! I'm eight!"

"Fine. Then I'll ask you again next year. Maybe by then you will have grown up."

"Oh...oh...oh...give me back Louisa's cape!"

THIRTEEN

I was surprised when, having just received the unsettling letter concerning physical touch from Chance Wood not twenty-four hours before, a new letter arrived. He, who had been so reticent to talk before, now wrote twice in a row without waiting for my response in between.

Dear Mrs. Smith,

I hope my previous letters have not caused you any undue distress. I am mindful of the fact I can at times come across as an abrupt man, possibly even cold. I do not wish to appear so any longer in your eyes. (Oh, my! What a very many sentences in a row that is to have all begin with that most egotistical "I"!)

Still, what I very much want to say here is that I have given much thought to your own letters. (And believe me when I say this to you, Mrs. Smith, there is very little else to do where I am but think.) If I have given you the impression I do not want your friendship, let me assure you here such is not the case. Indeed, I want it very much, and am hoping to return the favor tenfold. As a matter of fact,

I would consider it the greatest honor if you in turn would consider me as a repository for your own thoughts. Where you are concerned, anything you might say to me would be safe. After all, given my circumstances, who is there for me to tell?

I do so hope you will interpret this letter in the spirit in which it is intended. (There is that "I" again, but I don't imagine it can always be avoided!) Eagerly awaiting your response,

Chance Wood

I stared at the page in disbelief.

Who had taken my laconic prisoner and replaced him with this impostor, this cheerful talker? This was not the terse man I had come to know. Infuriating as the man I had come to know was, at least I knew what to expect from him: rudeness, invasiveness. But this?

Pushing aside my disbelief, I thought to take the letter to John. Was this not what we had been after? Did not Mr. Wood now appear to be in the process of becoming a different man, certainly a more cheerful and possibly better man, than the cold man who had written me back originally? Here was proof of the success of my efforts.

And yet, as I neared the open door to John's library, something stayed my forward progress. It was silly, I decided, to disturb John when my own meager project was a mere dwarf next to the giant of his career.

"Emma?" John called out to me as I was turning away. "I hear your feet and see your shadow there. Were you looking for me?"

I hastily put Chance's letter behind my back and entered John's library.

"Yes," I said, thinking inspirationally of some particular words Chance had written. "I wanted to ask you something."

"Yes?" John prompted, impatiently.

"The letters in and out of the prison," I said. "Doesn't someone read them to make sure, oh, I don't know, someone isn't telling prisoners how to escape?"

"What?" John laughed. "Are you worried about your modesty?"

I almost blushed at his mockery. There had certainly been nothing immodest about the letters I had written to Chance.

"Do not worry," he placated, misreading my distress. "Governor Croft has promised me he will not read any of your correspondence."

I was startled. "But why would he make such an exception?"

"Because I asked him to, of course. My wife is not a common woman, to be treated as though she might be just another suspicious character. You are free to say whatever you like." I must have still looked startled, for John added, "You keep forgetting, Emma. I am a persuasive man."

I apologized for disturbing John's work, thanked him for his time, and backed out of his office, Chance's letter still held behind my back.

It was good to know what Chance and I wrote to each other was safe. It was good to know, whatever passed between us, there was no one for him to tell; there was no one who would ever know.

FOURTEEN

I once asked John, who had tried his hand at both, with mixed results, what the difference was between writing comedy and tragedy. He replied that with the former you must find a way to ensure your intended audience will laugh; while with the latter, you desperately pray they do not.

So many words John had spoken to me concerning the writing life, as he saw it, came back to me now.

I sat at the escritoire in my bedroom, my desk arranged so I could peek out the mistily curtained French doors of the ground-floor room, the doors opening from the back of the house, the view taking in the borders of stocks and mignonette beyond.

As I tried to find the right note to strike in my response to Chance Wood's last letter, particularly loud in my mind's ear were John's words concerning how writing enabled one to live lives, for one reason or another, one could not otherwise indulge.

I pressed pen to lip, thinking.

I was aware of a disposition in myself to feel I knew Chance Wood far better than the sum of our correspondence would indicate, but it was impossible not to build up stories in my mind around what I knew and what he wrote. At times, I would think I could almost perceive extra unwritten words on the pages that simply were not there, as if there were a story surrounding the apparent story. I had a sense of Chance Wood doing the same thing: building more in his mind about what was between us than the mere words on paper. This was hardly surprising; he lived in a prison where there was little stimulation, and it was easy to understand how someone, in such a circumstance, might allow imagination to create an even more exciting correspondence than had thus transpired, sometimes jumping ahead in terms of emotion expressed because what went on in the mind was so real it felt it must surely have transpired in reality as well. Then I would remember John's words when he would say, of novels, that in the best ones you always had the sense there was more on the page than what your empirical senses told you. And Chance Wood *was* being more open now. He *was* writing letters that were more than just a single line or two. And yet I somehow sensed that, despite the new openness as evidenced in his last communication, should I place a foot wrong, he might bolt from me again.

Of course, the rational part of my mind wondered: Would that be such a bad thing? Did I really want to continue an association, to come closer to one who had the obvious power to unsettle me so?

But then, it was as though a sheer lightness, a silent laughing breeze blew through me. He was locked up in there, and I was free out here; what possible threat could he conceivably pose to me? Might it not be interesting to let him in just enough, just to see what new avenues of thought he might perchance lead me down?

Feeling surer of my actions than I had in days, I set pen to paper:

Dear Mr. Wood,

How wonderful it was, at long last, to receive a communication from your hand that exceeded two clipped lines! And yes, I do agree with your most recent suggestion: It would be nice to engage in an exchange of thoughts.

Odd, though, now we have reached this point of agreement, I am not certain where we should start. Perhaps you have some more specific idea? If so, I should be very happy to learn of it. Do you like politics? I am told that, for a woman, I have an unusual grasp. History? Literature? I have a smattering of both. Though I must confess my interests in music are mostly confined to knowing what I like, I can at least try to explain those likings coherently when called upon to do so, even if it is not in any sophisticated manner. We could even discuss games; I have been known to win at chess if I have sufficient reason to be certain my opponent should not mind so terribly much losing to me.

In any event, let me know which topics suit you. I can see where regularly utilizing this form of communication with a single correspondent naturally lends itself to a certain amount of chattering. Further, now I can fully appreciate how one can fall into trouble by creating a string of "I's"!

Sorry to end on such a seemingly silly note, but some days are more naturally given to silly notes than others.

As always, looking forward to hearing from you,

Mrs. John Smith

With a hand that was barely even shaking at all this time, I sealed the letter up and left it for Timmins to post.

FIFTEEN

John kept his promise.

He did keep asking me to marry him. He asked me again the year I turned nine, then ten, then eleven, and on and on.

I suppose, if it had been anyone else doing the asking, I might have found the persistence of the suit annoying. But it was John. And, if I was not inclined to say yes to his annual entreaties—*I am only nine!* I would tell him, *Only ten! Only eleven!*—I was equally disinclined to cause a permanent wound to one who was as close as any twin might be.

As we grew older, the previous status in our relationship began to shift. During my eighth year, in conjunction with his stretched-out physical form and his sudden impulse to throw proposals at me, he began to acquire a level of confidence previously unglimpsed. And, as sometimes happens with such acquired personality traits, each successive year saw a deepening of the quality in him, so that as his early teens turned into late teens and then twenty and twenty-one, his level of self-possession became such that it appeared nothing could derail him.

As also sometimes happens when one of a pair of friends undergoes such a change, the other is changed too. And so it was, as John's sun rose, mine went into a slight slope of decline. By the time I was eighteen, then, I was no longer in a position on the board from which I could think to turn him down any longer.

"Yes," was my simple answer, when he asked me the question for the eleventh time, on the exact date we celebrated my eighteenth birthday.

He took my gloved hand in both of his, confident smile spread wide.

"I knew," he said, "it was just a matter of time."

———————

Dear Mr. Wood,

A while back, you wrote that you thought I must be "an exceedingly lonely woman." I sought to ignore your words at the time, but now I feel the impulse to write and tell you how right you were.

I would not previously have characterized myself as "lonely." Indeed, I would have said, among the women in my circle, I am the most content of women. But I am beginning to think now perhaps that is not quite true. Oh, I am busy enough—God knows, I am always busy with one thing and another! But that is not perhaps the same, is it, as feeling true companionship with a kindred spirit, a like mind; or, if not necessarily a like mind, a mind that knows mine. There are moments when I feel, if I must spend another moment in society not of my own choosing, I will go mad.

There is an unusual corridor in my home. It connects the family side of the house from the more public rooms and is solid midnight wall on one side, all glass on the other. Sometimes, when I know I can steal a few moments undisturbed, I go there to sit on the tile floor.

I am not sure what else there is to say.

Mrs. John—

I crumpled up the sheet of paper, tore it to shreds between my fingers, tossed it on the fire, watched it burn.

When I woke in the morning, I told myself I had never written anything at all.

SIXTEEN

Dear Mrs. Smith,

May I now call you Emma? I feel as though I am about to know you so much better than I did previously, and I cannot think that Mrs. Smith, under these changed circumstances, remains the best term of address. Further, I cannot think what proprieties might be violated by my addressing you thus—should I receive your consent in doing so, of course—since I cannot imagine why another human being on the face of this planet should ever learn of it, save you and I.

I—I, I, I! One sentence ends with "I," while the next inevitably continues there, although in my mind, I must confess, they all too often recently begin and end with "you." I, too, like history and politics, and also know what I like when it comes to music. But are you quite certain, Emma, those are the topics on which you wish to spend your time with me? Is there nothing else that might matter to you more?

I suppose you must think me very forward now, but it does seem that, if we are limited to a few pages every now and again, we should

*not squander that blank space on topics that might adequately be
covered with others.*

*If you will agree to be Emma with me, I can now become with
you (and there the line ends for once on the word which it most
properly should),*

Chance

How in the world had he learned my given name?

SEVENTEEN

Dear Chance,

How odd it is to suddenly begin a letter to you in such a fashion, yet I do wish you to be comfortable in our exchanges, so I will try to get used to it.

Not talk of history or politics or music, though? What then shall we discuss? I am quite certain I am uncertain as to where I might begin.

Hmm...let us see...

My husband and I visited with friends, Joshua and Maeve Collins, for dinner and cards the other night and the hostess mistakenly served him a soup with mushrooms in it. As John told Maeve, "I am deathly allergic." Then he laughed. "Well, that is what Gammadge's cousin says"— Gammadge is a friend of ours—"but we all know how inaccurate the words of doctors can be. Suffice it to say, as a child, each time I ate a mushroom, I grew progressively sicker. According to Gammadge's cousin, it has reached a point where the next dose might kill me—something to do with a lapsed tolerance. I am not quite sure I understand the theory, but then, I have never

*been quite certain Gammadge's cousin does either." I thought
everyone knew John was deathly allergic and I cannot for the life
of me imagine this woman did not. But it is also equally
unimaginable, knowing of his condition, she should serve it to him
anyway. It is odd, really, how you naturally expect certain people
to have certain knowledge, just because they have seemingly been
on the periphery of one's life forever, and how surprising it is when
they do not.*

*Then conversation turned to a couple we know, Charles and
Constance Biltmore. Joshua said Charles had looked angry the last
time he saw him, Maeve mentioned Constance looked more worried
than usual the last time she had seen her. I find myself worrying
often about Constance. She seems to me to be a very good woman
and a very unhappy one. I do wish I could help her somehow, but,
given how many subjects are simply not to be talked about in polite
converse among women, I am at a loss as to how.*

*I am afraid I have never corresponded with someone I didn't
know before. Is this the sort of thing you had in mind?*

Emma

P.S. Do you, by any chance, play cards?

His reply came in the very next post.

Emma,

No.

Chance

I suppose another woman might have taken those three words, lined
up as they appeared on the page, and divined a second meaning from
the constellation of them. But I had never been another woman. For
my part, I chose to take them at face value.

And, of course, there was a postscript:

P.S. I do indeed play cards. I play them very well.

The spring-summer season had just opened at the Haymarket, the smell of beer and oranges just beginning to resettle on the air as the ladies promenaded in their court dresses, their feathers, their jewels, awaiting the signal that the green baize curtain was about to rise.

To all appearances, it was nice of the Jamisons, having taken a box for the season, to invite us to be their guests at the theater, but it soon became fairly obvious their motives had gone deeper than the mere pleasure of our company. For her part, Sara was bubbling over with her accomplishment. Having resolved back on New Year's Eve to conquer her burgeoning waistline, a glimpse at the new lines of her form whenever her green watered-silk dress peeked out from beneath her cloak revealed she had, against all odds, been successful. Paul had conquered his New Year's demon as well: His handkerchief was well positioned and, he was quick to point out, all through his own doing.

"But, of course, that is not the only thing I wished to discuss with you," Paul addressed his words to John as we took our seats in one of the private balconies lining both sides of the stage, Sara and I in the front row.

Sara leaned in closer to me so I could see her features clearly despite the low light offered by the candles and the weak lamps. "I do not mind so very much seeing another one of Mr. Ibsen's plays. But I do wish it were something other than *The Master Builder*. Why, over the last three years, what with traveling and all, I do believe I've seen it as many times."

"I quite agree," I whispered back. "I would much rather have seen *A Doll's House*. But I hesitated to say anything earlier."

"What is it with men and that play?" She opened her fan. "I cannot for the life of me understand why the play intrigues them so."

"—has to do with the effects of the Revolution on the Colonies." Paul's words came at me in midsentence, falling into the void left by Sara having cleared her mind of everything on it for the time being.

"It sounds," said John, assuming what I knew to be his diplomatic tone of voice, "like a truly fascinating plot. However, as your friend, I feel—"

"Yes, yes, I do know what you are about to say."

Now John's voice was openly amused. "Am I always so transparent?"

"Not transparent, perhaps, but your earnestness on certain topics is a fairly predictable commodity."

"Very well, then. Please, do tell me what I was going to say."

"You were going to say the writing life is not as easy as it might appear to outsiders; that anyone in possession of pen and sufficient paper in these times considers himself a potential novelist; that it's easy to want to start a book, but quite another thing to sit before the unforgiving, accusatory, gauntlet-throwing blank page day after day and feel impelled to prove oneself equal to the challenge." Paul paused. "Do I have the right of it?"

"In the main. But you left one thing out."

"Oh?"

"That publishers are only pleasantly supportive in novels."

Sara moved toward me once again, whispering, eyes glued to the stage. "I do not like this character very much," she said. "If I were Mr. Ibsen, I would find a way to have one of the other characters murder him. A shooting would do very well here."

Dear Chance,

Last night we were at the theater with another couple. The man half of the couple sought out my husband's advice about writing. I wonder, sometimes, how many people who have not tried it believe writing is as easy as accidentally cutting oneself with a knife. I wonder if people ever realize how hard it is to tell the truth in anything, whether in one's waking life or in writing.

Is this more like what you had in mind?

Emma

———————

Emma,

No.

Chance

———————

Although my parents did not reside far from us, it was rare for us to dine with them. So when my father sent a note saying they should like to come the next Sunday after church, it occurred to me it must have been months since we'd entertained them and so I sent an answer back saying, of course, we would love nothing better.

Well, "love" *was* a bit of an exaggeration.

As we waited for them to arrive, I felt a nervousness in my stomach.

What have I to be nervous about? I asked myself. Weston, who was probably the chief interest for their visit, would undoubtedly be well behaved as always. What indeed had I to be nervous about?

No sooner had Louisa entered than she commented, as she always did upon entering, that she had never had any liking for Timmins.

Well, at least we were in agreement about that, although I, living there as I did, would not have dared speak the thought aloud.

No sooner had dinner been completed, Weston having behaved himself admirably well, even treating my mother with an affection I could not see she had ever earned and pleasing my father by talking in a manly way of books he favored, than my mother indicated it must be time for Hannah to come and collect Weston so we adults might talk.

No sooner had Weston been collected, and we had settled ourselves on sofas around the fire in the dimly lit back parlor, than Louisa started with: "John, are you close to finishing your prison novel?"

"Well," he answered in a rather John-like fashion, "I am certainly closer to finishing than I was on the day I started."

Her look at him was nearly a squint, as though she suspected him of laughing at her.

"You novelists," she said slowly, consideringly, "you are very fond of word play, aren't you?"

I wondered, not for the first time, how it was possible we were related.

But John was clearly not bothered. On the contrary, he smiled back with innocence. "It is our profession."

Hearing some sort of cue in that, Louisa turned to me. "Are you still writing to that murderer?" she asked without preamble.

"My dear," my father said, "this isn't the time—"

"I never could understand"—Louisa spoke to John—"how you could let her do such a thing in the first place."

"Actually," I pointed out, as I had on the previous occasion when we had discussed this, "writing to the prisoner was John's idea."

I felt a curiously delicious sensation as I spoke those words, "writing to the prisoner." On one hand, I was openly discussing what I was doing. On the other, no one could possibly guess the contents of my correspondence.

"What is this 'let'?" John laughed. "Have you ever tried *not* to let Emma do what she wants and then seen the result?"

I liked his defense of me well enough, but could not see the truth in it. I had of late been experiencing a dawning awareness that everything I had done in life so far had only been possible through the sufferance of others. There was nothing, save for this budding and strange correspondence with Chance, of which I could truly say I was writing my own original story without the hand of anyone else guiding the tale.

"I simply do not understand," my mother addressed me, "why you wish to do such a dangerous and improper thing. What is to be gained by it?"

Slowly, with great patience, I endeavored to explain the original conception: How I wanted to become a better person, how John had thought I might make some poor wretch's life a little better.

"Yes," she said with impatience, "I see what is in it for the wretch. But what I do not, cannot understand, is: What is in it for you?"

Out loud, where the world could hear me, I said: "The good feeling granted by the opportunity of helping one less fortunate."

Inside, only to myself, I answered: *Real human contact.*

Then I surprised myself by adding, "But it does not matter. I have ended my correspondence with 'that murderer,' as you call him."

John's head snapped up, studying me closely. It was an uncomfortable scrutiny, one that made me feel like one of the brightly colored insects he collected or perhaps some new specimen of fish in his aquarium.

In the way of long-married couples, from the set of his jaw, from the look in his eyes, I could see his mind thinking, *She did not tell me that.* I could see his mind thinking, *She is telling them a lie.*

"That is a relief." Louisa settled back into the sofa. "But why then did you not say something before? And why, may I ask, did you stop?"

"Because," I sighed, as if it were true, "I realized I could do him no good."

And then John surprised me. "That's right," he said, his eyes still on me. "Emma and the prisoner have ceased their correspondence." Having backed my lie—perhaps he could see how torturous it was for me to talk to my mother and that a lie was a small fall from grace if it achieved peace from her—he turned to Louisa. "So, you see? You have been worrying about nothing. You have been worrying about a thing that is finished."

Before departing a short time later, Louisa made an oft-repeated request: that Weston come, on his own, to stay with them for a time.

As always, I found a polite excuse to avoid it.

"That is a wonderfully generous suggestion," I said, hoping my smile looked warm and genuine, "but he is at a place right now in his lessons with Nanny where I do not think it would be wise to disrupt their routine."

"What could a child possibly be learning in the nursery that is more important than what he could learn from me and his grandfather?"

"Nanny has begun teaching him what she knows of French and German and I am sure it will benefit him when he enters into business one day. You know none of us has ever had any facility with languages and one does always hear people saying these days what an advantage that can be."

"I suppose," Louisa conceded a touch suspiciously. "We would not want to interfere with any advantages Weston might obtain. Although I do think spending more time with us would also prove to his advantage."

I would be hard pressed to say exactly *why* I was always reluctant to have Weston spend time alone with them; they were certainly good enough to him whenever they were in company together. I suppose that, having had the disadvantage of Louisa's indifferent care in my youth, I did not want to expose Weston to the same.

"I am sure Emma knows best," my father addressed Louisa. "I am sure when the time is right, she will send our dear boy to us."

———

The part of my discussion with Louisa that had concerned my correspondence with Chance seemed like a worthwhile thing to discuss in a letter to him. After all, what could be more natural and worthwhile than letting him know what we had together had been somehow expanded in the world, having become the topic of dinner conversation with others?

But I could not tell him what had been said, did not want him to know that, even if it was only to avoid further aggravation with my mother, I had in a sense denied him.

So, instead I wrote:

Chance,

My parents came to dinner on Sunday. We had a lovely time . . .
Was this what you wanted—to know more about my family?

Emma

———

Emma,

   No.

Chance

———————

Chance,

   ...We went on an outing with the Meads and the Vaughns...

Emma

———————

Chance,

   ...Do you think you would like receiving books in prison? Do you think that would be allowed you? I only ask because I understand that Tolstoy's...

Emma

———————

Chance,

   ...Is this what you had in mind?...

Emma

———————

No.

No.

No.

Chance

Well, at least his responses were consistent.

EIGHTEEN

Chance,

I don't understand! What is it that you want from me?

Emma

Emma,

That you be yourself. That is all.

Chance

It was so easy when you think about it; so simple, really. With that one short line, that was all it took to send me right over the edge.

I thought about what I had said to myself—having told my mother what I got out of my correspondence was some kind of altruistic feeling—that what I wanted was real human contact.

There had been brief moments when I had believed Constance might be a person with whom I could have real human contact. And I did still worry about her, very much so. But I also realized any relationship between us could only ever run one way. Perhaps I could someday be of some small use to her, but, given the sadness and fear that seemed to be her life, I doubted she could ever offer the same to me.

The desire for real human contact—I realized now it went beyond this: I wanted to see another person for themselves; I wanted to be seen for myself.

———————

Chance,

As I think about what to put into a letter to you, what to put in if I am to reveal my true self, I look back upon the thirty-four years I have lived, and I wonder: Has there ever been one moment, one second, when I have been myself with another human being? And whose fault is it—the world's, for insisting a uniform facade is always preferable to individual reality? Or mine, for willingness to comply? My true self,—do I even know who that person is? Or am I so caught up in what I want the world to see—or is it what the world insists on seeing?—such a person does not even exist yet?

Who has never longed to be seen for her true self by the other? Are people so very different from one another that it should be conceivable one party should desire such a state while the other yet wishes to remain in hiding, sheltered behind the front of a public face? Will you ever reveal yourself to me?

Emma

———————

Emma,

Much better. However, you are still, for the most part, speaking in abstracts.

Chance

Chance,

If I tell you I am not sure how anything in my life came to be as it is now, is that better? *If I tell you I do not know how I ended up with the parents I have, it should not surprise you. But if I tell you I do not understand how I ended up with the so-called friends I keep, with my husband, with even my child, that I do not see where any of the world that surrounds me bears the stamp of my choice, is that the* better *you are after?*

Emma

Emma,

No, there is nothing "better" about it; but what you say is finally true nonetheless.

Chance

Chance,

Will you not talk at all of yourself?

Emma

Emma,

    No, not yet. But I will say I have more liking for you each day, more than I would have thought possible. I wish I could be the cause to make it "better" for you.

Chance

Chance,

    Sometimes I think if I could just go away for a little while . . .

Emma

Emma,

    You can always come here.

Chance

His words, despite their obvious sardonic tone, tempted me.

No, of course I do not mean they tempted me to physically go to him. How could I do that? But they tempted my mind and spirit, pulling me closer to him all the time.

In all my years of living, and so many of those years had felt long, no one had ever spoken to me as he spoke to me now, no one had ever taken such an interest in my every thought and feeling. True,

John was always studying me, and yet there was something scientific in his attention.

But this was different.

Chance's attention, so very different from my husband's, was like a sun shining down on the only cat left in the world. Chance did not ask how I was in order to make sure I was well enough to go on servicing his needs, go on running his household smoothly. He wanted to *know* me. More than a mere escape from my daily routine, more than a frisson of excitement at conducting a relationship that no one in the outside world really knew anything about, it was as though he wanted to live inside my skin.

And I wanted him there.

Some days, there was just one line, just one question to express what I was thinking.

Chance,

Are you familiar with the works of Mr. William Shakespeare?

Emma

———————

Emma,

I am not a scholar, as I am sure you have readily guessed. But, as with your music, I know something and of that something, I know what I like. I know some Shakespeare and like some of what I know. Why do you ask?

Chance

———————

Chance,

Do you know the 116th sonnet?

Emma

———————

Emma,

Of course—I read it in a collection from the prison library.

> Let me not to the marriage of true minds
> Admit impediments. Love is not love
> Which alters when it alteration finds,
> Or bends with the remover to remove:
> O no! it is an ever-fixed mark,
> That looks on tempests and is never shaken;
> It is the star to every wandering bark,
> Whose worth's unknown, although his height be taken.
> Love's not Time's fool, though rosy lips and cheeks
> Within his bending sickle's compass come;
> Love alters not with his brief hours and weeks,
> But bears it out even to the edge of doom.
> > If this be error, and upon me prov'd,
> > I never writ, nor no man ever lov'd.

It is the one that makes all the rest of them worth it. Well, save for the final couplet, which is rather weak. Again, why do you ask? Surely there can be no literal application to our current state. After all, we cannot possibly be tested by alteration since, having never seen each other in the first place, that measuring stick is removed. WHY DO YOU ASK?

Chance

———————

Chance,

It has to do with the very idea you raise: removal; the notion of bending "with the remover to remove."

Hettie Larwood—no, I know you do not know her; she is an annoying woman, and I suspect you should not like her if you did— brought an Arabian gentleman with her to dinner here the other night. From what I know of her, I would hazard a guess her social sponsorship of him had more to do with the novelty of possessing something no one else has, as opposed to any real Christian charity.

Be that as it may, considering how reticent he was in the beginning of the evening to discuss anything about himself, when Charles Biltmore, possibly still bitter over a loss at cards the evening before, pressed him to discuss his own religious beliefs, he waxed quite eloquent. The rest of us were rather taken aback at Charles's forwardness on a topic not usually broached, but the Arabian gentleman positively welcomed the opportunity to expound on a topic obviously quite dear to him.

He spoke of his religion as being the most sacred thing in his life. He said he had practiced it as far back as memory began, had lost so much through it, through challenges and persecutions, he could never envision letting it go now. "My investment," he said, "has been too great."

Then he referred to his God as Allah. But that was not the surprising part. Oh no. The surprising part was when he spoke of him as being "the Uncaused Cause, the Unmoved Mover of all things." Is that not an astoundingly beautiful evocation of the ineffable nature of purpose in this life?

Sometimes, lately, I begin to wonder if somehow you are the Uncaused Cause behind my life, the Unmoved Mover behind my actions? I feel myself doing certain things—holding my head a certain way, putting on certain articles of clothing, moving inside of my own skin—and I feel you there all the time now, watching me. Who are you really?

Emma

———————

Emma,

You are becoming strange on me again. Your last letter prates on quite skittishly before finally coming to rest at a point I can understand.

Still, you may have the right of it with your sonnet. You, yourself, I am coming to believe, are the "ever-fixed mark."

But never mind sonnets, never mind Muslims. Speaking of "possessing something no one else has," do you imagine any of these other fine ladies, the ones with whom you while away your social time, have in their possession an imprisoned man who believes himself to be falling in love with them?

I wonder, Emma, often: What do you look like when you are not wearing any clothes?

Chance

NINETEEN

His words shocked me, caused a sense of outrage. What man had ever spoken to me thus? Even my own husband had never said such things.

And then I remembered what I myself had wanted: a truth in human communication. Why should it be any different for him? He had indicated he wanted as much himself. So why should he not speak these things, if this was what he thought? Surely, he also felt, as I felt, the safety of the prison that separated us. That prison made it safe for us to say what we truly thought in a way we would never have been able to had we met in the normal fashion. The intimacy was a real thing, a breathing thing. Why not explore it, if we were both of a mind to? Surely, dealing truthfully with one another, which could only be achieved through greater intimacy, would bring me closer to my original goal of becoming better myself by making things better for him. Was that not the point of the exercise?

I wanted to write one thing that was true, even if he was the only one to ever hear it.

———————

August had come long and hot, the only thing that didn't feel new.

Straw matting had replaced what little carpeting there was on the floors, the furniture covered with cotton or muslin slipcovers.

And still it was too hot.

We had decided to spend the day at the park. True, without the cool areas of the carpetless floors, the drapes to keep out the sun and the shadows to hide in, we would be exposed to the worst of the heat. But at least we would not feel cooped up any longer.

Lucy packed a hamper for us, including a loaf of bread and a thick wedge of Stilton, Timmins insisted we each wear hats to keep out the sun, and John, declaring the day too humid for clear thought, put his revising pen down for once and consented to join us.

With Hannah along to keep an eye on Weston, who looked rather silly as did we all under Timmins's choice of hats, there was little for me to do once there. And so, as Hannah and Weston punted along in their little rower on the pond, I stretched out on a blanket under the tree next to John.

If given my choice, I would have kept more distance between us now, but such behavior on my part would have appeared, well, odd. True, we still shared the same bed, but somehow close quarters there were acceptably unavoidable. In waking life, however, in what was now my daily waking dream, such proximity was near intolerable. The closeness between us I had once prized had now been altered by a glimpse at something deeper.

Thankfully, John's eyes were closed against the rays of the sun that poked through the leaves as he lay on his back, legs crossed at the ankle, hat clasped in hands on chest as though awaiting burial, and so he did not catch the fleeting expression of distate I was unable to wholly prevent from forming. How I wished it were another man beside me now.

Without opening his eyes, a smile on his lips, he spoke.

"It has been some time since I heard you speak of your prisoner, not since I heard you tell your mother you were no longer writing him, in fact. Yet Timmins informs me you greatly look forward to the post each day."

Damn Timmins! Aloud, in a teasing voice, I said, "Hmm...I wonder what Timmins would do if the roles were reversed and *you* were the recipient of such missives?" To myself, however, I knew the answer.

"Oh, you know Timmins."

I did.

"He is just an old gossip. I am sure the situation would be the same."

It would not.

He opened one eye, squinting it as he tilted his head toward me. "You never answered my question. How is your prisoner doing?"

"Perhaps I didn't answer, because you did not expressly ask that." I spoke, pretending the pettishness in my voice was just that: pretense. "You did not ask anything, as a matter of fact. What you did was make a statement. There was no question mark I heard."

"Well, now, my dear, you can safely assume the question mark is officially there. How is your prisoner?"

I felt inexplicably deflated. "He is fine. He is in prison for a crime, as you have pointed out before, he may or may not have committed. He is expecting to be there for the rest of his life. How else would he be under such circumstances? He is fine."

"That is an awful lot of 'he,' Emma."

"I was merely trying to answer your query, once the question mark was brought to my attention, to the fullest extent possible. There is really nothing more to be said on the subject."

"Oh no?"

"Mummy!" Weston shouted from the rower. "Look how well I am doing it! Nanny says I am the captain now!"

"That's wonderful, darling!" I shouted back, fully content in the moment. It was the first such feeling I'd had in I knew not how long.

John rose up on his elbows, watching Weston row them on by. He lifted one hand to the side of his mouth, called out: "Just be careful, Captain, that your crew does not mutiny!"

I looked at my son. There was always at least one moment in

each day when it was yet surprising anew that something John and I had done together had somehow managed to create this perfect being.

John's next words stopped my sense of wonder.

"It seems strange to me, after these several months, you and your prisoner should still be corresponding, if anything more frequently than ever. Have you not succeeded yet in becoming 'a better person'?"

"If I did not know such a thing is not in your nature," I laughed, "I could swear you are jealous."

"Jealous? No. I am just wondering what is taking such a long time."

"Well, John, if you did not want it to take such a long time for me to become 'a better person,' then you should not have picked a prisoner who is serving a life sentence."

"It is to be my fault then?"

To this, I had no answer.

"Come!" I yelled to Weston instead. "There is another boat here hard aground and you are the only captain equipped to save her."

I rose to my feet, dusted off my skirts.

"Emma?" John reached up, grabbed on to my wrist. "I would like to see some of the prisoner's letters. Will you not show them to me?"

Despite the oppressive heat of the day, I felt a chill inside.

"I have thrown the letters away," I said. "As soon as they come in, I read them, and then I throw them away."

"Of course," he said, agreeably enough. "But surely you can save the next one for me?"

TWENTY

Even though I had told John I would save him Chance's next letter, the correspondence passing between us now was such a heated thing I knew I could not do what I had promised.

Chance had ended his last letter to me, *I wonder, Emma, often: What do you look like when you are not wearing any clothes?*

Well, I certainly could not show *that* to John.

I looked through my letters from Chance, searching for some of the more benign ones, but they were all dated. Having told John I had thrown all his letters out, I could not now produce a letter dated months before.

I realized the natural solution was to request Chance provide me with a few letters to show John, but I immediately rejected that idea. What I had created with Chance, despite the… *nature* of some of our correspondence, felt pure somehow. I could not now soil that purity by asking him to write something that would be a lie, even if it was to protect us. If one of us had to lie, it would be me. John was my husband. John was my problem.

But what was I to do?

With nerves shaking my hand, I practiced at forgery. But all attempts failed. Even disguising my handwriting, the individual letters that made up the words, even the tone, were still undeniably feminine. I could no more make myself into a man than I could make myself into a lion.

In a half-mad moment, I considered asking Paul Jamison for help. He wanted to see if he could be a novelist—then let him try his hand at this! But I knew insanity lay in such a scheme. Surely, I could not depend on someone from our inner circle, however ambitious, to keep such a secret.

Then I remembered John talking of a young novelist, one Harry Baldwin, whom he had met while in the company of Herbert George Wells. John said Mr. Wells was a great champion of Mr. Baldwin's work, indeed envisioned a successful future for Mr. Baldwin as a novelist, as successful perhaps as John's own. But, when John had tried to read Mr. Baldwin's work, he found he could not in good conscience lend his own support to the young man's career—to me, he referred to him as "that hack"—and an enmity had grown up between them. Unlike John, Mr. Baldwin had not been able to afford to leave his own career as a chemist in order to devote his full energies to writing and, as far as I knew, was still at the same apothecary. I resolved to seek him out there.

The odor in the apothecary, located in a questionable part of the East End, assaulted me, the smell of chemical compounds cloyingly sweet. Had I not known better, I would have thought I was in an opium den.

A haggard man came out from behind the counter to help me, a hank of greasy brown hair falling down over one tired gray eye. He looked badly in need of a decent meal.

"Mr. Harry Baldwin?" I asked.

He seemed at first greatly taken aback. Perhaps he thought me a creditor? But I quickly put his fears at rest as I set out my story.

Explaining I was the wife of John Smith, whom he had once met with Mr. Wells, I further explained I needed his help in a little joke I wanted to play on my husband. I had, in fact, concocted what John, in one of his looser moments, might rather scathingly refer to as a cock-and-bull story.

"You, of all people, Mr. Baldwin, must realize how smart novelists are. Well, my husband has given me the task of corresponding with a prisoner in Hollowgate." That was true enough. "But I find I have not the stomach to go on with the correspondence. It turns out the prisoner is too...crude for my sensibilities." I hated telling that lie about Chance, but if it served my end, I would do it. "And so I have cut off all communication between us. But now, as it happens, my husband has expressed an interest in seeing the letters. And I don't have any to show him!"

"So," said Mr. Baldwin, a sneaky grin coming for the first time to his face, "you want me to impersonate your prisoner?"

"Oh," I said brightly, "John was right: You *are* a smart man!"

"I am a very busy man too," he said, more sneakily yet. "Between my work here and my writing..."

"Of course!" I said, opening my reticule. Having anticipated this, I was well prepared. I pulled out several notes. "Do you think this a fair amount for, say, four letters? I do think if you sent one each week, it would be sufficient. If you do it properly, I would imagine my husband will grow bored with it by then..."

I could see Mr. Baldwin was thrilled at the prospect of playing a trick on my husband, whom he undoubtedly resented greatly. Seeing his pleasure at duping John, a part of me recognized it was wrong of me to deceive my husband in this fashion. But what choice did I have?

"But what shall I write in the letters?" Mr. Baldwin asked.

"Oh," I said, "you are a novelist. Surely you can imagine the kinds of things a prisoner would write about: write about the boredom, the awful food. I suppose you could write just a little bit about the loneliness too."

He laughed, a harsh sound. "I think I could manage that."

"Here," I said, producing some crude paper I had bought cheap.

It was as close as I could find to the prison stationery Chance used. "Use this."

I had thought of everything.

Within a week, the first letter arrived:

Dear Mrs. John Smith,

It is still boring here. The food is still lousy. Sometimes, I get lonely for the outside world.

Chance Wood

I suppose a more finance-conscious woman might resent that the generous sum that had been paid to Harry Baldwin for that letter had produced so few words, and those ones that had been virtually spoonfed to him. But it did not matter, since his meager note served my purpose perfectly:

John looked satisfied.

TWENTY-ONE

Perhaps it is hard for another person to believe, but I had never touched myself before.

Unknowable to anyone else; if such a thing is possible, more so to myself.

It was still the early part of a Sunday afternoon. We had just returned from church, the meal had yet to be laid out, and Weston was playing at our feet as John poked around at his desk. All during services, in front of God, all I could do was think about the other him, he who had become the Unseen Seer along with everything else he now was in my universe, always there with me, watching as I moved through a world that daily grew less and less real.

As I watched the child I had borne playing on the Turkish carpet that had once again replaced the straw matting, feeling as though I were at least one dimension removed from the scene, I felt a wave take me, an impulse more extreme than any I had known before.

On legs that had a slight tremor to them, I made my shaky way to my feet, one hand on the arm of the sofa for support.

"If you both will forgive me," I said, "but the weather is still hotter than normal for late September. I fear I dressed too warmly for church, and now I find I am feeling unwell."

"Mummy, you look so pale!"

John looked up abruptly, all solicitation. "Is there anything—?"

"No, I am sure I will be fine." I made my progress toward the door. "But perhaps you could eat today without me? I believe if I could just lie down quietly for a little while…"

I could not stop myself; I begged forgiveness one more time before I was gone.

———————

Slowly, I drew the drapes. The day had gone dark gray, prelude to a gathering storm; perhaps the storm would relieve the unnatural heat. Now, with the draperies shut, my bedroom became nearly dark as night.

I sat on the edge of the bed, oddly nervous; nervous as I might have been on my wedding night had I been granted the opportunity. The shadowed edges of the room's heavy furniture were still discernible; my hand, when I raised it to undo the buttons at the collar of my dress, still recognizably my own. The temptation was great to distance my mind's ownership of that hand, to imaginatively replace it with that of another. Closing my eyes, I gave in to the temptation, imagined a coarser hand in place of my smooth-skinned one, coarser but just as gentle—at least in the very beginning—all the same.

Would he move as slowly? I wondered. *Would he be as determined to take his time?*

My dress came down over my arms, the sudden shock of air chilling the tops of my breasts as they strained against the tightness of my undergarments.

Ties came undone; hands crossing each other at the neck, fingertips caressing the hollows between neck and shoulder.

Was the silk in the touched or the touch?

Hands moving around and slightly upward, as far as they could reach, to the sides of the neck, behind the ears and down the jawline, into the hollows again, over the edge of the shoulders, down arms, moving inward and upward, filling the hollow at the elbow—let all hollows be filled—and back up.

Then hands feathering down the corset with its bone and steel stays, each hand insinuating its way inside the top of the undergarment and cupping one soft breast, kneading, tracing circles round and round in ever-decreasing circumference until the target had at last been met. Touching, rubbing, and squeezing harder: Not only were the feelings in the areas touched a new thing in that it was such an extreme of feelings, but there was also an answering wetness and an echo—twinges? like a tuning fork, perhaps?—that was also entirely novel in its extreme. It was a novelty that silently screamed, *There is an answer. There is something to be known beyond the mere periphery, the mere hint of feeling.*

It was not a sensation I knew, not one I was familiar with. The hints I had known of all along, but not the reality.

Rising from the edge of the bed to unsteady feet. Slipping off shoes. Hands pushing dress the rest of the way off, removing undergarments, removing stockings.

Hands to breasts again, eyes shut tight, hands traveling down the center of the torso, over hips, briefly over buttocks . . .

Sitting down abruptly again, as though pushed.

An invisible hand against the chest, *my* chest, pushing me backward onto the downy plushness of the bedding.

I lifted my legs, set soles of feet to the top of the bedding, propelling myself backward until my head was at last among the pillows and there was room for my entire body to spread out.

Hands finding thighs, knees raised up, feeling another hollow, the hollow behind the knee, tracing the outline of the leg, around the foot, and back up the inner leg.

One hand back to nipple, the other hand pausing, stopped so close to the triangle of hair between the legs that one strong exhale of the held breath would force contact.

New territory; new geography to claim, to map out.

I released my breath.

Hand coming in contact with parts never touched before save for washing, parts that had no proper name of which the mind was aware.

Fingers parting hair, parting lips of skin, seeking out something they sensed was there although it had never known the touch of fingers, not ever. Something throbbing, pulsing out a signal to let the fingers know it was there. Ah! A knob—ripe, swollen, aching, surrounded by a warm moistness. Touching gently at first, in a form of awe, then rubbing faster and with greater pressure. Increasing wetness; a stronger signal.

The beginning of a tremor, the start of a shudder—which is greater? How would one ever know?

Sensation pushing reason away.

If Weston's birth was a physical pain beyond anything I had ever known to exist, this was an aching pleasure that reached beyond my powers of description.

Why, a small voice in my mind, my mind that refused to ever give up on reason entirely, wondered wryly, *have I not known of this existence before? Why have I only suspected it, suspecting with no clear answer?*

Hand moving faster. The other hand, the one that had been at the breast, traveling downward over the expanse of flesh that separated it from its mirror image, meeting at the center, curving around, seeking out the opening beyond, the opening that had only ever been filled before at another's insistence, at another's choice, now demanding something for itself.

Inserting one cautious finger, then two, body now working with hands, riding them.

The preliminary heartbeat of an explosion unique in that it was unique to the person experiencing it.

Fragmenting. Shattering.

At the very last, I had to raise one knuckled fist to my mouth and bite down hard; failure to do so, and my scream would have roused the house.

Breathing began to return to normal; clenched jaw released knuckle.

I put my fingers to my nose and inhaled; this was I. I placed my fingers on my tongue and closed my mouth around the taste; this was me.

It was the most joyous moment of discovery; it was the loneliest moment of my life.

For no matter what, I could not escape the fact I was entirely alone.

Crossing quickly to the wardrobe, I removed a wrap, sashed it around my waist, and crawled back into bed.

————————

"Emma?"

John came upon me, lying beneath the covers. The occasional aftershocks I was still experiencing, I can only imagine he perceived as a cold, perhaps an oncoming ague.

I could not speak.

Gingerly, John sat down beside me. "Are you unwell? Should I send for Gammadge's cousin?"

I struggled to find my voice; I really did not want to be seen by Gammadge's cousin. "No," I said. "It is just a chill. I am sure I will be fine soon." I bit my lip. "John?"

"Yes?"

"Could you hold me for a moment?" I felt so starkly alone. "I am sure I will feel better in a moment, if only you could just hold me."

He looked puzzled, but gently, very gently, he moved forward to comply. "If that is what you want, my dear, if that would make you happy."

But as I sat there with his arms around me and with my head on his shoulder, it did not make me happy. It was not what I wanted.

————————

I did not know why, could not understand my own reasoning if there even was any, but I told Chance about it. In a letter, too honest for me to even record here, a letter shaped by both the wonder and the loneliness of self-discovery, I told him all about it. *Let it be,* I thought, *that one true thing.*

TWENTY-TWO

I did not hear anything back from him.

Why was I surprised? Could I really expect to reveal such naked things about myself to another human being and have them still wish to look upon me, still wish to know me?

The clock ticked. Hours turned into days; I looked for the post, haunted the brass letter slot. Yet still the clock ticked, indifferent, stopping for nothing. Days turned into a week and then two; two more letters came from Harry Baldwin writing as Chance Wood; still silence from the real one. I looked at my servants, my acquaintances, my family, my husband, even my child, and I saw nothing. Everywhere I looked, I saw him, saw myself as I had revealed myself, opened myself to him.

Time was mocking me. Time was saying, *You fool.* Time was saying, *What did you hope to accomplish?*

I could not stand it any longer. On the

fifteenth day, having heard nothing, I wrote to him again. I did not even bother with a salutation.

> *It is lonely out here on the limb. Where have you gone?*

It was the betrayal that stung more than anything, the sense that I had been enticed out to a point and then left there, abandoned where I had thought to grasp on to a waiting hand.

In my anger, no longer recalling what the word "discretion" meant, having no heed for reticence, I went on. I spoke my mind. If I was laughed at, made a sport by one who had invited my confidence, I no longer cared.

> *That—my heart—is a door that has slammed shut. If you wish to see it again, you will have to drag it out. And, frankly, I don't think you will.*

I did not bother to sign it. Surely, there would be no mistaking the sender.

———————

When his reply did finally come, two days later, with me still reclining in my dressing gown when Lucy brought it, unable in my depression to raise myself from my bed, it blew my world wide open.

> *Emma,*
>
> *You are not alone; never doubt that. Never see your heart again? If I must use my teeth to devour the stone and skin that separates me from that which beats within you, then it will be a minor effort required of me indeed.*
>
> *I do not remember: Have I said yet that I love you? That you are all I think about now? Odd, since it is so very true, I cannot believe I have only spoken it within my own mind and not to you. Odder still, it should be so true and yet, apparently, somehow you know it not.*

There comes a point where I do not know what we have said aloud here to each other and what we have yet kept back for ourselves.

Did I remember to say it this time? Already, I forget. Regardless, I love you, Emma. I think now that I have always loved you.

Chance

TWENTY-THREE

L ove" seemed such an extreme word for what little others, looking from outside, might see of what lay between us. It was a word that shocked me when I first read it on the page. And yet, in that instant of shock, there was recognition.

How could what was between us be anything else?

I was his mirror; he was my confessor.

It was the only way I could explain to myself how we had found ourselves at such a place in time.

When I wrote to him about this new theory of mine, he countered that while he could fully comprehend how he functioned as my confessor—since it was obvious so many of the things I now shared with him on a daily basis were things I had never shared with anyone else before—he had trouble grasping how I was his mirror.

I thought how like an ornamental mirror I

was with him: When candelabra were lit, the mirror's gilded frame caused him to glitter more brightly, the reflected image—him— set off at best advantage. But that seemed too fanciful, so instead I wrote:

> *It is that you like the reflection you see when you look inside me. It is, in some ways, drastically different from how the rest of the world views you. In me, you see possibilities of yourself you had not been aware of in quite such a way before. And, at the risk of repeating myself, you like that.*

The smile was evident in his reply. Not even having a clue as to what that smile might really look like, I saw it plain as day.

> *Well,* he wrote, smiling, *that is certainly true enough.*

———

It was hard to believe, at times, my life could still proceed with any degree of normalcy at all; and yet it did. I could not stop the turning of the leaves; nor, I found, did I want to. Time, inexplicably, felt as though it were suddenly on my side. It seemed that, if I could just be patient, my heart's desire would somehow become mine. Wait, plant one foot in front of the other, allow the nights to stack up—and then . . . and then . . . what?

I did not know, was not ready to wrap my mind just yet around how such a tomorrow might ultimately be achieved.

In the meantime, there were still the days between now and that nebulously distant tomorrow to get through. There were decisions about menus to be settled, a son to keep in smiles, and a husband who, having finished the draft of his prison novel, was now at loose ends.

Ah, my husband.

Having previously approved of his intent on a career in writing and of the domestic bliss that a husband's contentment with his daily work would provide, I now longed for the days when he was a mere employee, however high-ranking, of merchants. True, then we had not even the dream of the wealth that was our accustomed lot now, but the advantage of his old job was that he did have to leave and go to work every day.

As it was...

"Emma, what shall we do today?"

I had been hearing such words each day for the last month, words I thought might drive me mad. Odd that a man who had no trouble dreaming up all sorts of occupying tasks for a myriad cast of imaginary characters should not be able to occupy his own mind during the daylight hours once he had completed building a boat for those characters and setting them out to sea.

And so, we visited friends; we had friends visit us. We went out to the country; we shopped in the city. We played with Weston to the point where, really, he probably would have preferred a slight holiday from us.

There had been a time, very early on in John's writing career, when I was sadly wakened to the inherent loneliness of living with a writer. Oh, to be sure, if I wanted companionship, I need no longer go outside the home to seek it. If I wanted someone to share something with, all I need do was go to his library door and someone would be there.

Except I didn't, because there wasn't.

True, John was not an ogre about interruptions if they came at an acceptable time. But even if on the surface it appeared as though he were responding to my words, answering a query, he was no more with me than, say, I was with Lucy as she puttered around the house, removing draperies that needed to be cleaned. You could say whenever John was working on a project, we didn't really live in the same house at all.

Now, however, I longed for the solitude that had once been a torment.

There was no time even to write to Chance. Before, when John had been hard at work on his novel, he had rarely noticed anything amiss. Now, he would not fail to do so should he be allowed to see how much space on blank paper was filled with the thoughts that passed between myself and the prisoner.

I found myself urging him to take up his pen.

"Emma, what shall we do today?"

I cleared my throat. When I did speak, my words sounded carefully formed even to my own ears. "You know, John, now the last book is at the publisher's and you await their verdict, that does not necessarily mean you must twiddle your thumbs at their pleasure."

"What do you mean?"

"How about if you were to begin a *new* project?"

"Are you sure it is not simply that you have grown used to having me out of your hair? And now, I am back in it, you seek to find a way to extricate me again?"

Seeing the aghast expression on my face, he laughed.

"No," he said, "I am sure that is not the case. No, I do know you have always had my best interests in mind. Still,"—he paused, considering—"although I am a bit restless of this *holiday* of mine, I am not altogether sure I am ready to give it up in favor of returning to work just yet."

And so, he was not to be rushed.

As I tried to figure out how else to occupy John's time, so he would not spend so much time occupying mine, Timmins brought in the post.

Ever since I had employed the ruse of Harry Baldwin, I took special care to pick up the post each day myself, so I could keep back Chance's letters, showing John only the three that had come from Harry. A fourth had never come, despite that a few weeks had gone by since the third, not to mention the fact I had paid for four. I had given it up as lost money.

"Ah," John said now, flipping through the letters. "You have another letter from your prisoner."

Dear God! I thought; for once hoping, praying, it was not from Chance.

"Here." John extended the envelope. "Why don't we read it together?"

I hoped he did not see my hand tremble as I took the letter. But then I saw right away, from the writing on the envelope, it was not my Chance.

And so, John read over my shoulder:

Dear Mrs. John Smith,

It is still boring here. The food is still lousy. Sometimes, I get lonely for the outside world…

Chance Wood

"Huh," John said, ripping the letter in half, "I can see now why you just throw these away. He is not the most original man, is he, your prisoner?" John yawned. "I do not think you need to show me any more letters. It is sufficient one of us be bored. So," he finished, "what shall we do today?"

And so I was free again from the prying eyes of my husband and yet the task of occupying that husband continued.

Now the only way I could find any peace in my own home was to rise before everyone else in the morning. The evenings were out because my husband, as much in love with reading the created worlds of others as he was in creating them himself, sat up long into the dark hours of these nights, catching up on what he had not had sufficient time for when he was still laboring over the perfection of his own novel globe.

The very early morning was all that was still left to me now.

The bathroom was crammed full with twin upholstered chairs in tapestries whose chief colors were mauve and forest, with a vanity and a large cupboard to contain all the linens, with ornate lighting fixtures—Argand burners with tubular wicks, the whale oil in the lamps giving off a light beneath the glass shades that was clear, bright, and smokeless—and with gilt-framed pictures on the walls.

And a mirror, of course, a very large mirror from which I had spent years avoiding my naked reflection.

The bathroom, and in particular its mirror, seemed like the perfect place to go in the morning, when one needed to hide in solitude from a world not yet waking.

As I stood before the mirror, looking at the places on my body my hands had learned how to touch in the dark, I realized I did not know this woman; but then, I had not known the one who had come before her either.

It was not an unattractive picture, this gilt-edged reflection, the very attractiveness of it accusing me for having shunned the sight of it for so long. The curled hair, wherever it grew, was still dark, still had the shining remnant stamp of youth left on it. The skin, never exposed to any sunlight, was pale, but not unhealthily so. The breasts were full, the circles around the nipples large, brown, the nipples themselves erect with tiny bumps of excitement raised on the skin that encircled them. The waist was smaller than it had been since my late girlhood, due to the lack of appetite for food and excess of energy brought about by my heightened awareness these last several months. The legs appeared surprisingly long and shapely for the body, considering I was not a tall woman. The hips, the lower stomach—both gave some evidence of time. But what of that? I was a thirty-four-year-old lady who had once pushed a baby out into the world. There was nothing to be ashamed of in the evidence of those facts.

And then there was the inverted triangle of black hair, the triangle I had spent so much time and energy over the course of my lifetime studiously ignoring.

I imagined him behind me now, entering me. My breath came faster and I turned my eyes away from the reflection, but then I imagined him, still behind me, forcing my face forward, making me look at him, at us, at what I was doing.

Afterward, as I leaned against the wall, still panting as I rested my forehead on the back of my hand, I heard my household begin to stir as Weston called to me.

Somehow, this had to stop.

TWENTY-FOUR

I began to let myself imagine what it would be like if he were ever to be released, should he ever somehow escape his prison. I knew it could not happen, *would* never happen, but I liked to think on it just the same.

———

No one who has ever seen pictures of the house of Mr. Charles Dickens can doubt there is money to be made at novel-writing. While I would not try to put John's success on a level with that of Mr. Dickens, nor was our home—lovely as it was—as grand as his, John was at least on the next tier down; and so, had done quite well indeed.

John had not always been a writer, of course. When we were first married, he had been employed by two merchants and had remained so for the first five years of our union. But then, one night, when the moon was particularly bright and we had taken a summer fancy to discuss unfulfilled dreams, I learned of his secret desire.

This lunar revelation shocked me in that it was so far from what he did in his everyday working life; and, further, in that it should be possible after knowing another human being for so many years to still be surprised at the knowledge that one might not know the other person completely at all.

In fact, I was so shocked by his words I never even thought to raise any unfulfilled dreams of my own.

It was my support of this very thing—this folly, as some thought it—for which I might hear John's friends comment on his good fortune in marrying me. As Joshua Collins put it, in a less gallant moment, "If my wife could not depend upon my income being a steady guarantee, she would stop at nothing to rid herself of me in favor of a more sure thing."

The day after the moonlight talk, we set about, jointly, to see what we might do to secure John's dream.

Of course, it is very easy to say one wishes to be a writer, as more and more people seem to be saying all the time; it is yet another, if John's experience was anything to go by, to actually take the first step on the road that leads to that ultimate destination, keeping one's eye on the goal at every moment so one can sometimes even ignore the daily pain and grind of putting one tedious foot in front of the other until the goal is achieved.

First, John needed to decide what sort of writer he wished to become.

"A novelist, of course," he answered me, as if there were no other options worth considering.

When pressed, he added, "Why, what else could I possibly be? A biographer? I did not throw over a successful career so I might record for posterity what someone else wishes the world to believe of him. A historian? Even worse; history is being rewritten every moment, rewritten even as we speak. Why should I wish to play a part in the creation of a perpetual lie? No, dear, the novel is the only place for me, the only place I will be able to go where I can find truths."

———

"It is not so much that the reader needs to be persuaded that he—or she, as it were—would behave in the exact same way as the protagonist if faced with the same set of circumstances. It is merely that they must believe with all their hearts that the protagonist, faced with the situation as it is set out, believes him- or herself to have no other choice." John paused, glanced down the length of the table for my approval. "Is that not right, dear? Is that not what I am forever saying, at any rate?"

I did not know about the *rightness* of it, but I certainly did know it was one of the select comments on the writing life he was forever saying. I proceeded to say as much but in what I hoped was a lovingly chiding way.

It was our turn to host the Jamisons and the Larwoods for dinner, and Paul Jamison, determined to see his own novel-writing project succeed, had been pressuring John for advice. We had invited the Biltmores as well, but Charles had sent late word they were not coming.

To call it a dinner was not perhaps an accurate description. Well, it was from the men's point of view; for no amount of talk could stem their interest in the food, from the turtle soup through the Manchester pudding.

We women, on the other hand, were the ones challenging the notion of it being a real dinner. For between Hettie, who had never been known to eat, Sara, who now no longer would eat, and I, who no longer could eat—well, fresh platters made from the leavings on our plates would have sufficed any three other women as a completely satisfying meal.

I wondered what Chance would think of these people, were it not impossible for him to meet them.

"I do not know much about characters in novels," said Sara, studiously avoiding the chocolate ice, the syllabub, the trifle, although she spoke so quietly that, the men still talking of their own pet topics, it was just Hettie and I who heard her.

"Nor I," added Hettie in a rather hot whisper. "But I do know about the behavior of real people in the real world."

Since there were just the six of us for dinner, we had forsaken alternate-gender seating in favor of the three men clustered down at one end of the table while we hens were at the other.

I was sure Hettie had some gossip she wished us to dig out of her. A cool eyebrow cocked in her general direction was sufficient enticement to get her talking. Not that I cared what she might have to say so very much, but it would help pass the evening.

"Maeve Collins is with child … again!" she burst out with it.

"No!" Sara and I gasped, although my guess would have been that, when she herself learned the news, Maeve's gasp must surely have been louder.

"But I thought …" Sara started, stopped short of any indelicacy.

But, yes, she was right. We had all indeed *thought* …

Having borne a new child every eighteen months, like clockwork, over the course of a twelve-year span, no one had been much surprised when one day Maeve just stopped. Most of us, in fact, although we would only say so in our own hearts, could not quite understand why she had not found a way to stop sooner. The only one who did indeed seem surprised by the stem in the flow of new Collinses was Joshua himself.

"I do miss the sound of new feet on the carpeting," Joshua said after one year passed, after two, after five. "New feet make a house a home."

But Maeve, having nearly died after the eighth, did not look as though she missed little feet at all. On the contrary, the only thing she had appeared to miss for years was her sherry or Madeira if there was not quite a generous amount of it on the table anywhere she happened to dine.

Well, really, who could blame her? Even with a full staff to tend to the children as they grew up, it was still her body that needs must be twisted out of shape anew with each pregnancy.

"What will Maeve do?" I asked.

"Do?" asked Hettie.

"What *can* she do?" asked Sara.

We all knew there was only one answer.

I thought of Constance. Why had they not come? I felt guilty I had not gone back again to visit her after that first time, but there had just been something so forbidding in Charles when he had come in upon us. He was pleasant enough, on the surface, but it was like the juicy skin on a game bird, underneath which the meat had gone dry and hard. I shuddered to think what it must be like for Constance, living with such a man.

Gently, I pushed open the door to Weston's room, saw the figures of his nursery rhymes dancing on the walls.

John and I had been married nearly ten years before I became pregnant with Weston.

Naturally, as month followed month, and despairing year followed hopeful year, we grew to accept we would never have children. So when, late in my twenty-seventh year, I found myself feeling queasy at all hours of the day and night, and with certain odors beginning to drive me nearly mad, I began to question both my physical and emotional well-being.

"You women really amaze me sometimes." Dr. Stephen Gammadge all but laughed in my face. "Why, you are with child, Mrs. Smith!"

So began one of the happiest periods of our married life.

That is not to say the pregnancy was an easy one. If there was a complication or discomfort, it seemed I must have it. Yet I kept my eyes on the goal: At last, at long unbelievable last, we were to have a child.

Labor, when it did come, was worse than anything I had ever imagined.

Oh, true, I did have some minor inkling. But a minor inkling and the actuality of experiencing more pain than one has ever felt in one's entire life are two very different things. John would say the inability of mere words to transmit the essence of certain experiences is at the heart of the writer's daily waking dilemma and, having tried to share experience in an epistolary fashion with Chance Wood, I could only agree to the challenge, ever doubting the success.

I learned a lot when my child was born, learned things, feelings I had never known before. I had not wished to ever lose control like that in front of others, but the biggest piece of learning I came away with from birthing Weston was that everyone screams in the end. Children may scream at the beginning of the story—that is, of course, if by God's grace they survive their journey into a new world—but we, all of us who give life, still scream in the end.

My water had broken when I'd lain down to sleep. Sixteen hours later I was wondering, with what little was left of my mind, if I would have felt differently had I not been robbed of sleep, if I would have been stronger, more equipped to bear what I no longer felt I could. I am told there are some women who do not seem to mind it so terribly, would rather push out an eight-pound baby through an opening that sometimes balks at having a husband enter it, than have a rotten tooth extracted.

Sixteen hours of pain is a long time.

There were times when I thought I might be ripped in half, times when I begged those in attendance, *Can you not find another way?* I really had done my part, had really been quite a good sport. *Can you not find another way?* Surely, having done everything I could possibly do, they must surely be able to find another, some other, any other way.

My bright ideas earned me knowing laughter, nothing more.

And so the pain went on.

I don't imagine I had ever, previous to that midafternoon when I finally pushed Weston out, pictured myself with my naked knees pulled back close to my face in a position I could never have imagined assuming, not in a thousand years. You can only fight the pain for so long; in the end, it carries you through.

But then, as suddenly as the pain had started sixteen hours before, it stopped.

One moment, all I could think of was my own searing pain; and in the next, following hard upon a rush of blood and fluid and sheer life, all I could think about was him.

Do I mean to say in that instant I ceased to be a selfish person?

Surely not.

But, in that instant, the axis of my whole world tilted in such a way nothing would ever be the same again.

It cost me much to bring Weston into this confusing world. And, once he was in that world, it was impossible for me to imagine myself ever living in it again without him.

The night owned a strong moon, which made its presence known through breaks in the draperies as I pulled the door gently closed behind me now. Stealing across the room, I lowered myself down onto the chair by my son's bed, a child's bed fit for a tiny prince.

In the shadows, I could see some toys had not been put away, remnants of an incomplete cleanup, but also remnants of a childhood day well spent.

How beautiful he was in sleep! Perhaps even more so than when animated. Awake, one could see what he was in any moment; in repose, the whole history of the past was there, all the potential of the future.

Surely, even if I was as yet the sun to him, his father would determine far more about that future than I would, if only by example. And here was a most peculiar thought: Would I *like* the man my son would become? Stranger still, an obvious answer did not come readily to mind.

One thing was certain: He would have some latitude for choice; maybe not as much as he would like—perhaps no one ever gets that, except possibly over in America—but he would certainly have more room to maneuver things to his own liking than, say, poor Maeve Collins.

I realized with shock I had somehow managed to grow a hard kernel of resentment toward my son for having a freer future than my own.

I looked closely at him, seeing his features as well as I could in the partially moonlit room: I knew the softness of those cheeks so well; even without touching them, I could feel the impress of them against my own.

No, I did not resent him after all. On the contrary, I wanted him to have every opportunity for his happiness that there could be available to him. The problem was, I wanted the same thing for myself.

I rose from the small chair, touched my lips to his forehead, inhaled the familiar smell that was actually painful in how ineffably dear it was to me. As I closed the door behind me, one last thought occurred: What would Chance think of my son? Surely, he would love him as I did.

———————

John was asleep on a recamier in the sitting room, an open book facedown on his lap.

I tiptoed past him into the bedroom beyond and the escritoire, still seeing that strong moon, now just a little bit lower. It had been so long since I had written to Chance; it felt as though letting the silence stretch out any longer would risk the loss of the dream. If I had to walk to where he was and deliver it myself, I would do so now.

Dear Chance,

It has been so long since I last wrote to you, or heard news from you, I should doubt that anything has existed between us were it not for one small circumstance.

Here is the thing:

I find, of late, that your image is everywhere I look. If I sit down to dinner with family or friends, you are there. If I shop or go for a stroll, you are there. Even if I go to church, yet you are there in the shadows. Odd, is it not, since I haven't a clue as to what your true features are. I do not even know how old you are! And yet I cannot escape you. I wake up in the morning and you wake with me; I close my eyes at night and, even in sleep, you refuse to let me go. I might be more embarrassed at declaring my feelings so boldly to you, were it not for the cold comfort of knowing I will never have to look you in the eye and own those feelings.

And yet, here is the other thing:

Also, of late, I find a picture of you as a living, breathing part of my life—and not just this phantom correspondent to whom I pour out my deepest feelings—emerges as a very possible, even probable, thing. Now, I ask you: Why would I think that? Do you have any idea? Yet, odd as it is, I see us traveling abroad together, see your hand in mine.

Do you think I am losing my mind?

Emma

There were times, countless times, when I wished to ask him for details concerning his own wife's death, his marriage, but I knew better, knew that was a scab best not played with. Besides, I also told myself, countless times, it was best I not know.

At war with myself—the desire for knowledge competing with the fear of knowledge—I kept such curiosity to myself.

TWENTY-FIVE

I began to let myself imagine his release in greater detail. I imagined us living together. Where? I knew not. The images were still somewhat hazy, save for the concrete presence of the faceless man beside me. Naturally, John had no place in this picture. But Weston did. Whenever I pictured this timeless vision, Weston was always there with Chance and I, playing happily in the background.

It was a fantasy that pleased me greatly.

———————

John's sisters had doted on Weston from the moment he was born. It was not that they didn't have children of their own. Indeed, between Ruth, Elizabeth, and Victoria, they had eleven! But the youngest was already eighteen and so it fell to Weston to be the petted one.

It had been growing more difficult, of late,

to listen to the sisters prate on about things of consequence to them, things that seemed of little consequence to me. But they were John's family. If they were used to coming on Wednesdays, what excuse was there to act inhospitable?

I poured tea, handed the first cup to Ruth. The oldest of the sisters, Ruth, already a grandmother, behaved and looked more like John's mother than his sister.

"You know, Emma," Ruth whispered once Lucy had exited the room, "it is odd but I swear Weston looks more like your maid every day."

Knowing well my son no more resembled me than I—oh, I don't know—resembled a tiger, I could not help but laugh, plus I also knew Ruth's penchant for teasing anywhere she thought her words might have effect.

"If you want to nettle me," I said, still laughing as I took in her surprised features, "you will have to try harder. I do not mind my son looking like the maid. She is a very pretty maid."

"Still," put in Elizabeth, auburn locks bobbing nervously, "you don't want people mistaking *your* son for the maid's. Too common."

"I shouldn't worry about that too much if I were you," I said. "Your brother outgrew his own boyhood curls. The same will happen to Weston and then he will no longer look like the maid. He will be a handsome young man. And," I added, laughing again, "when that happens, he will be beyond your reach for petting."

Victoria adjusted her skirts around a body that remained skinny as a girl's even after having borne six children. "Yes, he will be handsome," she said, "just like John. You always did find John handsome, did you not?"

"Mmm," I said noncommittally in answer to her rhetorical question.

I heard Ruth call to Weston, who had been playing happily under the watchful eye of Hannah.

"Go to your aunt," Hannah advised him now.

But before he could make it there, he was waylaid by Victoria's thin arms. "Never mind Aunt Ruth," she said. "She only wants to ask you about what you are learning. Come, tell *me* the important news." Here her dark eyes flashed. "Tell *me* what you have been *playing*."

"Mummy and I—"

"Never mind Aunt Victoria," said Ruth, grabbing on to him. "Tell me what Nanny has been teaching you."

I did not hear what Weston said. Having seen everyone had tea and biscuits, my mind turned to wondering over John's attractiveness.

I supposed, really, I had always thought him handsome enough. Society looked upon a man who cut as fine a figure as he did with great favor; still more so now that he had earned his own fortune. Was it possible I was just accepting the common barometer as my own?

"Is Diana's Katherine still troubling her?" Elizabeth asked with real concern.

Katherine was the eldest child of Diana, Ruth's middle daughter. Katherine's father had been so determined she would be a boy that, until a real boy was born five years later, he had treated her as one. Now she was fourteen, they still could not break her of habits acquired when she thought her say might one day be worth something.

"I believe Diana despairs of her," said Ruth, "and, frankly, I cannot say I blame her."

"It would help," said Elizabeth gently, "would it not, if Katherine's father did not find the situation so humorous?"

"It would indeed," said Ruth. "I have tried to warn Anthony, but he fails to listen. There is no more I can do."

I doubted Ruth would ever leave it at that.

"You are lucky to only have sons," Ruth said to Elizabeth. "Daughters can only bring one grief. Is that not right, Victoria?"

I could have pointed out we had all of us been daughters once. But it would have taken energy to raise such an objection; and, for such relative trifles—not to mention the trifles of relatives—I simply no longer had any.

"Oh, I don't know." Victoria tried to be diplomatic. "I rather think my four sons have given me just as many difficulties as my two daughters." She nuzzled Weston's curls; she had not yet let him escape her embraces. "But you will never bring your parents grief, will you, dearest boy?"

All earnestness, he looked her straight in the eyes and shook his head.

We all laughed.

"I didn't think so," said Victoria. "There was never a better boy who ever lived."

———————

Chance's reply to the questions of my previous letter arrived just as I was seeing my sisters-in-law out. It was all I could do not to hasten their departure in a way that might cause undue curiosity. As it was...

"You seem in rather a hurry all of a sudden," Ruth observed.

"Oh," I said, trying on a smile, wishing them down the street already, wishing them gone, "perhaps I am. You three have so well pointed out the virtues of my son I now feel the need to spend time with him myself."

It was a small lie, really, and one I hoped she would accept.

But what did it matter, since, having shut the door upon her and the others, I did not even waste time in seeking out a more private place to read, though a part of me said such a course of action would be wiser. Who cared if someone came upon me, saw me reading? Who cared if someone saw the expressions on my face? With my back pressed against the door, I was able to finally slit open the envelope and...

1. *You can picture me, because you know me without seeing me.*

2. *You think it is possible—probable? surely one of the two—we will meet one day, because all things* are *possible, as long as we draw breath. Was it not you who first brought up Mr. Shakespeare? Do you not remember your* Macbeth? *Macbeth thought he was in the clear, that Birnam Wood could not ever come to Dunsinane— what? a forest move?—but he was wrong. He thought, if only man not of woman born could slay him, then he was safe again; and again he was wrong. There is nothing you can dream up that is not possible; that is one thing I know for cold certain.*

3. *No, Emma, you are not insane. Not unless, when you picture us together in the flesh, when you picture us traveling together or*

picture your hand in mine, you fail to picture me naked and on top of you. Such an omission might signal an unsound mind.

Love,

Chance

P.S. Wishes may not in fact be horses, and so, we must make our own opportunity.

TWENTY-SIX

The pursuits that had previously occupied my spare hours now no longer felt open to me.

Needlepoint?

I no longer had the patience.

Music?

Let somebody else play.

My mind was caught in the gossamer of a web I was continually spinning. There seemed to be no way in which to free my feet from the sticky stuff that kept them from moving very far.

But that was all right:

I had no desire to be free.

It was my choice not to be free.

"Emma?"

"Yes?"

I was in our bedroom, in my nightclothes,

legs indecorously draped over the arm of a gentleman's chair, my naked feet tattooing their own dance in the air. I could scarcely be bothered to look up from my reading in order to see what it was John wanted from me.

Of late, I had taken to reading novels featuring heroines who bore the same name as I as if perchance therein might lie insight. But I was grasping at a thing not there. Flaubert's creation was even less self-aware than I, although I admired the author's practice at the art of leaving out, while Austen's was in the main too nice.

"Have you seen the book I was reading? I was sure I put it down around here somewhere."

"How should I know where it is? You are the one who placed it down."

He was quiet for a moment. "You have changed," he said.

Now, at that, I finally looked up. My words were sharp: "How do you mean?"

He looked at me, considering. "You did not used to be so abrupt with me. There was a time, I am almost certain, when you would have set down your own reading in order to help me search for mine."

"Are you not capable of searching for yourself?" I forced a smile I did not feel into the harshness of my words. "Are my eyes so very much better able to see?"

"I do not know about 'better' on their own, but formerly, you would not have minded adding yours to the aid of mine."

I put down my book with no small amount of peevishness. "Very well, John. If that is what you require."

"It is not a matter of what I require."

"Then *what*? For God's sake, what is it you want from me?"

"I just wanted my book, Emma. But it does not matter now. I no longer feel in the mood for reading."

———

I felt a movement inside me, like a phantom presence, reaching, stabbing all the way up into my womb.

It had become habit for me now—ritual, perhaps?—to imagine

myself with him before the rest of the household rose. I performed this ritual in the bathroom. It was not perhaps the most romantic place, but it was certainly the safest. There, I would read his letters over again, letters I knew were a mistake to keep.

What, after all, could I offer in explanation for the passion behind his words or the fact they were clearly intended for an auditor who welcomed their intimacy? What could I say, to explain the difference, both in handwriting and in content, between these and the letters I had hired Harry Baldwin to write?

No, there was nothing I could say in my own defense. They were what they were, naked, and still I would not give them up. Instead, I kept the best ones attached to the undersides of the drawers of my vanities, both in the bedroom and the bath. But there were getting to be too many of them; soon, I would need new hiding places.

Why did I feel the need to hide them in such a criminal fashion? Did I not trust my husband?

That is a strange question, difficult to answer.

Previously, I would have said I trusted my husband with everything. But I had come to learn that was false. I had not trusted him in the past. I had trusted neither him nor myself with my truest thoughts, not as I trusted Chance now.

Did I believe my husband capable of spying on me, of reading my correspondence without permission if, say, he were to come across a letter while looking in my escritoire for an extra pen?

Again, previously, I would have said no.

But now?

Now I often found myself, when my mind was not totally filled with Chance, thinking on that scientific mind of my husband's: how he liked to know things, how he liked to take apart the things he knew.

For safety's sake, even if it was a risky form of safety, I haunted the letter slot and, after several readings, carefully attached the letters to the undersides of the drawers. And so, in the still-dark hours of the mornings, I had Chance's words and, through my hands, his hands.

I wanted to place my fingers under his nose, invite him to sniff, tell him I had been thinking of him even before my mind knew I was awake.

As foolish as that was, perhaps, to lay myself open so bare to another human being in a letter, I could not keep it from him. I wanted him to know.

If he should turn away from me then, would it crush me?

Undoubtedly.

But the obverse of that coin, to continue on with what I was doing in oblivion, was also an impossibility. If he should turn away from me, then it would prove he was not what I wanted. And this I could not believe possible, not when I myself wanted him with a physical hunger that was greater than anything my body had ever felt before.

To confess the extremes of my passion was not enough, however. I did not want him merely to know how my body was affected; I wanted him to see into my mind, my heart, and my soul as well. To that end, I shared with him something I had come across in my recent readings. Perhaps it came from one of the Emma novels I had been reading, but I did not think so. Try as I could, I was unable to recall the source.

It did not matter. I wrote:

Do you know what the real definition of vertigo is?
It is not the fear of falling.
It is the fear of wanting to fall.

TWENTY-SEVEN

E mma!"

Waving a newspaper in the air, John stormed into the music room, where I had been seated at the piano, not playing.

"What is the meaning of this?" he demanded.

"What...?" I half rose from the bench, reached for the paper.

He snatched the newspaper back. I had never seen him so angry before. But then he must have changed his mind, for he thrust it at me, almost under my nose.

"Here," he said. "Read it. Then perhaps you can explain it to me."

It looked to be the start of a new serialized story in the local paper. The byline was Harry Baldwin. The story was called "A Caged Love."

"Dear Mrs. Stephen Jones,

   "It is still boring here. The food is still lousy. Sometimes, I get lonely for the outside world.

"Your Prisoner"

And Mrs. Stephen Jones wrote back:

"Dear My Prisoner,

   "I would do anything, if it were in my power, to relieve your boredom, satisfy your hunger, banish your loneliness.

"Mrs. Stephen Jones"

The next letter from Mrs. Jones's prisoner was exactly the same, but Mrs. Jones's reply was different.

"Dear My Prisoner,

   "I should like to send you something that will help to relieve your boredom. Perhaps you would like something from my undergarments . . ."

I had read enough.

   This was bad, very bad. How in the world was I going to explain this? Harry Baldwin had turned the task I had given him into a public farce.

   A farce! I thought, with an almost hysterical relief. Therein lay my answer.

   Surprising myself as much as John, I laughed. "You always said Mr. Baldwin was a hack," I said. "This confirms it." I tried to hand the pages back to him, dismissing the ridiculous matter, but he shook his head.

   "Who cares if he is a hack?" John asked, mystified. "What is he doing writing a story with a character called Your Prisoner, using the very lines you showed me in those letters?"

"Are they the same lines?" I glanced at them again, seemingly unconcerned. "No," I said finally, as though I'd puzzled through the problem and reached a satisfying conclusion, "I don't think so. I'm pretty sure *my* prisoner has a fondness for the ellipsis Mr. Baldwin lacks. I'm sure if I had kept the letters, you would realize they are very different."

"But the contents, Emma! The contents are virtually the same!"

"Are they?" I said again. "But why should that be surprising? After all, you are the one who is always saying there is no such thing in writing as an original idea; that anytime a writer thinks he *has* hit on an original idea, chances are at the very same moment there is a little man writing in China who has been struck by the same idea and the race is then on to see who will publish first."

Then I put my hand to my cheek, as though struck by a horrifying idea.

"Oh, dear," I said. "You don't suppose this is somehow the beginning of a prison novel Mr. Baldwin is writing, a possible rival for your own?"

"I can't imagine that hack could write anything good enough to rival a dog's scribblings," John said, "let alone mine. But you are clearly right: This is just some sort of bizarre coincidence. What else could it be? There is no way Baldwin could ever have seen Chance Wood's letters. And you, my dear, would never write anything as tawdry as this. Be that as it may, you are probably also right; the unfortunate Baldwin is trying to at last achieve success by writing some sort of bizarre allegorical tale about prisons. Who knows? Maybe he even fancies he can beat me to publication. Well, we shall see about *that*."

Now here was a new worry.

"Are you planning on paying Mr. Baldwin a visit," I asked, hoping I did not sound as nervous as I felt, "in order to confront him?"

I had a horrifying image of John seeking out Mr. Baldwin as I had done, questioning him until the chemist broke down and told him all. I knew it would not take much. Really, if John were to just offer him a few banknotes, that would be all it would take. And then... and then what?

John would come back to me, even angrier than he had been just a few minutes before. He would want to know why I had hired someone else, a veritable enemy of his, to write false letters, rather than showing him the real ones that still came.

And then...

"Oh, no," said John, smiling, "I would not give him the satisfaction. I plan to act as Apollo: I will strike from afar."

I suppose I should have asked more about what he had in mind, but I was so relieved to have averted disaster, at least for the moment, I counted my winnings and left it at that.

TWENTY-EIGHT

Will you be requiring anything** more at the moment, ladies?"

I was in Sommers Tea Room with Hettie Larwood, the coral wallpaper, overcrowded with French flowers and scrolls, giving me the start of a headache Hettie would no doubt finish. Our table was situated by a window, so if the conversation lagged at least I would be amused watching the world go by. It was already cool enough outside that my proximity to the glass gave me a chill, but it was somehow comforting to see autumn had reliably come, other people were still capable of getting themselves from here to there. Sometimes, it seemed not a wonder there was so much violence in the world, but that there was so little.

Tea and cakes had just been placed before us. I knew Hettie would never touch the cakes, and I, my mind nearly wholly preoccupied with imaginary events not in the room around me, imagining myself walking outside that window with Chance's hand in mine, was equally disinclined.

Hettie looked down her long nose at the tray of fruit tarts, macaroons, and fairy cakes, as if they were dangerous enemies against the Crown.

"Have you heard any news of Maeve lately?" I asked, hoping to avert one of Hettie's diatribes relating consumption to religion and the betterment of mankind.

"I did, as a matter of fact, just yesterday. I am sorry to report she is not looking well at all. Surprising, since she has had so much experience."

For once, I could not hold my tongue. "Perhaps it is that repeated experience that has tired her out. I do not think any of us would like to go through what she has. It is, after all is said and done, still her body."

"Why, what a peculiar idea!"

"Sometimes, it just seems as though we should have more say."

She looked at me piercingly. "You have very strange ideas. Still, if you must give voice to them, it is probably best that you do so with me. You would not wish the wrong people to hear you."

Before I could respond, she leaned forward, eyes unnaturally bright. When she did speak, despite her excitement, she kept her voice low.

"Did you not hear what happened at the Biltmores' the other night?"

I did know that some members of our mutual acquaintance had dined there Saturday last, but John and I, although invited, had not been among their number. Perhaps I should have forced myself to attend, given my concerns for Constance; and it was certainly a rare enough thing to be asked there. But Weston had been mildly feverish and I had pleaded off going. The real truth of the matter was that there were times when the continual social whirl became too tiresome for words. Now that there was Chance, I took such society to be a rude disruption of the interior world I shared with him.

"No, I have heard nothing," I said.

If a whisper could squeal with delight, Hettie somehow succeeded at it with her next utterance. "Constance got carried away!"

"How do you mean?"

"She did not eat enough at supper; I fear the wine went straight to her head."

I did not say anything at this. Maeve's tendency to overindulge may have been marked and yet gone unremarked, but this was the first I had heard of Constance traversing a similarly dangerous row.

"And that's not all," Hettie added. "After the men rejoined us, she was actually seen *flirting* with Captain Brimley!"

Captain Brimley? He was so feminine, that hardly seemed notable.

"I do not think Charles liked it one bit," Hettie continued. "In fact, I happen to know he did not."

"How can you be so sure?"

"Because he rather roughly hurried her from the room. I do not know that anyone else heard, but I happened to be leaving the room myself at that point, and heading in generally the same direction, and I overheard Constance say she did not care if Captain Brimley was not well thought of by the men; to her, his company was superior."

"And Charles?"

"Oh, I never saw him so furious before." Then she shrugged mildly, returning her attention to the teacup as though a stage curtain had abruptly been pulled on a performance.

"What did he do?" I demanded.

"Do? Why, nothing." She stirred a cup that no longer needed stirring. "He saw me then, didn't he? Dropped his grip on her wrist just as quick as you please." More useless stirring. "But I'll tell you what."

And here she leaned forward again, gleam back full force.

"It wouldn't surprise me one bit if Constance found herself on the way to the country very soon . . . nor if she stayed there a very long time."

I removed my cloak, took the ceramic pin out of my hat, tossed all three items onto the bench in the entry hall. Looking in the mirror above the bench, I attempted to set my unruly hair to rights. Glancing at the door, I saw the door text I'd made for our home, as was my duty as lady of the house, so many years before: "Thou, God, Seest Me."

On the way home, I had thought about how unfair Constance's fate seemed. Would we be invited out to visit after a certain amount of time? It would be good if we were.

An unfair fate, yes; and yet I cannot say it surprised me. After all, what else, I wondered ruefully, was there for a decent husband to do with a wife who had grown unruly? The Brontës might have shoved her away in some attic. At least, where Charles was taking her, she'd enjoy the fresh air.

I tried to tell myself that, at any rate.

And yet I could not help but feel a sense of uneasy guilt. If I had tried harder to talk to her. If I had somehow tried harder to get her to talk to me...

"Emma," said John, coming upon me, "I see you are back."

Still thinking of Constance, my answer was somewhat absent: "Yes."

"Did you *enjoy* Hettie's company?"

Hettie had previously been a joke between us, as married couples everywhere join forces to use the common thread of low-thinking about others to strengthen the bond between them. Knowing I had not been the best of company for him of late, seeing the lifeline of Hettie, I grabbed it.

"You know as well as I do," I said, "that 'Hettie' and 'enjoy' are two words that have never belonged in the same sentence together."

His smile made evident that after all these years he appreciated my wit.

He led me toward his library. "Come and talk with me for a moment."

This invitation was like something from our past. It seemed it had been a long time since he had casually sought out my conversation, a long time since I felt open to him. There had been a time, a once upon a time that now seemed so long ago, when it felt as though we talked of everything.

The somberness of thinking how just one small misstep had cost Constance her freedom made me realize how close by disaster always walked. And yet, I would not say it was fear that made me respond to my husband so. Rather, it was a wistful longing for a simpler time. And, in longing for it, somehow feeling freed to give in to it.

"Is there something in particular you wish to discuss?" I asked, with an earnest cheerfulness that should have triggered any trained ear into knowing that much of my tone of the past months had been false.

"Tell me, what gossip had Hettie today?"

I took a seat on a velvet sofa in the corner. "Surely, *that* cannot be what you wish to discuss!"

"Oh, but it is!" he answered, taking a seat across from me and leaning forward with no small show of eagerness, elbows on knees. "Tell me, what awful things had she to say about our mutual friends?"

"But this is so unlike you! And Hettie was too mean-spirited; her words do not bear repeating,"—I held up a hand to forestall any further pressure—"not even to you." Before he could speak again, I carried on. "Now *you* must tell *me* something: What has gotten into you?"

"Oh but this is like me now, my dear Emma. This is the new me."

"The new you?"

"Yes. And, as always, it is all your doing."

"*My* doing?"

He cocked a hand behind one ear. "Do we now have an echo in here? Yes, your doing. You did say I should start on a new novel, did you not?"

"Well, several weeks ago, I did say—"

"Yes, and it was excellent advice."

"Why then did you not heed it right away?"

"Because, my dear, sometimes it takes even a man of my superior intelligence a while to catch on to the sheer brilliance of an idea."

" 'Sheer brilliance'? I must say I do like that. But what does this all have to do with gossip and dreadful Hettie Larwood?"

"It is simply this."

Enchanted by his enthusiasm, as I waited in the midst of his dramatic pause, I was momentarily transported back to that earlier time in our relationship, a time when the future seemed all possibility and hope.

"I have selected the topic of my next book," he said, "and am ready to proceed. It is very different from anything I have done before."

"And what," I asked, still twinkling in the past, "is to be the topic?"

"Why, gossip, of course. I'm going to do a novel of social gossip."

I settled back in my seat, deflated. "If that is what you wish to do..." I was flabbergasted. "Why in the world would you want to do that?"

"Because it will be different? Because it will be a challenge unlike those I've set for myself before?" He shrugged, as if perhaps even he did not know his own mind. "I suppose it is that with the previous books, I have taken on single issues—war; prison reform—but this will offer me the chance to take things apart that are part of a far bigger canvas."

"Yes, I'm sure another novel of social gossip is exactly what the world needs."

"Oh, do not look so disappointed, Emma. It is a capital idea, as I'm sure you'll come to see in time. It was that serial of Harry Baldwin's in the paper that put me in mind of it."

I looked at the fish in the aquarium. Despite their comfortable surroundings, they looked to be doing none too well.

"How so?" I asked.

"I have been doing some thinking. You had said perhaps Baldwin was trying to write his own novel of prison reform, to rival mine, but I have concluded that is not the case."

"Oh?"

"I believe Baldwin is doing something about gossip, using the epistolary form as his device. And it is my intention, my dear, to get there first."

TWENTY-NINE

It would be a mistake to overidentify me with any one of my characters. While it is true there is a part of me in each of them—I, after all, create them; put the words in their mouths— they are none of them wholly me any more than I am wholly one of them. Unfortunately, people cannot ever be depended upon to keep the creator separate from the creation."

Thus spake John, at any rate.

How truly easy it had become to find fault, to pick at the stitches until the entire piece of needlework began to unravel.

———————

Sara Jamison first made me aware of this tendency on the part of human beings to, when in a state of wanting out of a marital relationship, look for fault to find in the other. Now, her words returned to devil me.

It had been two years previous. Since this was well before her resolution, Sara had helped herself to a clutch of biscuits.

"Did you hear Daisy Carter the other night at dinner?" she asked, the words coming out in a slight mumble around the remnants of food she had yet to swallow. Sara really did have the most revolting manners.

"No," I said. "What was I supposed to hear?"

"Why, her criticisms of Henry. It is one thing for women to criticize husbands when they are out of the room, but I heard her doing it"—she paused, leaning forward—*"while we were all still at table."*

"Perhaps she was only teasing. Wives will do that, you know."

"Oh," she sighed, settling back in her seat but not before grabbing another biscuit. "You are too kind. Sometimes I wonder if you can possibly be so naïve."

"What do you mean?"

"Why, it is obvious why Daisy can no longer leave off criticizing Henry, no matter who is there to hear her do so."

"And why is that?"

"She has taken a lover." More chewing, more talking around crumbs. "Or she means to."

"How do you know that? Has she said something to you about it?"

"I am the perfect confidante for anybody's secrets. But no," she admitted, "of course she didn't say anything to me. I know simply from observing her. In these matters, I have superior powers of observation."

"How impressive. I cannot say I knew this about you before— that you possess a talent for sniffing out adultery or would-be adultery."

"Nevertheless, it is true."

"It must be very convenient for you. I hope Paul knows of your talent. It would seem an unfair advantage goes to you if he does not."

"Do not worry about Paul. He knows better than to stray very far. But, back to Daisy, it is easy to see the way it is with her."

"And how is that?" I must say, she had piqued my interest.

Eagerly, Sara leaned forward, whispering, as if what she was about to divulge were some sort of priceless recipe someone might wish to steal.

"There are two very reliable ways to spot an unfaithful wife," she said.

I leaned forward to meet her now, playing my own part well.

"Yes," I whispered back, a coconspirator, "and they are...?"

"The first way is quite simple: If a woman only praises her husband, then you have very good cause to be suspicious. Well, except for you, of course, who has always done so, most women do not speak well of their husbands at all times. Oh, no. There must be a perfect balance struck."

"A balance?"

"Yes. Say on Monday you—well, no, on second thought, let's not use you; *you* are a very bad example." She thought for a moment. "Fine," she said at last. "Let us create an imaginary woman. We'll call her Mary."

"All right," I agreed.

"Let us say," Sara went on, "on Monday, Mary praises her husband in public for being a fine man of business. Let us say further on Tuesday, she tells you how ill he manages the household finances. Mary, you see, like most women, neither blindly praises her husband, nor does she shred him every chance she gets. Mary is obviously a faithful wife."

"I see," I said, even though I really did not see yet at all.

"The second way is when a woman who has had no problems striking a balance before begins to find fault with everything. The way he dresses is no longer right and his appearance is displeasing; he makes too little money, he makes too much but doesn't spend it or earn it properly; his voice grates, being either too loud or mousy soft; he is not attentive enough or he is smothering. In short, he is no longer right in any way, because he has become all wrong. And what is more, he cannot win. A new game has been set up all around him while he wasn't looking, he doesn't know the rules, no one is going to tell him the rules and, even if they did, he no longer possesses the requisite skills to win."

"The requisite skills being?"

"Being *the o—ther*. While you cannot truly fault a man for being what he is not, for that is in fact shaped by what he unavoidably is, the husband of an unfaithful wife is not the lover. He simply cannot win."

"Cannot it be that," I objected, "like Hettie, one of these women who only find fault is merely dissatisfied with the world in general? Must such a woman always be an example of a tigress on the prowl?"

"You do have a point about Hettie," she conceded. "But the formula works with almost everyone else."

"And that is how you tell an unfaithful wife?" I asked. "She is always either wholly one thing or another?"

Sara relaxed back onto the cushioned sofa, smiling, finally satisfied.

"*Ex—act—ly,*" she said.

———

I thought of Sara Jamison's words now, how she had claimed herself to be "the perfect confidante for anybody's secrets."

How I wished that were true!

How I longed for somebody, *anybody,* to talk to about Chance.

But who was there for me to tell?

The one person I might previously have gone to with a confidence—John—*Well,* I snorted, *he was out.*

And who else might there be? My sisters-in-law?

No.

Maeve? Hettie?

No and no.

Louisa?

God, no.

I had the feeling there might have been a time, a missed opportunity, when Constance and I might have become friends of a different sort from what we had previously been, the kind of friends that might actually speak the truth to each other from time to time.

But she was away, wherever Charles had sent her. She was no longer available to me and I had the sense she might never be again.

There was only one person who could help me, who could talk to me about my feelings for Chance, and that was Chance himself.

———

Chance wrote back:

> *So what of that?*
> *Fall, Emma.*
> *Fall.*
> *I will catch you.*

THIRTY

In my distress over Constance, in my general distress over everything, I went to see Lady Collins.

A servant led me to her in the conservatory, a bright room, the centerpiece of which was an elaborate birdcage, a miniature aviary with pagodas on a Japanesque stand.

"Emma!" She set down the book she had been reading, *The Emperor's Candlesticks,* by Baroness Orczy. "How lovely! When one gets to be as old as I, one is rarely fortunate enough to receive unexpected guests."

"I am sure that is not the case," I said, taking a seat close by her.

"You are very kind, my dear. But, tell me, what brings you here?"

"I am concerned about Constance," I said.

"Oh, I see," she said with some sadness. "Yes, I have heard of Constance's trouble."

"What do you make of it?" I could not stop myself from asking.

"Make of it? I am not sure what you mean."

"Do you think it is... right?"

She thought for a long moment. "No," she said finally, "it is not right."

Hearing that confirmation gave me an odd peace.

"What can be done about it?" I asked.

"Done?" she echoed. "I'm afraid there is nothing to be done. We must simply wait and hope the situation resolves itself to a happy conclusion."

"I see."

"I keep thinking the times have changed since I was a married woman, but then something like this happens, and I realize how far we have to go. But tell me," she brightened, "how has your resolution been progressing?"

I told her about the letter-writing with Chance. I did not tell her about the content of the letters.

"What a marvelous thing!" she exclaimed. "I am sure John is right, that your doing this is a great good. And you are very fortunate to have a husband who trusts you. Can you imagine any of the other men encouraging their wives so? Indeed, can you imagine Charles allowing poor Constance to engage in regular correspondence with anybody?"

Rather than answer her rhetorical question with a response that could only sadden us, I turned the conversation to an area of personal interest.

"Do you remember, Lady Collins, when Hollowgate Prison was built?"

"What a peculiar thing to ask! But yes, of course I remember it. It was meant to be some kind of wonderful thing, a place of reform."

"You make the building of the prison sound like a hopeful thing."

"It was, in a way. It is important for people to believe they can make positive changes in their times."

"And how has it turned out?"

"Oh." She looked less energetic now. "Well. Things that are started out hopefully have a nasty habit of turning out to be not so impressive in the end. You try to create something novel, only to realize you have created the same thing you had before with merely a different appearance."

I saw her stifle a yawn.

"I am sorry," I said, rising. "I do not wish to overstay my welcome."

"You can never do that, my dear, but I suppose I am tired now. Please do come again. I would like to hear more about how your progress at becoming a better person is going. It is so worthwhile, despite the odds against it, to seek to make positive change."

Her words recalled me to my original purpose and I saw clearly, as I said my good-byes and walked out the door, how far I had strayed from it. What would the world think if it could read the letters that passed between Chance and myself?

The walls would come down. In fear of what would be perceived as a cancer infecting us in turn infecting the whole around us, we would be excised.

Yet I could not give it up, could not give *him* up.

And, besides, even if my original intent had been to be a better person, and I had somehow strayed from that, I did indeed—I was certain of it!—make life better for *him*.

He certainly made life better for me.

Was there not some positive value in that?

THIRTY-ONE

Perhaps I could talk to Katherine," I had suggested to Ruth the day before, Lady Collins's words concerning the importance of the individual to make positive change still ringing in my ears as we watched Weston playing on the floor, absorbed in some game involving a wooden train. When asked the rules, he gave an explanation neither of us could understand, which caused him some exasperation. Secretly, I thought some of his games for which he claimed rules had indeed no rules.

She may not have quite sniffed, but only just barely.

"I did grow up mostly in the society of your brother," I pointed out. "And while I never became quite so, well, *grubby*"—even I winced over the word—"as Katherine, I do know something of the appeal of boys' games."

"I suppose...hmm...if you really think you might help..."

And so, I found myself on the last Thursday in November, freezing in the park beside my grubby grandniece, who did not appear to mind the frigid air in the slightest.

To say Katherine was grubby was no exaggeration. On the contrary, she was Perrault's Cinderella but without the air of a victim and with a decidedly boyish touch. Her long auburn hair was wild with lack of attention, her dress a mass of wrinkles and stains that almost prevented the viewer becoming aware of the fineness of its cut, the quality of its fabric. Her face bore its usual quantity of smudges from pursuits best not, based on past experience, queried about too closely. I did, however, suspect there might have been a garden toad or two involved.

She was tall, too, infuriatingly so, already besting me by a good head.

"I know Grandmother must have put you up to this," she said, striding manfully beside me as I drew my cape tighter. There was no longer a leaf remaining on a tree and the park had all the stark beauty the opposite of overripeness always presents. "So I will not hold whatever you may say against you, whatever those things you might say might be."

"That is very open-minded of you, if confusingly put," I said, careful not to smile at her earnestness. "Still, I shall endeavor not to give you too much cause for offense."

"I would appreciate that greatly." Her seriousness would not be dented. "I only wish Mother and Grandmother would be more careful."

"Well, Ruth and Diana do only have your best interests at heart."

"Now that, straight off, I cannot believe. They have their *own* best interests at heart."

"Do you honestly believe that is quite fair?"

She tossed her head. "Fair has nothing to do with anything from their viewpoint. Why, then, should it from mine?"

"Because," I suggested mildly, "you are perhaps a fairer person?"

"Well, that is true enough."

I placed a hand gently on her arm. My hand was quite cold, while her arm, even without the benefit of a cape over her dress, for she would not be bothered with one, was warm indeed.

"Why do you not tell me what is wrong?"

"Oh, Aunt Emma!" She groaned aloud. And, for once at least, she sounded like a young girl. "They do not want me to do *anything*! They do not want me to play with the boy who lives on the property next to ours. They say he is too inclined to do things involving toads"—I knew it!—"and that, after I play with him, my clothes always smell so."

"Do they have any other objections to him, aside from the toads?"

"Only that he is not a girl."

"Perhaps you could find a compromise: the boy minus the toads...?"

She gave this a long moment's thought. Then: "You mean because the smell would not give me away and I could then carry on with him?"

Rather than even risking a nod of the head, since I did not want to appear to be giving her license to disobey, I kept silent.

"Yes," she said, "I can see you are right. Sometimes it is better to let the other side believe they have won the battle. Then, while they are resting confident in their glory, you sneak in and win the war."

"Is there anything else wrong?" I prompted.

"They say Jonathan is to be the scholar in the family. They do not like it when I look at his things, in particular his books."

"Ah, I see."

"They say that when *I* look at his books, it somehow interferes with his ability to learn from them."

Jonathan, sweet enough but slow, was rather dim for a boy-child. Katherine, on the other hand, was brighter than any two boys I had ever met combined. He was bound to find her skills with his books intimidating to say the least.

But one should never look to be less bright.

Had my own parents had a son in addition to me, I might have been no better off than poor Maeve or Hettie, neither of whom had ever been known to pick up a book, unless of course it was to move someone else's out of the way so they might sit down.

"Is it my fault, Aunt Emma, that I am smart?"

"No, dear. Never blame yourself for that."

"Then what must I do?"

I sighed. I did not want to tell her to become less than herself. How awful must it be, I thought, for a girl as bright as Katherine to be compelled to play second in anything! It was just barely tolerable for her right now, I could see, while their five-year age difference held Jonathan at a lowly nine. But, as the years turned and he was groomed to assume his position as son and heir, whatever power she had by being the elder now would shrink as if it were nothing. Still, it was not in me to counsel her on a path of self-diminishment.

I grabbed her hands in mine. Even through my gloves, they were like ice. Apparently, the cold had finally caught up with her.

Looking her in the eye, I spoke with fervor: "Do nothing."

"But—"

"Do nothing differently, but go about your business as you have always done. There is absolutely nothing wrong with being an intelligent girl. Your light must not be made to grow dim merely so that your brother's may be perceived to burn more brightly by comparison."

"But Mother and Grandmother say...they keep saying..."

I had never seen Katherine, our most stalwart Katherine, at a loss for words. Yet now, she struggled to speak her mind.

"What is it?" I rubbed her hands. "What do they keep saying?"

It came out at last in a rush.

"...that it is my duty as a daughter; it is my role and I must accept it."

Duty!

There it was. There it always was.

I myself felt increasingly bound by the knots of my several duties. I had not necessarily marked them as I acquired them over the course of a lifetime. But I knew them all too well now. I had started with the one Katherine was experiencing: the strangulation of the duty of a daughter. But then it was possible Katherine, being Katherine, might escape the other two that yet held me. There was my duty as a wife and my duty as a mother. The way I looked at it, these days, as far as the world that thought it knew me was concerned, I was always an extension of others: Edward and Louisa's daughter, John's wife, Weston's mother. But I was starting to gag on it. The part of daughter—I felt I could not escape. I was born to it. Weston, on the other hand, well, I could not see ever wanting to escape that small, vulnerable demand.

On the other hand—or the third hand, really—there was John. Could not he get along without me?

But none of this thinking on my own troubles would help Katherine. And, dwelling on them, when there was no exit in sight, would probably only hurt me.

I hugged her to me, pressed my cool cheek against her soft, warm one.

"Duty is an overrated concept," I said gently, "one best left to knights and characters in books. Make your own path, Katherine. Let no one hinder you."

THIRTY-TWO

"What have you done, Aunt Emma?"

Diana flung her wrap at Timmins. Stunned for once, he folded it over his arm, disappearing into one of the shadows where I swore he lived.

Of all John's relatives, Diana was the prettiest, her blond hair worn in twisted coils down her back; her dark blue eyes more the color of a gemstone than anything made as part of a human being by nature. In her presence, one could never escape the feeling of having been gazed down upon by some Olympian judge…and found wanting. Her husband had petted her to the point where the only thing she was good for was pouting her full lips, as if there were a mathematical relationship between how far that lower lip went out and the likelihood of getting whatever she wanted.

Well, and there was also her talent for demanding whatever she wanted when that became necessary, of course. She was very good at that too.

"Would you like some tea?" I asked.

"What I would *like* is for you not to meddle in my family's affairs."

"What has Katherine done to displease you now? Has she caught some more toads? Got dirt stains on a pretty dress, perhaps?"

"Are you laughing at the situation, Aunt Emma?"

I said nothing, having not laughed at anything yet or even smiled.

"No, it is much worse than that," Diana said.

"Much worse? Please," I gestured to the sofa, taking a seat myself.

Were failure to sit not such a blatant act of rudeness, I suspect she would have remained standing in order to have that much more of an advantage over me. As it was, she rejected my implied offer of intimacy by seating herself at the far end, leaving me alone in the middle.

"What has Katherine done?" I prompted again.

"It is not what she has done."

"Oh?"

"It is what she *hasn't* done."

"Well, I did assume that, that being the only alternative."

She eyed me sharply, but with a small gleam of appreciation. "Do you know that you are sometimes an annoying woman, Aunt Emma?"

I could not hold back a smile. "Your uncle has commented so, many times, and under similar circumstances."

At that, she turned completely sour again. "No, Aunt Emma, they cannot have been *similar circumstances,* of that I am most certain."

"Very well, then. I'm happy to take you at your word on it."

"These *circumstances* are not light at all."

"No, I can see that they are not."

"Would you stop being so agreeable?" she nearly shouted.

"Yes," I spoke evenly. "Why don't you get to the point?"

"The *point is* that Katherine, of late, my fourteen-year-old daughter Katherine, has taken to walking around the house in... *clean clothes*."

"Oh, my! That is a dreadful situation!"

"Please take your hand away from your face, Aunt Emma. False horror does not suit you."

I said nothing.

"It is a dreadful situation," she went on. "I do not trust this new Katherine. Why, there was even a ribbon in her hair the other day."

This time, I kept my "oh, my" to myself.

"I know this does not seem like anything serious to you, but so far, all you have had to raise is one small boy."

"Do you have any idea why she might change so suddenly?"

"I thought, at first, it might have something to do with the boy next door, Martin. I thought perhaps she fancied him. They've known each other for ages. You, of all people, should know what that's like."

"And?" I prompted with terseness. A part of me, a very strong part, did not want to see Katherine's life take the same turn mine had.

But Diana did not seem to notice my mood's turn from light to dark.

"So I spoke with Martin's mother. She said they'd hardly seen Katherine at all lately."

I relaxed back into the sofa. "A dead end then," I said.

"It would appear so, yes."

She was silent for a moment.

I prompted her one last time. "What else do you think it might be?"

"*You*. Katherine was fine until you spoke with her. Well, no, she wasn't fine, but we did know what we had on our hands. But now..."

I did not think it fair to blame me for the changes in her child, but I could see little good would be served in saying so.

"What is it that worries you the most?" I asked.

"I think I am worried the most, silly as it sounds, of not knowing what to worry about."

"What do you want me to do? I have known you a long time. You did not come here today just to lay blame." A slight untruth.

"Make it as though whatever you said to her never happened."

"I do not know if I can ever do that," I said, "but I will take responsibility for her myself."

It was all I could do to keep myself from sighing with relief as I closed the door behind her. Of course I cared about Katherine; she was my favorite among all the nieces and nephews, the child of my heart; indeed, had Weston never been born, I would have undoubtedly continued to lavish attention on my grandniece to the point of embarrassment.

I should have, if nothing else, welcomed the diversion from my own obsession. But the truth was that I barely felt as though I could afford the charity of a thought diverted elsewhere.

A whole part of an afternoon when I had to divide my thoughts of Chance with thoughts of someone, *anyone,* else was quite enough.

I was so tempted to answer that inviting letter of his. I wanted to dare him:

Fine. Then catch me.

But that was not a letter I was ready to write.

THIRTY-THREE

Unwilling, unready, to let myself fall completely, I sought for something else to write Chance about. It occurred to me, while he had often pressed me for details of my own daily existence, he had spoken precious little of his own. Except for one reference to borrowing a book from the prison library and another reference to having little to do in prison but think, he had told me nothing. But when I tried to ask him what it was like, for the first time in a very long time I felt him shut a door in my face. He shut it gently, but he shut it just the same.

> *No. I will not tell you what it is like where I am. I would not want you to ever learn what it is like to be in here. I love you far too much to wish on you such awful knowledge.*

Perhaps I should have acceded to his wishes, but him saying no to me like that was a weird sort of encouragement, urging me on. If he thought my sensibilities too delicate for me to have knowledge of the baser side of human existence, he was wrong. Anything that had to do with his personal existence was something I wanted to know.

And yet, if he would not tell me, how was I to find out?

I waited until John was away from home for a bit and stole into his library. His desk was covered with research for his new novel of gossip, which I pushed aside in disgust. It was not what I was looking for; it did not interest me. I was sure, somewhere, he would have notes from his research at Hollowgate. Until the prison novel was finally published, he would keep everything so he could make last-minute changes.

Having found nothing on top, I began searching through the drawers of the desk. In the first drawer I opened, there was a notebook with a title on the cover: *The Experiment*. Perhaps this was it? But when I opened it, I saw it had entries, like a diary, the first one dated 1 January 1899. That wasn't it. John had started working on the prison novel long before that. The line of the first entry caught my attention: *A person can wait years for an opportunity—look for it, hope for it, work for it—and then, suddenly, serendipity drops just the perfect opportunity in one's lap....*

The words piqued my curiosity. What was John talking about here? But this was not what I had come for. And if I did not get on with the business I *had* come here for, John would return or Timmins would show up, and all my snooping would be for naught. I put the notebook back.

At last, in the second drawer, I found what I wanted. If I was going to get through it all, I was going to need to skim some of it.

John wrote: *Pre-Norman dungeons and strongrooms: brutality, corruption, thoughtlessness, neglect. Today: brutality, corruption, thoughtlessness, neglect!*

I sincerely hoped it was not so for Chance.

Benefit of clergy: immunity from death penalty for clergy. By 1600s, even women holding no clerical office were claiming it; abolished in 1827.

John wrote: *Are prisoners to be allowed no mercies?*

Early 1800s: men and women herded together in dungeons—gaol fever, smallpox rampant. To correct that, some prisons went solitary.

John wrote: *Being alone and insane is so much better than being in company and ill—ha!*

Statistics going back to 1857: Approximately 116 murders a year.

Chance had accounted for one of those. He was one in 116. But no: There could not be so many people like him.

Sir Edmund du Cane: introduced separate confinement. Work must be unpleasant, unconstructive; perhaps prisoner should pick oakum, uselessly unraveling old rope, or he might work the crank or treadwheel.

John wrote: *Solitude is more terrible for some than the more immediate pain of the whip. Prison creates criminals! It is a wonder they do not all go insane! Du Cane—the man was mad! All, including pretrial detainees, are treated the same, as though they are already guilty. Unfair madness!*

The Gladstone Report: 1895—Questioned the separate system of Sir Edmund: demanded more elasticity for individual prisoners. Committee recommended abolishment of unproductive labor. Books should be made more widely available. Oakum-picking should be used only as a last resort. The act was to go into effect in 1898.

I could picture John muttering as he wrote: *This is the dabbling of dilettantes! They worry about oakum-picking as if it is the thing in most need of change!* He agreed, at great length, with the report insofar as the system should be more elastic, but *they haven't moved quickly enough!*

The architecture of prisons: Most English prisons, Hollowgate among them, now built on the model plan of Millbank and Pentonville; at Pentonville, faces covered with masks when outside of cells. The layout is that of a giant starfish, the whole covering seven acres, with just over five hundred cells, the individual halls of the prison radiating from the center. Each hall is composed of several tiers of cells, the outer walls on one side, open balconies on the other. Each cell measures thirteen by seven by nine feet high, the walls being lime-whitened brickwork above a colored dado. The flooring is wood or stone. The window, high up in the outer wall and either heavily barred or formed by several small panes fixed in a steel sash, is opposite the door, a sliding panel letting in fresh air. Each cell has a plank bed, bedding, and mattress; a wooden stool; a corner washstand with enamel utensils; two wooden shelves. Sometimes, instead of a stool, there is a chair and wooden table. There is also a slate, pencil, and cleaning materials; the water closets are on the landings. There is a bell for emergencies. Between the main halls are the recreation grounds, the workshops, and the laundry. There is a Protestant church, sometimes a Roman Catholic chapel, and Jewish synagogue. There is a separate wing for women with only female officers. There are eight hours of labor and an hour of exercise.

And then there was a contradiction. In another part of John's notes, it mentioned Millbank resembling a six-pointed star. Which, then, did Chance reside in: a sprawling starfish or a six-pointed star? It seemed important to know.

Something about *Dickens and Thackeray watching a Swiss valet, François Courvoisier, swing.*

John wrote: *Secular reading should be available. It is not enough to place a Bible in every cell and overload them with religious tracts. Reading prevents crime! It is not enough to distribute the inevitable copy of* Robinson Crusoe. *With more educated people finding themselves in prison all the time, it must be recognized that certain temperaments require more than four walls and a Bible. Reading raises pride in a man!*

John wrote: *Too much done to the convict v. too much done for the convict. HOW DO YOU MORALLY REFORM THE AVERAGE CRIMINAL?*

How, I wondered, indeed?

I replaced everything in John's library exactly as I had found it, went to my bedroom, and wrote to Chance. I could now picture where he lived, what his daily life was like.

> *I understand prisons now have far better libraries than they previously had. I hope that alleviates the tedium somewhat. Have you read anything interesting lately? I do not like to think of you being bored...*

Chance wrote back:

> *Have you been doing* research, *Emma? Yes, there is a library here. When I am done with a book, I leave it at my cell door before going out to work; when I return, the schoolmaster has left another,*

preferably not one I had last time. I am sometimes allowed foreign-instruction books and I have read some French and Spanish. But usually the reading material is not so thrilling. One grows tired of reading Nicholson's "Carpentry."

But I do not want to talk about where I am. I would much rather talk about where you are . . .

THIRTY-FOUR

I wrote now with neither salutation nor signature:

> *I have a little riddle for you: What do you
> call it when you can't go forward and you can
> no longer go back?*

Chance responded in kind:

> *Us.*

So, if nothing else, we were of a single mind now.

———————

But even I, in my desperation to possess something that was unpossessable, if such a word ex-
ists, could not spend the entirety of my time
chasing after a chimera.

And so, having given my promise to Diana,
I began to spend more time in the company of
my grandniece Katherine.

"Do you really think," John said, as I finished preparations to go out, "a fourteen-year-old girl is the best companion for a woman of your years?"

I fixed the sash of the hat under my chin, trying not to bristle at the perceived censure in John's tone, when, I told myself, in reality, what he was probably doing was merely the same thing he was always doing: taking a thing apart to see what it was composed of.

"I do not know if she is the best companion for me," I said, willing to be saucy about it, "but when taken in comparison with the female members of *your* family, *I* am certainly the best companion for *her*."

"Very well, then." He smiled his indulgence, sobering an instant later. "But please, do not stay out too late. You know there was that unfortunate break-in recently at the Palmers'. I fear times are changing, even for us. I should not like to see you harmed in any way by those changes."

———————

"What would you like to do this afternoon?" Katherine kicked at the soft white powder that had accumulated on the walkway beneath our feet. I could see, through the puffs of breath that sent up smoke signals in front of her face as she spoke, that the tip of her nose was red.

"I do not know, Katherine." Something about the responsibility I now felt for my grandniece made me speak in more overly formal tones than I would normally have done.

"'I do not know, Katherine,'" she mimicked me. But there was no malice in it, and I had to join in her laughter.

"Very well, *Miss* Katherine," I said, "can you think of something you would particularly like to do?"

"*I* don't know." She kicked at the snow some more. "I suppose we could always go shopping for something like, say, *a hat*. I am sure if, later, I were to tell Mummy we had spent the afternoon doing *that, that* being the *that* about the *hat*," she giggled, "she would be most pleased with us."

"And is that what you would like to do most—please your mother?"

She made a face. "Who, Aunt Emma, do you think you are talking to?"

Then her features brightened as she gazed at something up ahead.

"What?" I asked.

"I *do* know what I want to do!"

"And that is?" I followed to where she was pointing. At the very end of her finger, it seemed, was the prison.

Hollowgate.

All of that brick, the color of dried blood. It was impossible to see over the walls of that fortresslike structure.

Once my initial horror passed, perspective shifted yet again, so now, instead of appearing to be right on top of us, the prison was returned to its proper position: about a hundred paces ahead.

"You want to go to prison?" I asked, my voice in my own ears an unwelcome mix of stridency and skepticism.

"No, I don't want to *go* to prison. Although, I must confess, it would be nice to get inside one of those places and see how things are really done."

"I highly doubt you would find it as 'nice' as you seem to think."

"Well, that is fine, since that is not what I was after."

"Then, what do you want?"

"Oh, I am not even entirely sure myself," she said, her forward steps drawing both of us onward. "But how will we know until we find out?"

With that, she took off, running on ahead.

I caught her up just outside the one forbidding door, the main entrance: massive oak; iron-bound. It felt as though a person could find oneself inside as a result of any one of a number of things, but that there was only one way one could ever get out.

"What can you be thinking of?" I asked, as she raised her fist to knock on the door as if it were merely someone's home.

"I want to see the inside," she said, excitement brightening her eyes, her color high. "Perhaps they will let us see the women's section. Would you not like to know how those poor wretches live?"

I found her curiosity unattractive and yet a part of me felt it too. But then, having gone through John's prison notes, I had some idea.

"This is not an *entertainment*," I admonished. "We cannot just knock and wait for the sentry to let us enter, with the hopes of satisfying our unfeminine curiosity."

Unused to being admonished by me, Katherine looked stung. But, before I could think what to do, the fortress door was pushed open and a woman emerged, crying, before the door was pulled to and locked again behind her. I would not normally make personal inquiries of a stranger, but it seemed I had never seen anyone more woebegone.

"Excuse me, miss," I said to the woman, who may have been a few years younger than me. "Can I help you with something?"

She looked up abruptly, tears making deep tracks in a face that may once have been pretty, before time and worry and life had gotten the better of her. Her hair, dull and lifeless, was a fright, like something birds would be at home in. For a moment, she looked as though she might be grateful for concern shown by another human being, but then bitterness settled hard onto her features.

"What can you do to help?" she demanded, as if somehow her situation were my fault. "My Jacob's in there,"—she pointed behind her, a movement like a stabbing—"and I'm stuck out here. I get to see him once every three months, 'cause that's all *they'll* allow."

"I imagine it must be very dreadful for you," I said.

"You can't imagine *nothing*," she spat. "I write to him, but he don't write back. Well, he can't write, can he? So I write to him for three months at a time, hoping someone in there reads him my letters, and then I get to come here, just once every three months, so we can talk. What kind of marriage is that, do you think?"

I shook my head. It sounded awful.

"I'm truly sorry," I said, thinking all the while on the inside about how much more fortunate I was than this woman. My life would never be like her life. Even if I could not visit him, as she was able to visit her own husband, at least the man I wrote to was able to write me back.

"Can you tell me something?" I asked.

She was surprised. "You want *me* to tell *you* something?"

"Yes," I said. "I cannot see inside the prison walls from here. Can you tell me: Is the prison shaped like a starfish or like a six-pointed star?"

Temporarily distracted from her own troubles, she peered at me with a certain down-looking satisfaction, as though I might be insane.

She slowly drew out each word: "It's...a...six-...pointed... star."

"Oh," I said, "how wonderful." Hastily, I reached into my reticule, extracted crumpled banknotes. "Please," I offered, as though making a tithe in church. "Perhaps you can get some more writing paper with it."

She glanced reluctantly at my hand for a moment, then seemed embarrassed. "Thank you, ma'am." She looked down as she used her raw hand to slip the notes from my gloved one, before moving away.

"Aunt Emma," Katherine said, calling me back to remembering that I had not been alone with the prisoner Jacob's wife, "why should it matter if the prison is in the shape of a starfish or if it is a six-pointed star?"

"Because," I said, speaking my thoughts aloud, "a six-pointed star is a more hopeful thing; you might imagine it in the sky or perched all shiny at the top of a tree, but a starfish is something you would find only at the bottom of the ocean."

"I'm afraid that Mother is right."

"And how is that?"

"In your own way, you are a peculiar woman."

I thought of her curiosity to see how the women inside the prison lived.

"Then we are a pair." I smiled.

THIRTY-FIVE

Once again, another year was nearing the end. This one had started out with my resolve to be "a better person." The very phrase now mocked me. And yet, there were times, when I was wholly in the present, in the way my mind seemed to connect with Chance's, twining around each other, I did feel better.

Katherine also made me feel better, in an out-of-breath, exhilarated kind of way.

Thinking on Constance, still away, did not make me feel better.

Christmas was yet two weeks hence, but there was snow on the ground, and the soft whiteness of it, in contrast to the strong gold and red and green decorations coming at one from all directions as one bustled past the shops, invited the wistful thought that an abundance of festivity could somehow heal.

I could have kept to the carriage the whole way, but I had sent it on, preferring to walk a bit. Despite the bracing chill, it was a good decision, for I got the chance to hear the carolers sing a hymn to Jesus outside the sweet shop.

Somehow, it seemed like a good omen.

———————

I was still removing my gloves in the foyer when Lucy handed me the post. When I saw the familiar handwriting, I dropped my gloves and the rest of the letters on the hall bench, retreating to the back parlor for some privacy. When I had come in the front door, I had been thinking how thirsty I was. But I forgot thirst now, forgot base comfort.

There was no salutation, the letter opening like an abrupt love-making. Well, for a long time now, such formalities had been only an occasional thing on both our parts. Odder was the absence of a loving signature.

Chance wrote:

> I have heard rumor that, in honor of the clean slate a new century holds forth, Queen Victoria has proposed to release some prisoners on a general pardon, those she feels pose no further threat to society at large. Apparently, Herbert John Gladstone, the chief Liberal whip, has placed this petition before her, claiming such a move would be in her best interests, that it would make her appear young, vital, progressive, *again*. But prisoners need a sponsor, someone who is willing to write Her Majesty on the prisoner's behalf. I cannot help but wonder if you, in turn, would be willing to petition her for me.

I remembered John's prison research notes and his referring to Gladstone's work in the area as the dabbling of dilettantes. What would he say of this new idea of the chief Liberal whip?

But that was a mere distraction.

The only time in my life I had ever experienced such an over-whelming change of fate had been upon learning I was pregnant with Weston. At the time, everyone assumed, "You must be so happy," as if there could only ever be a single emotional reaction to a thing. But I had spent nearly ten years living with the increasingly positive belief I would never have a child, had accepted this fate. And so, upon learning my fate had changed, I experienced almost every emotion imaginable: confusion, worry, even anger this had not happened earlier; relief, wonder, joy, and finally—blessedly—happiness.

This was like that in some ways.

I had been so certain, despite my day and night dreams, Chance and I could never meet, *would* never meet, I had never allowed myself the luxury of believing such a meeting might really happen.

And now the impossible had become possible!

Unlike the mixed emotions I had felt upon learning of my pregnancy, however, my emotions now were all on the positive side of the ledger: giddy disbelief, wonder, joy, all of it made possible by—best of all—hope.

If anyone could have seen me in that moment, they would have seen a woman with a smile so uncomplicated, a woman so overcome with elation, there were glittering tears in her eyes.

If anyone could have seen me in the next instant, they would have seen a contrastingly different display of emotion: suspicion, doubt, as I realized what Chance was asking me to do for him and the thought occurred to me for the first time:

Could it be possible that Chance had merely set out to use me?

THIRTY-SIX

Hard on the heels of that initial giddiness and first suspicion came a new thought: For so long, I had dreamed of Chance's release. And yet, now that the dream was a reality before me, how could I possibly act on it?

My life, for as long as I could remember at times, had been with my husband. To fantasize about a thing was one thing, but to actually have it happen? What would having Chance loose in the world do to my relationship with my husband? What would it do to my life? For, surely, once he was free, I could not resist the desire to see him, be with him.

And there came another thought, an ugly one, causing me to think myself very small-minded indeed: I had always imagined Chance, when I day- and night-dreamed about a life together, as being a handsome man, even if he had always been faceless in those imaginings. But what if the dream and reality failed to align?

What if Chance Wood was, in fact, a fat man? An ugly man? Would I still feel about him as I had formerly done?

Then I thought on his letters to me, all the many miles of words we had written between us, and I realized it did not matter a single bit what he looked like. If he was fat, I would still love him. If he was ugly, well, I would still love him that way too.

I returned again, reluctantly, to the notion that Chance had originally, somehow, set out to use me all along. Was such a thing possible? Could he have made up everything, most importantly his feelings, with a goal in sight?

I did not want to believe it.

I remembered the Arabian gentleman whom Hettie Larwood had brought to our table—it now seemed so very long ago—and how he spoke of being unable to give up his religion because of what he had invested in it, and I could not believe it.

Besides, he could not have forecast in advance that the queen would make her stunning century-turning decision.

As for the threat to my marriage, I was suddenly heedless of it. If it was possible for him to be free—*Chance free!*—for me to finally be with him, I could not stop myself from reaching now for that dream.

And so, the following day, for the first time believing the impossible might be possible, I took out my sketchpad. It had been some months since I had felt moved to draw anything, not even for Weston's amusement, but now I had a specific object in mind.

Women of my age and class were expected to have *accomplishments*—indeed, it was one of the ways that, when we were younger, we were judged in terms of suitability for marriage—but I, much to Louisa's everlasting chagrin and Father's amusement, was sadly lacking on most of refinement's fronts. True, no one ever asked me to sing more quietly in church, and Weston was sure my voice was the sweetest in all creation, but, with an off-key note here and there, no one ever asked me to sing louder either. And, while we did keep a piano for the entertainment of any company in the music room, Weston was the only one foolish enough to regularly entreat me to play. It is one of the most peculiar joys of having a child that one's voice is elevated to that of an angel of God; one's instrumental capacity, no matter how ploddingly rudimentary, raised to pitch-perfect status.

I could not do needlework very well either, but I did try regularly, since it was expected.

But I could draw. The one thing I could do was pencil sketches that showed both a precision of hand and a wealth of imagination, since I was equally adept at rendering what was in fact in the physical world before me or whatever I might conjure up in my own mind.

That vase on that table? I could have it done for you in seconds. A griffin? Done with equal ease. Even if I did not know the exact description of the mythic beast, just the word would be sufficient for me to put down on paper something that would satisfy the picture you had of it in your own mind's eye.

Now, as I sat in a corset-backed chair before my easel, the December sun streamed in from behind. I had set up my easel in the long corridor, facing the solid wall of midnight so that the sun would not blind me, so that all I faced was blank wall, nothing to disturb or influence inspiration. What I had not counted on was that the sun at my back, coming straight through the long wall of windows as it did, would make the heat behind me feel like the hottest of August.

I shrugged off my sense of a place too warm.

My object was to draw Chance as near as possible to what I imagined him to be. *If—when?—I finally set eyes on him for the first time,* I wondered as I sketched furiously, *will reality blend into line with my creation?*

I sketched, trying to push down thought, not wanting to examine thoughts I knew lay just beneath the surface. Did I really and truly *want* him free? An odd question, that. But everything that had gone before had been possible, to my way of thinking, due to one solid assumption: He was never going to be free. It was safe to say to him what I wanted, explore with him what I wanted, it was safe to let another human being talk to me in ways I wanted to be talked to and explored in ways no one had before, *only* because I knew we were never going to see each other.

But what now?

I pushed thought down, continued sketching.

Considering that I had been thinking on this subject for nearly a year now, it took relatively few minutes for me to pencil something I found to be acceptably true.

I studied my work, recognizing at once that I had drawn Chance exactly as I wanted him to be.

"It is a handsome drawing," said John, startling me out of my reverie, blocking the light.

There had been a time, many times, when we had gone on picnics together and other outings, times that were as recent as just two years past. John would work, occasionally glancing up with a word of praise about whatever I was drawing. Now his words of praise were as gall and wormwood to me.

John tilted his head at a slight angle, considering. "He looks rather like you," he said. "A much larger, much more masculine you to be sure, but you all the same. Still, I like it. Who is he meant to be?"

"He is no one," I lied, the prevarication costing me much, "just someone I made up in my head."

"So you say. But he looks so much like you," John pressed, studying the drawing more closely. "Is he another, darker side of yourself, perhaps, something I've never seen?"

To this, I had no answer.

I wrote Chance about a major concern I had:

> *Do you really think it will be allowed for a woman to sponsor the release of a male prisoner?*

And Chance wrote back, turning the major into the minor:

> *You have lived with your husband for how many years? Surely, you can now copy his hand so that no one could ever tell the difference.*

It turned out Chance was right. Previously, I had hired Harry Baldwin to write those letters, because I could not disguise my hand enough to fool my husband. But I could, I discovered now with practice, impersonate my husband's hand well enough to fool someone else.

I studied the handiwork of my signature before folding the letter—*John Smith*—and concluded it was good.

THIRTY-SEVEN

I wondered about the turn of previous centuries. Had there similarly been this feeling of standing on the edge of monumental change, as though one single turn of the earth, one single tick of the clock, would tumble all over into a world drastically different from the world that had been there just a second before?

There were those who predicted that with the turning of the twin nines of the present year to double aughts, all hell would break loose. Most, however, just thought it a grand excuse for a party even bigger than the queen's Diamond Jubilee. Regardless of where one stood on the matter—thinking hell was inevitable or that the party was going to be heaven on Earth—it was impossible to remain indifferent or apart; for, should one try to do so, one or both factions would surely pull one back in.

As for the queen's own recent behavior, the general public was divided on that as well. Some thought it admirable, though they sincerely hoped none of the prisoners, upon release, settled near them. The other half merely laughed behind their hands. What need, they asked, had a monarch who had straddled the throne for sixty-three years to attempt to appear young, vital, progressive? At this point, if Her Majesty wanted to literally take everyone's heads off, there were few who would be inclined to stop her.

John himself thought it the height of folly.

"What can she possibly hope to gain by this?" he asked.

We were in his library, having just put Weston to sleep and having finished a light dinner, a dinner I had been unable to eat, despite the fact that Cook, at John's encouragement, had prepared my favorite things. There was a small fire going, but it was insufficient to warm me.

"Whatever can you mean?" I countered. "Isn't it you who is always talking about how many possibly innocent men you met during the course of your prison visits? Have you changed your mind on that?"

"No, not at all. But opening up the gates and just letting prisoners leave willy-nilly, based on whether or not they have received some kind of sponsorship, is hardly a sound basis for reforming the system."

"Oh? And how would you go about it?"

"Well, to begin with, I would not have committed to the prisons those who do not belong there in the first place."

"It must be nice," I could not resist observing, "to always be confident one would choose rightly given any set of circumstances."

"Yes, Emma,"—he spoke with a rather insufferable smugness—"it is."

"Very well, then. Let us imagine you do not control all of the strings from beginning to end in this hypothetical juridical universe."

"My, but you are determined that we have an intelligent discussion tonight, aren't you?"

"But then let us suppose that—abracadabra!—you are suddenly queen." And here I flourished my hands in the air.

"Oh my." He laughed. "You are bestowing large favors tonight."

I reflected on how there had once been a time when his words would have charmed me, when I would have basked in the glow of his good-natured appreciation, evidence of a high regard. And even now, looking at how the fire warmed his features, I could see we were good together in our own way. I could see mind interlocking with mind to form a single piece.

But where was the heat I felt with Chance? With Chance, there was real passion, a different kind of interlocking. With John, however good some of our moments might be, it was a mental exercise, coldly executed.

I shook off that ill humor.

"Imagine you are queen," I said, "and you find yourself armed with the knowledge that, in your own prisons, there are those who do not belong there. Now, then: What do you do?"

I was truly curious. I did so want to know what John, with all his ideals concerning prison reform, would do if he had the power.

"Nothing," he said.

"What?"

"Nothing. I do nothing."

"But I don't understand."

"Well, I'm certainly not going to just start letting people out, now, am I? After all, unless I am willing to see the country go to the time and expense of having each case retried, and having them retried in a just fashion, I cannot know who is truly guilty or who is innocent. To simply start freeing people runs the risk that the wrong people would be set free."

"So, then, you would keep innocent people imprisoned alongside the guilty because it is more convenient to do so?"

"That is a hard way to put it, but yes, that is exactly what I mean. We all have to pay certain prices, Emma, to ensure the solidity of the society we have created."

"Perhaps. Although, I must say, I do not see that it is ever you who is paying the price."

––––––––––

Chance wrote:

I can offer you nothing upon my release. But I do not want you to run away from me. Not like you did before, when you tried to take your heart back.

In the final analysis, it did not matter what John thought he would do in her position, for the queen, as part of her fin de siècle celebration, released select prisoners, among whom numbered the one I—acting as my husband—had sponsored.

———————

By the time Chance was finally released from Hollowgate, it was I who was in a prison, one of my own making.

THIRTY-EIGHT

We were thirty-two for Christmas dinner that year.

Well, thirty-two adults, that is, including my parents, plus the small children, plus Katherine. The children would eat their dinner crowded into Weston's nursery, rejoining us afterward. Katherine, caught between worlds, would dine with us. Her mother had wished it otherwise, but it was my home and my choice. Katherine looked so charming in her sapphire silk dress, the color creating a strong impression when combined with that flame of hair; so mature, really, I wondered how Diana could dress her so and then try to force her back down with the children.

The tree was the tallest we had ever had. Adorning it were cotton-batting ornaments with fruits, vegetables, Santas, and angels, sprinkled with sparkles of ground glass and mica—they looked as if they'd just come in from the snow. There were also several Dresdens—miniature cardboard ornaments made in Germany, embossed in silver and gold in the shapes of schools of fish, steamboats.

Spirits were running high in general with everyone enjoying the feast, looking forward to the parlor games that would be played later. For myself, I found the turkey tough, the pudding cold, the sweet too sweet. John, on the other side of a silver epergne displaying holly for the season, took obvious pleasure in carving whatever he was carving, expounding on the writing life to Ruth's husband, Joseph Lowry, as he did so.

When John had first taken up novel-writing, none of his family was supportive. All that changed, of course, with the meteoric rising of John's success. Now they were eager to hear everything he had to say on the subject. It was as though he were a palace pet who had been trained to do some extraordinary trick no one else could quite under-stand the workings of. And John, a human being and thus no stranger to the call of vanity, was happy to oblige them with discussions of his craft.

"Over the years," John informed a rapt Joseph and company now, "I've changed the way I do things. In the beginning, I used to write my novels straight through, sequentially, event following upon event. But I found myself growing stale."

"So what do you do differently?" Joseph asked, accepting a serv-ing of vegetables from one of the extra help we'd brought in for the occasion.

"Oh, I still start at the beginning." John paused, listened. "What is that noise?" He looked down the table at me and the others fol-lowed his lead. "Emma, are you tapping your foot?"

Until he said something, I had not realized that was exactly what I had been doing: tapping my foot, impatiently, wishing the minutes away, wishing time to speed up so that the moment of Chance's release might finally be here.

Blushing now, I shrugged.

Shaking off his annoyance with me, John turned back to Joseph. "As I was saying, I still start at the beginning. But as soon as I know how it is to start, then I immediately write the ending."

"How strange," said Peter Newcombe, Victoria's husband.

"Not really," said John. "After all, it is not the same effect if the writer knows the ending as it would be if the other crucial partner in the compact, the reader, did. For the latter, such knowledge would be a spoiler."

"And for the former?" prompted Luke Osborne, Elizabeth's husband.

"Oh," John spoke with relish, "that puts me at the kind of advantage I most enjoy. I have set up the target, I know where the bull's-eye is because I myself have placed it there, the mark remaining fixed from the very start, and all I need do is find a way to make all my arrows fly for that red center. After I've loosed them, they can arc in all kinds of different directions, so long as they ultimately find their way home."

"And you feel as though you have control of the whole enterprise the entire time?" pressed Joseph.

"Oh, yes," said John, at last sitting down himself and raising a glass to toast the assembly. "To control." He looked directly at me, seated all the way down the table from him, and raised his glass just a hair higher. "To total control."

———————

"John has been reluctant to discuss the subject of his new book with anyone," Ruth observed after dinner as we watched the children play with the few trinkets they had been allowed to open. By "anyone," I knew she meant Joseph, that Joseph must surely be frustrated, and that he had pressed Ruth into service as his spy. "Has he even told *you* about it?" she asked, as though the implicit taunt in her words might draw me out.

"Of course he has," I said, smoothing out my skirts. "But you know your brother's habits. He will not discuss the specifics of the manuscript itself until it is published."

"Can you not give us the barest hint of a hint?" wheedled Elizabeth.

"Very well," I said. "I suppose it cannot hurt you to know that the subject matter he has chosen to tackle this time is gossip."

"Gossip?" asked Victoria. "What about gossip?"

"I am afraid," I said, "I have already summed up all I know."

"Surely Uncle John tells you more than that," said Diana.

I ignored her. "Katherine," I called.

She looked up from where she had been helping her younger twin cousins, Sophia and Sally, figure out the charms of a nutcracker.

"Come and talk to me," I said, rising up from the sofa.

I waited for Diana's objection as I watched Katherine walk toward me, but Diana must have felt the need to remain on her best behavior, even if we were family.

"Did you enjoy eating dinner with us this year?" I asked.

"Very much so," Katherine answered. "It is a nice change from watching the others fight over who is to be served first, who has received the most dessert, and who is really the oldest."

"They fight over who is the oldest?" I laughed as we exited the room.

Linking arms, we slowly walked the length of the black-and-white-tiled corridor, with its many windows to our left side. Even this area had not escaped Lucy's decorative excesses, urged on by John's holiday zeal—the two really were quite a pair, when it came to such things. We had no destination, but were merely promenading, as we might have done outside had it been daytime and warm.

"Yes," answered Katherine. "The two oldest boys argue about that every year. Sometimes," she admitted, "in the days when I still ate with them"—as if that were so long ago!—"I joined in."

I laughed. "How strange. I thought only old women played that game."

We were interrupted by the sound of running feet.

"Mummy!" Weston exclaimed, coming to a stop, the color high on his cheeks, his breath quick.

"Slow down." I put a hand on his arm. "What is so exciting?"

"Grandmother said if I come stay with them for a while, she will *even* see the servants take me skating!"

I felt a vague sense of unease, a cold hand reaching out for my heart.

"I'm sure such a trip would be wonderful," I said, faltering, "but you cannot leave us now."

"But why ever not?"

"Because it is too close to the New Year." I forced a bright smile. "How can I possibly face the new century alone without my best boy?"

Thankfully, he did not point out that I would not be alone; I would be with my husband. Instead, showing that rare depth of compassion young children sometimes possess, he placed a reassuring small hand on my arm.

"Of course, you are right," he spoke with grave seriousness. "I could not leave you alone on such an important occasion."

Then, turning from graveness to instant sunniness, also with the mercurial nature of small children, he exclaimed, "I'm going to go see what sweets are left!" And he scampered merrily away.

I turned to my grandniece.

In the warm glow given off from the flames of the red and green holiday candles in their gilded sconces, Katherine cut a rather adult figure. In such lighting, and in her sapphire-colored silk dress, it was easy to mistake her for a young woman far older than her years. The light shimmering in her eyes, off her hair, she was possibility itself.

I wondered what her future would bring.

"I cannot believe you told them all about it," accused John, flinging his tie across the bedroom we shared.

"I told them nothing of any importance," I said, unwilling to be cowed.

"Then why did Joseph press me for details of what gossip might be contained in my new book? Can you answer me that?"

I may not have been tall, but I made the most of what I had.

"They are *your* family," I pointed out. "Surely, by now, you must be aware of how, well, *relentless* they can be."

"Yes, it is true, they have been relentless since the beginning of memory. But," he pointed out, "you have never before shown signs of being willing to be swayed by them. Or by anyone else, for that matter."

I couldn't very well point out that I no longer cared, and that this was why I had revealed as much as I had to his sisters, now, could I?

"Perhaps they just overwhelmed me," I sighed.

There had been a time when I had thought John and I so well

suited to each other. In many ways, I thought, I was the only woman who was intelligent enough for him. But I had come to learn that, in John's eyes, "my husband" = "the man who takes care of me," while "my wife" = "my possession." I no longer wanted to be possessed, unless it was my choice to be so.

THIRTY-NINE

31 December 1899

It was almost the new century.

In the previous year, a lot had happened, as Joshua Collins would no doubt tell me were I to attend his annual New Year's party. As John would no doubt inform one and all, the writers and artists had made their share of contributions as well.

But did I really want to attend Joshua's annual party?

Of course, I kept forgetting that with Maeve's advancing condition, the location for the annual gathering would be moved to a new venue: the Larwoods' austere table. Joshua, not one to sit home and hold his wife's hand through any of her confinements, would no doubt be there. Regardless of venue or guests present, did I really want to attend anybody's holiday party this year?

I would rather die first.

I wanted to spend this last night of the year, this last night of the century, thinking of what the morrow would bring.

I had not, of course, told John of Chance's impending release. And, as he was no longer going to the prison, caught up as he was with his new race to beat Harry Baldwin to the publishing finish line, there was little chance he would learn of it. True, he would probably notice, via Timmins's ever watchful eye, that there was no longer a steady trickle of letters between me and the prisoner he had arranged for me to correspond with. But I had an answer prepared against the moment when his inquisitive mind might question me about it.

I would tell him a year was quite a long time for one to work at becoming a better person; that, in my case, I thought it had been going on long enough. I would lie through my teeth and say the prisoner and I no longer had anything to add to the dialogue between us.

Perhaps it would be enough. Perhaps John would attribute it to the flighty inconstancy that is woman, the whim to take up a cause and leave it just as abruptly. I did not see it as presenting any great problem. I only knew that this year, of all years, I did not feel up to merriment.

In truth, I had become, even to myself, somewhat blurry around the edges. It was as though I had been drawn in pastels and then someone else had come along with an eraser, smudging the outline between me and the concrete world.

Between worlds—that was where I was—waiting for one century to tick over into the next, so that my old life could end and, with a single release, my new life begin.

"I do not feel well," I told my husband, when he came upon me in front of my vanity and inquired as to why I was not dressed yet. "I am not feeling quite myself this evening."

His face showed concern. "Do you wish me to call the doctor?"

"Oh, no. I am sure all I need is a little rest. You know, each year the holidays seem to absorb so much more energy. I think just a little time apart from everybody is what I need." I had a sudden inspiration. "You could go yourself," I suggested brightly.

"Oh, no," he declined. "I could never do that."

He seated himself on the edge of the bed behind me, watching me in the mirror as he removed his coat.

"Very well," he said, removing his tie as well. "If we are to stay in and be homebodies, what shall we do to amuse ourselves?" He rose and took a few steps forward, filling the mirror behind me, as he placed one hand on my shoulder. "It is, after all, a significant New Year."

Well, I might have supposed it would come down to this, I thought, keeping my mind and body separate as the latter endured the piston thrust of my husband as he moved above me, his eyes shut on some experience wholly different in every way from what I was experiencing.

I did not want my body to be there, promised myself that, somehow, this would be the last time.

But tonight it had been unavoidable. True, having pled myself too sickly to go to the party, I should have been able to escape this as well. But avoidance would have meant being required to keep John conversationally satisfied all night, and that I could not do.

I marveled that there had been a time when I fancied I enjoyed these couplings, even when there had also been times when things had been a little stale. Was it possible my feelings could have changed so, the feelings of nearly half a lifetime, after one relatively short year?

Oh but they had changed.

How I longed to have the person above me be he whom I had never seen before. How I longed to know what that would be like. Would I feel differently, were I to be performing this same act with a different man?

My mind wanted to be in the next year already, did not want to be where it still was, and anything that kept me there was an agony. It had taken all of my resources when, earlier, over a light supper John had asked Timmins to bring up to our room, he insisted we play the resolution game.

"Come," he had said, tilting his wineglass at me when I tried to demur, "if we were out this evening you would. Feeling slightly ill is no excuse for a weakness of resolve," he added, his own pleasure in his play on words evident.

"Very well, then," I said. "But why don't you go first?"

"All right." He set his glass down, reached for my hand. "I know that, in the last year, I have been too preoccupied. I have not lived up to my resolution of last year. Therefore, I hereby resolve to redouble my efforts to make my wife the happiest woman in the world. In short, my dear, I am stealing your resolution from last year: I *will* be a better person."

I was touched by his words, but surely not in any way he could have imagined. They frightened me, taunting me with their abject goodness.

Of course, no evening could be complete, certainly not such a momentous one, without a lesson from my husband.

"I have been doing some research into this wonderful thing we have each year, the New Year. Did you know, my dear..."

I did not, I thought, nor did I care, my mind retreating from his wearying recitation on the history of New Year's, returning only as he was finishing up with...

"And on the previous turn of the century, when 1799 became 1800, no less than Josephine Bonaparte wrote that for two whole years the fortune-tellers in France had been making predictions. And, you know, Josephine set great store by fortune-tellers, given that one did predict, after all, that she would one day both lose a husband and be queen."

"How fascinating," I said, hoping his sharp eye did not catch my yawn.

"Do you not see, Emma? Historically speaking, people have superstitiously believed the dawning of a New Year brings with it momentous change; a new century, even more. God knows what people will do at the next millennium."

"So, you are saying people are superstitious and silly?"

"No. I am saying they are *right*." There was a gleam in his eye. "When we wake up tomorrow morning, everything will look the same and yet nothing will be. But it is only with the passage of time that later generations will look back and mark just how great those changes were. Of course, it is all ironic," he went on with a shrug, "since in truth the first day of the new century, its turning, will not technically occur until 1901."

I could not conceal a second yawn.

"I am sorry, my dear. I am tiring you." He raised his glass again. "And you never did say: What is your resolution to be?"

Reflecting on the goodness of his resolution, and my inability to match it in kind, I did the only thing I could do:

I seduced my own husband.

"Are you sure?" he asked, with the appearance of sensitivity, but more out of form, I suspected, as he initially rose above me.

But it was a way to avoid having to speak myself, having to commit to a single path.

In my own mind, however, I did wonder at what my resolve might be. There was still time to change, I told myself, time to switch everything around so my prospects lay in a different direction than the one I had set myself on. Would I do it? Could I do it? After all, I had a whole life here, a life that had taken me, well, a *lifetime* to build. Surely, I would not risk throwing that all away—throwing *Weston* away—for something that felt to be as great a part of creation, of imagination, as it was of reality.

Would I?

As my husband continued to thrust into me, I did something I had never allowed myself to do before: I pretended he was someone else.

Once Chance was free, what would my life become? When would we first be together? How often? What would it be like?

I couldn't even imagine.

———————

Later, as John was drifting off to sleep, he drowsily asked one last time, rolling over: "You never did say: What is your resolution for the New Year, the new century?"

"Never mind that now." I patted his shoulder. "Sleep."

I rolled over in the other direction.

Tomorrow, the prisoners would be freed.

FORTY

It was a month since his release and I had not heard from him. But the silence had not stopped me from thinking about him, had not halted expectation.

———————

My dress was purple with cranberry and emerald flowers, and a swirly vinelike design throughout in a deeper shade of purple so dark as to nearly be blue. The garnet of my earbobs brought out the cranberry in the dress.

I had lost weight, so much so that my dress now hung on me, but I had not previously noticed how great was the loss. I had somehow reconvinced myself I was still eating the same as always, despite John's comments, despite John's insistence Cook only prepare the things I liked best.

I saw John depart in the carriage, taking

little note of how damp I was getting as I watched him pull away in the rain.

Did I sense, even then, I would somehow be safer on this night if he remained?

John was on his way to a meeting with his editor. While his editor resided on an estate only miles distant, they had built up a custom, when a manuscript needed more than usual attention, of working through the night. The final points of the prison manuscript were now ready to be gone over and John had said I should not look for him until, at the very earliest, late in the afternoon of the following day.

"I am not sure what more Connor can add to the subject at this point," he said, referring to his editor by given name.

In point of fact, John always did say his editor was as much an architect of his creations as he was the shepherd that guided them.

"And do try to eat something, dearest" were John's last words to me. "You've grown frightfully thin."

I did not know whether to be touched or irritated at his repeated concern.

As I reentered the house, Timmins glanced meaningfully at the outline my damp dress made of my figure.

"Madam," he spoke, "you will catch your death of cold." He paused, pursing his lips, before adding, "If you do not put on more clothes."

Could he know something?

"Of course, you are right as always, Timmins." I laughed. "Although there are times when, it seems to me, you are worse than Nanny."

As I closed the bedroom door behind me, a man emerged from the shadows. Surprisingly, I did not start at this. Although I had never seen him before, immediately I knew it was him.

How long I had waited for this!

And yet, how strange he looked in my bedroom. It was almost as though one had come upon a painting one had looked at day after day, year after year, to discover that another artist had stolen in like a thief in the night, only this time, the thief had added something rather than taking something away, added to a previously pastoral scene an indelible figure that no amount of turpentine could ever remove.

Where there used to just be my large bedroom, with its fireplace, heavy draperies, and French windows, there *he* was; where there used to be my vanity, chair, and full-length mirror, there *he* was; where there used to be my armoire, writing desk, and four-poster bed, there *he* was—and would now forever remain, I well knew, no matter what I might do to try to eradicate his memory from my surroundings.

How different this room would now be for me forever. It was as though he took up all the space of any room he was in, erasing everything else.

It was particularly strange to see him standing there not far from my writing desk, the place from where I had written him so many times, only able to guess at what my correspondent might look like.

Still, somehow, despite the strangeness of it, the intrusion of it, it was just as I had imagined it, so many times.

"How did you get in here?" I asked, but then I saw the open French door.

"My husband—" I began again, but he cut me off.

"—is not coming back for hours. I heard you see him off in his carriage."

Somehow, I had expected a darker man, but the size of him was as I had imagined. Somehow, perversely, I had expected him to be a male version of myself, only substantially larger, with dark hair and eyes, pale skin.

Well, I had gotten the substantially larger part right, at any rate.

Was he taller than John? I could not tell. Perhaps not. Certainly, he was broader, the hint of a muscular form beneath his clothes that John's own patrician form would never be a match for.

Without realizing I had done so, I had moved across the room, coming to stand beside him near the open window.

I could see his features clearly now: an abundance of brown hair thicker than the fashionable norm, hazel eyes beneath brows that had a slight sardonic arch, proud cheekbones, determined jaw, generous lips surrounding teeth whose only flaw was a slight gap between the front two. Involuntarily, I reached a single finger toward those lips.

He slammed me against the wall so hard it raised a lump, but, even startled as I was at the abruptness of his action, I didn't notice it at the time, nor would I have done the next day had not John, pausing to caress my head on his way out, remarked upon it.

I wore neither corset nor extra skirts beneath my thin dress. What would have been the point any longer? I was ready. Nowadays I was always ready.

He pushed up my dress.

"You surprise me," he said, commenting on my lack of skirts. Brusquely, he pushed my lone undergarment aside. "Perhaps next time, you will not even wear this?"

I felt his hands beneath my thighs. For the briefest second, I thought he might use his fingers to see if I was ready, but he did not. And why would he? He must have known, as he lifted me upward and onto him, that I wanted this as much as he did; that in my anxiousness to live this moment, I was living it too quickly, moving through it too fast, nearly beyond it before it had even properly begun.

As I felt him straining, pounding inside me, I moved the velvet curtain back, tilting my eyes up and to the side.

It was odd really; as much as I had wanted this, as much as I wanted this now, it was as though I had to remove at least part of myself from it; it was as though I felt that if I gave myself over to it too completely, I would lose it that much quicker. And so, a distant part of my mind registered that the rain had stopped and with it the humidity that had been with us for so long had finally fallen, the fog had lifted, revealing a scattering of diamonds of varying brilliance embedded against an inky velvet sky.

He moved faster and faster, catching me back, capturing all of me, and I raced to remain where he was.

When it was over, it was as though we were frozen there like some bizarre tableau, our upper bodies still clothed, he with even his traveling cloak still on, my naked legs yet wrapped around his hips, his damp forehead—damp with remnants of the rain? with sweat?— pressed downward to mine, eyes shutting out the world.

"Madam?" I heard Timmins knock on the door. "Are you all right?"

I struggled to rein in my breathing, heart still pumping so wildly I was sure he could hear it through my chest, through the door.

"Fine, Timmins."

"Are you sure, madam? I thought I heard a loud bang. Are you sure you did not fall?"

"Of course I am sure, Timmins. I merely dropped my hair-brush."

"Very good, madam."

But I did not hear him move down the hall right away. Like a spider, it seemed, he waited for the opposing chess player to make a move.

"Good night, Timmins," I said, command in my voice, hoping not to betray the trembling, the tiny aftershocks I kept experiencing as I locked eyes with Chance Wood, unable to tear my gaze away.

Finally, at last, I heard Timmins retreat.

"You are even more beautiful than I imagined you would be based on your writings, Emma."

Even though he had spoken earlier, it was as though I were hearing his voice for the very first time. I would have expected, based on his previous life and crimes, to hear a lowborn voice, with something of the street in it, something *rough* even, despite the somewhat cultured tone of his letters.

But I was wrong.

Rather, he spoke well, his voice possessed of a rich timbre, a seeming confidence, as though he knew me completely even though, for all intents and purposes, he had only just met me. Competing with the confidence was a surprising vulnerability. The mix was exhilarating. It was also terrifying.

I wanted to ask him why he had been silent for the month since his release, what his plans were, what our plans were.

But he did not give me the chance.

Gently, he eased me down off him. Gently, he led me over to the dark bed, the bed I had only ever before shared with my husband.

"Lie with me awhile?" he asked, gently pulling me down.

And here was another strange thing: Even though we had just made love in a way in which I never had before, with an almost violent intimacy previously foreign to me—in that it was not just the other wanting to create that driving thrust but me chasing after it as well—now that it came to a point of some more, well, *normal* activity, I felt a shyness overtake me.

And yet, I could not refuse him.

Slowly, he undressed me, pulling the pins from my hair, holding it out of the way with one hand as he undid the back of my still-damp dress with the other. When I was naked, I did not flinch from his gaze. Nor would I permit him to assist me while I undressed him, a thing I had never done before; previously, I had helped a man put on clothes—a tie added here, a jacket there—but I had never sought to take them away.

Now, as we lay together beneath the canopy, we had the luxury of time untempered by urgency, time in which to explore every inch of each other as we had not before.

As he rose up above me, I took in his naked chest, as broad as I had imagined it beneath his clothes and as hairless as my own, his tapered waist with a smattering of hair extending from his navel down to the thatch surrounding his manhood; took in the deep and jagged scar on the back of the right hand as it reached to caress my breast; took in the indelible pale imprint on the wedding finger of a ring no longer there.

"Have you missed me, Emma?" he asked, wavering above me.

"Oh, yes."

"But you knew that I would come?"

I answered directly as he entered me: "Yes."

Before, the first time, I could have told myself of it, when reflecting later, I had been taken by surprise; that even though I had expected him, had in fact been expecting him daily for the past month, my reactions had been involuntary, no different really from the conditioned responses a man called Pavlov had been able to elicit from dogs in some preliminary experiments John had been telling me about. I could have pled temporary insanity, and I might have even believed it myself.

But not now.

Now what we did had such deliberation to it, passion having been relegated to a handmaid's role where it waited upon conquest, that the truth and the intent of what we were doing could no longer be denied.

What had started out on paper, quite possibly no more than the jottings of a middle-aged woman and an imprisoned man looking for a little diversion, had crossed the line over into the real world. I was no longer writing a parallel life for myself, a fantasy.

Fantasy now existed as reality.

And now that they were one and the same, I tried to rein rational thought to the romance at hand. What about this man was so compelling? It was not that he was so extraordinarily good-looking, although he was certainly handsome enough, despite that one flaw in his teeth. No, it was nothing so common as appearances. It was the energy he gave off. It was the way he filled the whole room, nay, the whole universe. It was that I could feel him wanting to possess me body and soul, not for his own mere happiness, but because he wanted to live inside me. He was an irresistible sun.

My mind halted at the impossible task of putting into mental words what it was about him that owned me so and I let my body and spirit take over where my mind had left off.

Each time I tilted my hips upward to meet him, as though I were trying to push myself into him in the same way he was pushing into me, I felt as though I were making a choice, over and over again.

It was a second-by-second revelation: After months of imagining his hands through my hands, these were now *his* hands, his real hands, upon me. It was his body inside me. It was his heart I felt beating next to mine. And when the world shattered apart, into a million tiny pieces of unimaginable sensation before reintegrating, it was with an awe-inspiring power, a revelation like nothing I had ever achieved on my own. It was like its own religion.

Sometime later, I lay on the bed and watched him go, no talk of when he might return, of when I might see him again. After all, now that he had gained his freedom, who knew but that he might not want to leave the area altogether... start fresh... start fresh without me.

It was not something I wanted to think about: the future. I had, for today, gotten what I had most wanted.

Well, I tried to tell myself that, at any rate.

In fact, as I lay there in one spot, my cheek resting on the comfort of my lightly clenched hand, my mind ranged over the possibilities of the whole wide world. I could almost feel that world spinning around me, spinning faster and faster even as my mind spun from place to place, like a bird looking for and not finding just the right branch to light down upon.

I would not have believed it if someone told me I would be able to sleep that night, but sleep I did.

Hours later—it was still night, but I could not say what time—I woke with a start. The rain had started up again and the wind was hammering at the open window, making a rattling sound as drops splattered against the floor. Hurrying to shut it, I saw there was now a small puddle where Chance and I had stood mere hours before.

Chance! What had I done?

Bending my head to the sheets, I inhaled the scent of us, of what we had done, coming off the linen in an unmistakable aroma of human earth and sexual life. I wanted to bury my nose further, summon up the night, ignore time.

But the side of me—a side that was growing smaller all the time—that was still practical, shrieked, *No!*

If I could inhale us so easily, anyone else—Lucy coming to change the bedding, my husband coming home too early—would surely be able to do so as well; smell us and know the masculine part of the smell was not that of my husband.

Locking the door on the desires of my heart, I whipped the sheets off the bed, the purple dress I had worn before still tangled among them. Realizing I was still naked, I dropped my bundle long enough to put on a dressing gown, then reclaimed it, setting off through the house.

I don't know what I could have been thinking, save to get the evidence off the bed and out of my bedroom as quickly as possible, but I found myself tiptoeing through the pantry and the kitchen with its big vatlike sinks, big enough for when John entertained dozens of his literary and political acquaintances. What was I thinking, that I would go downstairs to the laundry or use the vatlike sinks right there, that I would somehow wash out the sheets myself and not be noticed?

"Can I help you with something, madam?"

I nearly leapt out of my skin.

"Timmins," I spoke, hand to chest, awkwardly clutching the soiled items in the other, "you startled me."

"I am sorry, madam." He did not sound sorry in the slightest.

Had he been upstairs in his room above the kitchen, prowling around when he heard me down here? The fact that he was in his own bedtime clothes should have comforted me somehow, made me feel as though we were at least on equal footing. But it did not. In fact, I felt myself, as he peered at me closely, to be at a distinct disadvantage.

"Is something wrong, Timmins?" I finally asked.

"It's just that...Perhaps it's not my place to say, but..." He looked at me closer still. "Before, earlier this evening, you dropped your hairbrush..."

One hand flew to my hair, and yet in an instant I regretted the impulse. Did he see my horror? It was all I could do to keep myself from coming up with a sniveling alibi with which to appease the butler as to why I was disheveled.

"Shall I send Lucy to attend to it, madam? I thought you must be dressing it when you dropped your brush, but perhaps seeing the master off in his carriage disturbed it more than you thought."

"That's quite all right, Timmins. I can manage myself this evening. No need to bother Lucy. Already it grows late."

"As you wish, madam."

Still he stood there. Why would he not leave?

"Was there something else you required this evening, madam?"

"Hmm?"

He looked pointedly at the soiled sheets and dress I yet held so desperately. "Did you need those attended to?"

He held his arms out to receive them. Why should this feel like such a trap?

"Oh," I laughed, the laugh sounding a tinny note even in my own ears, "that. While I was getting ready to retire, I happened to spill a bottle of lotion on the sheets. It got on my dress as well and made a great mess."

His eyebrows asked why I had not summoned a servant to remove the bedding; why I had not, at the very least, if I had not wanted to disturb anyone else, just left it in the corner for one of the maids to attend to in the morning? But he would never ask such a question outright. And I would never—could never—answer it.

He pried the items from my grasp.

Helplessly I watched them go. What else could I do?

"I'll see that these are attended to first thing in the morning, madam, your dress returned to you just as soon as it is clean again. Surely, you need fresh sheets?"

I had no choice. Meekly, I went with him to the linen closet, where he started to make noises about waking Lucy again.

"That is all right, Timmins." I took the sheets from him. "I can surely manage on my own for one evening."

FORTY-ONE

The light was blinding me.

Hand instinctively moved up to shield my eyes as I awoke, squinting against the brightness of a new day. After a month of dreary darkness, the sun had made a triumphant return.

Through my slit eyes, I saw it was John who had drawn the drapes. For some reason, I drew the bedclothes more tightly around me.

He was early, very early. I had not expected to see him before evening. Had he been asleep beside me these last few hours and I unaware?

"How was your evening with Connor?" I asked, preempting him from asking me anything.

"It was fine," he said, removing his jacket, exchanging stale clothes for fresh, his actions bringing the realization that he must have just come in.

"How was he?"

"Connor was as he always is: polite, formal.

He, of course, wanted to change a few things in the manuscript, some major, some minor."

"Who won?" I asked, rising on my side, bending my elbow against the bed so I could support my head on my open hand.

"Do you even need to ask?" He smiled his most confident smile.

Of course I hadn't needed to ask. Of course John had won.

He shrugged. "I let him have a few minor details, just so he could save face, so he could later claim to have had control of the situation. But every major point, I carried. Naturally."

"Congratulations," I said, striving for a warmth I did not feel.

He shrugged again. "It is just business. And what did you do while I was away?"

What could I say?

"Nothing of any great consequence," I answered. "I read mostly."

"What is this doing all the way over here?"

I looked over to see what he was talking about. Dangling from his hand was a garnet earbob, one of the pair I had been wearing the day before.

"Did you fling it over for some reason while you were preparing for bed last night?" he continued. "Perhaps you decided it no longer suits?"

How close he had come to hitting the mark.

From my position now, lying on my stomach crossways on the bed, I could see the reflection of myself in the gilt-framed mirror across the room, could see the bruised look of my own lips even as he spoke.

I listened with only half an ear as he moved about the room, having already sped ahead to the next topic, but my mind was no longer on his words:

How close he had come to hitting the mark.

FORTY-TWO

I did stop and wonder, now Chance and I had finally made love, if that would be an ending to it for me.

Was this all I had been after, a taste of something...*different* from what I had known all my life? Had I just been looking for some sort of physical excitement? And now I had experienced it, would I be able to return to the contentment of my previous life?

I could not believe I was even asking myself these questions.

Of course, what I wanted with Chance had to do with more than two naked bodies moving against each other, seeking release.

Although, God knows, it was that too.

But it was also something beyond. It was also two naked minds moving against each other, seeking release. The two, our bodies and our thoughts, were an intertwined thing.

As for the Why of it—*Why this man? Why not some other man?*—who can really answer such a question? It is like being called upon to answer why one loves chocolate.

It was This Man because, for whatever reason, I was most myself with him.

It was This Man because, if I could have, I would have burrowed under his very skin to know him better.

What can I say?

He was original. He did not bore me.

I began to play the "What if?" game.

What if I had met Chance sooner? What if I had met Chance before my marriage to John?

Of course, such a game was pointless, as I well knew. But knowing a thing, and keeping myself from becoming obsessed about it anyway, had become two very different things. It had become impossible, the very idea that I could stop my mind and heart from meandering, racing down any of the streets and narrow alleys where they seemed bent to go.

So what if I was not wholly certain of what Chance's plans might be, now he had been released. We did steal time together, if only very occasionally, now.

In my weaker moments, I worried he might go his way without me; that he might decide I was not worth the risk, not worth the bother. But then, I would strengthen again. I would think, *That is not possible. It is not possible that I should feel what I do, the depth of what I do, and have there be no return. I could not possibly love like this alone.*

And so, as to the first question: What if I had met Chance sooner?

I attempted to chase down the answer with the same energetic mind-frame with which I might attack any intellectual pursuit. But I am afraid all my cogitations on the subject yielded precious little. Where might I have met a Chance Wood? Despite the fact his writings revealed a sharp mind, despite the fact he spoke in a voice far more refined in sound than I had suspected, the actual handwriting itself *was* crude, his dress that of a member of, at the very best, the slightly disadvantaged classes. There was nowhere in my world I might have encountered him in which we might have been on an equal footing, might have had the opportunity to develop more of a relationship than me requesting some service from him; a service he would have been obliged to grudgingly provide. I would ever be a lady, he would be thought by no one to be a gentleman, and any conversations we might have would be cast in stone in advance by the fraternal twinship of those facts.

As to the second question: What if, somehow, I had met him before my marriage to John?

But that, I found, was an equally preposterous proposition. Even had I met him in time, so to speak, I would probably have been too young then to appreciate the worth of the encounter. Would I, confronted with someone of such visibly inferior rank, have had the foresight to see what lay beneath? Would I have been better than Cathy with Heathcliff? Further, would I have had the strength to face off against my parents, against the whole of society, for the sake of it? It rankled me that I could not say with certainty, and I was yet wise enough to recognize this was an answer in itself.

No, it was just as well our relationship had developed as it had. Meeting facelessly, we had been afforded the opportunity to develop a bond without prejudice based on appearances. Meeting over time, we had enjoyed the luxury of having that bond strengthened without fearing the world.

Ah, time, though!

Now we had time, stolen moments of time together, but time itself had become a trickster, a mirror that kept rushing forward and then drawing back. Before, last year, had dragged on interminably by comparison with what was presently going on. Now time sped forward on wings that moved so quickly, I could not keep up with it. It was as though I were flying, airborne from one meeting to the next, with occasional full stops whenever life intruded.

And that life.

So many of the things that occupied my mind previously were now disappearing like so many inessential layers of clothing in a tropical climate. My mind was now a more heated thing than ever, and I could no more populate it with the concerns of Hettie Larwood, Sara Jamison, Maeve Collins, any and every woman I had ever known and their individual plights, or John, than I could sprout true wings and fly permanently to where I longed to be.

Let them clamor for my attention, let them need what they might, I could no longer hear them.

The beating of my own wings as I raced against time and space had simply grown too loud.

Shakespeare was right, I thought: "O brave new world," indeed.

FORTY-THREE

John **read to me from** the *Daily Telegraph*: "It says here Queen Victoria has sent tin boxes of chocolate to each of the soldiers in the African campaigns and that each box will have her portrait on the lid. It is meant to serve as her Christmas present to them. Well," he said, refolding the paper, tossing down his glasses in disgust, "that sounds about as effective as her idea to set prisoners free."

He looked at me for my reaction, but all I could manage was a vague "Is it not late for the newspapers to still be writing of Christmas?"

I took up my teacup and excused myself to the music room, sat down at a piano I had no intention of playing.

Now that Chance was free, the thought suddenly occurred to me, as an unwelcome visitor come to stay indefinitely: Never mind the idea of him possibly one day deciding to go off without me—might he not find somebody else now? Right here? Someone freer to attend his every need?

I could not bear the thought of it.

It was as though dawn and sunset had come at the same instant, and my head was spinning with it such that I could not choose which direction to look: the coming light or the coming dark.

One moment, I was all elation, all "O brave new world"; and the next, I was obsessed with the easier possibilities that another woman, *almost any other woman,* might afford him.

Did he see that too? Was he already planning something that might take him away from me?

I could not bear not knowing the truth, but I could not bring myself to risk losing what little I had by asking questions that might push him away.

So I held my tongue, held it against everything I wanted to know: how he spent his time, where he went, what he did when we were not together.

How had he acquired that wound on the back of his hand? When had he taken off his wedding ring, and what had become of it? Why had he killed his wife? And how? John had said it was a knife....

But no, I would tell myself, as I had done countless times before, I did not want to know, not really, the truth of what had happened with his wife. I certainly did not want to think about him having once been with another woman, however it might have ended. And, finally, I told myself, whatever had gone on with Chance and Felicia, however she might have died, whatever he might have done, I was sure now it was because he'd had no other choice.

Was it that I trusted him so much?

I am not sure that is precisely right.

I think now that, having invested so much, I was scared *not* to trust him. I think now that I was scared that if I questioned things too closely, I might learn he was not the man I needed for him to be.

FORTY-FOUR

Katherine running away should have taken me more by surprise, but somehow it did not. It was as though we had all been waiting for a long time for things to go badly for her; it was just a matter of time.

The letter came from her in the same post that contained the latest letter from Chance. Even though he was free now, we were not free to meet as often as we would like. Indeed, it felt as though we could hardly be together enough at all.

One day, when the weather was warmer than expected, John insisted we go out for a stroll. No sooner had we stepped outside, however, than I saw Chance standing across the street. *What is he doing there?* I wondered, praying all the while John shouldn't see him. As John led me down the street, I couldn't help but glance over my shoulder and, when I did, it was like torture. It was like seeing Chance trapped behind a glass such that I could not talk to him or hear him, could not touch him or be touched. I wanted to shake off the one and run to the other, but I could not. It was indeed so frustrating, immediately I begged John to return us to the house. Safe inside again, I began to wonder if there might not be a way for Chance and I to be together more...*permanently*.

For the time being, however, Chance and I found we must still content ourselves with epistolary communication to fill up the time apart.

So that Timmins, and, by extension, John, would not grow suspicious of a correspondence continuing between Chance and I far too frequently and for far too long, he now wrote my address on the envelope using the other hand, varying the paper he wrote on, so his letters no longer looked the same way twice. For myself, I wrote to him at the new address he'd provided, in a neighborhood I'd never been in, using his real name if I knew I'd be able to sneak out to post it myself and a false female name—he'd told his landlady he sometimes received letters for his widowed sister, now living on the streets—when I knew I would not.

But for once, something was able to distract me from my single-minded pursuit of Chance.

Venice, 15 March 1900

Dearest Aunt Emma,

It is much colder here than I had imagined, but it must be all the water that keeps it so.

I would not have run away, but I saw no other choice. I did investigate them all, but in the end, this was the only path I saw. I have fallen in love with one of the young men under Captain Brimley's command. When I tried to explain to Mother and Daddy about Hugh, they laughed. They said an officer was not suitable husband material for me, even were I not too young. I do know I am very young in years—but did not Romeo and Juliet love eternally and die tragically when much the same age?—and Hugh himself at eighteen really seems no older (I think he is already years older than Romeo and Juliet ever lived to be), but I think it is possible very early on to know what one wants. Isn't that what happened to you?

(I must confess here, Hugh still does believe I am sixteen.) Please,
Aunt Emma, I do not want you, of all people, to worry about us
overmuch. Hugh is amazingly resourceful. We have not had to
struggle so far hardly at all. I am sure once the spring definitively
comes and I am no longer so cold, I will like it here very much.
Please be happy for me. And please do not tell Mother or Daddy
where I am. I do not wish to cause them any harm. But if they knew,
they would only come after me. And I really did only leave because I
knew that, if I stayed, they would probably make me marry someone
horrible, someone not of my own choosing. I could not bear that.

Love,
Katherine

I pressed the envelope to my lips. It was almost possible to smell the
salty air of the canal on the thin paper. Of course, I had never been to
Venice myself, but I had seen pictures in books.

So my grandniece, recently turned fifteen, had been brave
enough to do what I had not the nerve for. In some ways, it made me
feel small by comparison: that she had been willing to forfeit family,
friends, *comfort,* in order to pursue that which she held most dear.
Reading between the lines, I could see a world of discomfort and fear.
But there was also resolution there, a bravery I could not help but
admire.

Well, good for her, was all that I could think.

I supposed I should have been more concerned with Katherine's
well-being. Did she really know this Hugh? Did either of them really
understand what a lifetime commitment to love meant? How would
they eat? How would they sleep?

And then there was the matter of her age. As old as she might be
for her age, she was still in fact very young.

I had wanted opportunities for Katherine that I had never had.
Was she closing the door on those opportunities by this early marriage? Or was she seizing opportunity, by choosing to love where and
how she wanted?

I wondered how she and Hugh would exist without money....

It is a sign of my own preoccupation that none of these thoughts
stayed in my mind for long. Truthfully, I think a part of me was

relieved I would no longer have Katherine to worry about. After all, when she was here, between her father's coddling and her mother's coldness, I had come to feel as though she were my responsibility. Now that she had decided to leave, however...

I turned my attention to the other letter that had come. The envelope, with that strange writing on it, was a feminine color such that the sender could be a woman with cheap tastes. That did not matter to me, though, as I tore it open, prepared to be swept away. It was, in the end, where I wanted to be.

My Dearest Emma...

That was all it took.

FORTY-FIVE

It was then I realized I loved him to distraction. Before, when I had heard that phrase, I had never known what it meant.

And now I did.

Before, I always had separate boxes for the various areas of my life. Here is my husband. Here is my child. Here are my friends. But now I was consumed with him, by him, he was everything, every moment of my waking and sleeping. He had spilled over into all the other boxes, refilling them so fully that the previous inhabitants had all been pushed aside.

And I did now have the brave example of my grandniece before me.

Was there some way I might get out of my predicament? Now that he was—miraculously!—free, was there not some way I might find my way to a life with him?

I chewed on this bone until it became white and dry in my mouth.

What, I finally concluded, *could I possibly have been think-ing of?*

There simply was no solution.

———————

"Perhaps there is, Emma." Chance whispered the words, leaning across the narrow table at Sommers Tea Room to do so. "Are you quite certain you have thought of everything?"

It felt odd, seeing him with that feminine French wallpaper be-hind him, but he had said he wanted to know what my "life without him" was like, and, peculiarly enough, Sommers was as representa-tive of this as anything else. He certainly could not come to my home; he certainly could not go visit my friends. Still, anyone I knew might come upon us here—a sister-in-law, a woman friend, since men did not often come here—and this act nearly qualified as being the most foolish risk we had committed yet. After all, I could not even pass him off as one of our set, if someone claimed later to have seen us, since his dress was so, well, shabby. And further to be talking about what we were talking of…

"I cannot just *go* to live with the man I love," I whispered back.

He leaned back in his chair, folded his arms in a very ungentle-manly fashion, legs stretched out in a posture not normally seen in Sommers.

"Why not?" he asked coolly.

"Because," I said, with more decisiveness than I would have imagined possible, given who I was with, given how much I feared losing him.

Fortunately, he chose not to take offense at my tone, chose not to press me for a more reasoned explanation; but rather, leaned forward again, re-creating the sense of intimacy I hated ever now to lose.

"Since you say you cannot just come live with me, and I see I must accept that—at least, for now—perhaps we might discuss alter-natives?"

Even though he had presented it as a question, I knew it was not.

"Very well," I conceded.

"What about divorce?"

True, husbands were known to divorce their wives. "So—what then exactly?" I asked. "Allow John to catch me out, so he would be forced to file suit against me for criminal conversation?"

He merely raised his eyebrows at me, encouraging me to go on.

True, it was within John's means to afford such a costly civil suit, I explained, and yet, it hardly seemed within the bounds of any of our characters to be party to one. "Not to mention," I added, "that you, named as the seducer, would be required by law to pay restitution to John for what you have stolen from him."

Neither of us spoke the words aloud—that given Chance's lack of funds, such a legal notion was absurd—but it hung in the air; the fact of the matter was, he quite simply could not afford me.

"Please direct me," I asked, so he would perhaps be persuaded to think the only thing preventing the adoption of this course was not just his relative poverty, "how would I contrive such a thing? Leave letters where John might find them?" I had told Chance before that I kept his letters, all of them, in various hiding places around my house. "Allow Lucy to see something she shouldn't, that she might give evidence at trial?"

His eyes spoke my own feelings. The idea was absurd.

"Not to mention"—and here now he seemed determined to help me talk my way out of this path—"the public embarrassment that would be sure to attach itself like a barnacle to all concerned." He put a hand to his cheek in mock womanish horror. "Good God! What would your mother say?"

Truthfully, I had long ago given off worrying about what Louisa had to say about anything. But that by no means meant I wanted to hear any of it.

"And," I finished up for us, "even if John were to divorce me, I would be left with no money to live on." Which was completely true. Although a settlement at the time of our marriage would have provided a fund that could not be touched, one that I would be able to use now for Weston and myself, I had foolishly—romantically—refused one. Romanticize in haste; repent seventeen years later.

So divorce was not a possibility. Which was really fine, since I didn't have the stomach for open displays of pronouncement anyway.

Chance spoke. "I have heard, of late, rumors of an alternative to divorce."

"Oh?"

"Yes. Apparently, in some circles, 'wife-selling,' inspired by a reference in one of Mr. Hardy's novels, has taken hold."

Every time he made a literary reference, or clearly understood one of mine, it caught me back, given the appearance of his clothes.

"It sounds somehow…Scandinavian," I said. "How does this 'wife-selling' work?"

Chance proceeded to explain that the highest bidder in such a suit might be the wife's lover, the entire proceedings viewed as an entertainment as well as an agreeable way for all parties to resolve their dispute without becoming mired in the legal system, this despite the fact that the sales themselves were prohibited by law. At any rate, it was difficult to picture John, with his well-developed sense of propriety, taking part in such an undignified play. Nor did I particularly relish the notion of myself as chattel, despite the fact that, as a wife, I pretty much well was. As for Chance, again, even had he the inclination, he certainly did not have the funds.

"So," Chance sighed, a rare sound, "no divorce; no wife-selling."

Well, I supposed, thinking to myself, *I could just pack my things and leave, couldn't I?*

What—leave the only world I had ever known? Leave my home? Leave my son?

The first two would be easy enough. But the last? Such a thing was impossible.

There was nowhere to go.

Chance must have seen the look of despair that crossed my face then, for he reached across the table, covering my clenched fist with his hand.

"Do not worry so much, Emma. I am sure there is a very simple solution; we merely have not arrived at it yet."

I so wanted to believe he was right. Impulsively, acting as though there were not a whole roomful of people around me, I moved to cover his reassuring hand with my other one.

But I snatched it back, directly I heard the questioning "Emma?" spoken in Constance Biltmore's tentative voice.

Apparently, Constance was finally back from her stay in the country.

Despite Chance's reassurances about there being a solution out there somewhere, I remained convinced there was nowhere for us to go, that we were already all we could ever hope to possibly become.

In my despair, trapped inside a box I had helped to build up around myself on all six sides, I retreated, making the box yet smaller still. I took to my bed, claiming vague and incapacitating ailments. It was some time before something occurred that made me want to rise up again.

FORTY-SIX

The nice thing about people thinking you've gone insane is that, suddenly, erratic behavior requires no explanation.

Lie in bed for a week? Why not. Who is there who will say anything, provided such a retreat appears to have a calming effect?

I could no longer be depended upon to have anyone's best interests at heart, my own included. Did I want good things for my child? Of course I did. But I wanted things for myself now too.

Need had replaced desire.

———

It was lonely, though, at times, lonely being the only one who knew what passed between Chance and myself, as if it somehow were not real, as if having one other person besides we two who knew the whole story *would* make it real.

But who?

Then something happened to stir me from my self-obsession.

Lucy, perhaps not seeing me as I lay so quietly beneath the sheets, came into the room. As she worked, I heard a sound I had never heard from her before: She was crying.

"Lucy?"

She turned with a start and I now saw her red-rimmed eyes, the tears streaking her face.

"Madam." She put her hand to her chest. "I thought you were out...."

"What's wrong?" I asked gently. "Tell me what is the matter."

"I am...I am...I am with child!"

Oh no. The vague horrors I had always felt regarding Lucy's possible ill future had now come home.

"Who...?" I asked.

"I...I...I cannot say."

Why? I wondered. Why would she not be able to tell me?

She sniffed again. "Are you going to throw me out?" she asked.

I thought about what she was asking. Surely, in almost any other household, that would be the result.

I rose from my bed, walked over, put my arms around her, let her rest her head gently against the white cotton of my nightgown.

"Let us not talk of this now, Lucy. For now, let this be our secret."

———

I turned once more to Lady Collins for counsel. The servant this time led me to the back parlor, where Lady Collins half lay on a Chesterfield, a book in her hands. I saw her place it to one side.

"*The Experiences of Loveday Brooke, Lady Detective.*" I read the title upside down. "By Catherine L. Pirkis. Is it any good?"

"I am up to 'The Ghost of Fountain Lane.'"

"What is it about?"

"A forged check and, well, a ghost, of course."

"But is it any good?" I asked again.

"It is, I suppose, better than Kipling," she said. "One grows tired of Kipling." As usual, Lady Collins was not one for polite small talk. "But, surely, you did not come here today to talk to me about books, did you?"

"I have a friend," I said, reluctant to admit I was talking about my own household, "who has discovered one of her maids is with child."

"How awful for the poor girl!"

"Yes. I thought so too."

"She will probably find herself on the streets without a reference."

"That is what usually happens, isn't it?"

"Of course. Unfortunately, of course."

A part of my mind was thinking that when the time came it was no longer suitable for me to keep Lucy in my household—after all, what kind of an influence on Weston would her expectant presence be?—perhaps sympathetic Lady Collins might take her in.

"The problem is," I proceeded delicately, "my friend asked her maid who the father of the child was and the maid said she could not answer."

"Oh dear!"

"Why do you say that?"

"Because, obviously, the father must be someone in the household, either another servant or..."

I thought of the only men in our household: John and Timmins. I thought about how much Lucy and John seemed to share in common, both in physical appearance and mutual love of things like an excess of Christmas decorations. Most of all, I thought on how I could not picture any woman willingly lying with Timmins.

Lady Collins was surely right: Why would Lucy refuse to tell me the identity of the father? The only possible reason could be that she was certain that such knowledge would prove devastating to me. It was shaming to think on, that my maid felt the need to protect my feelings.

I must have been silent for too long, because now Lady Collins was studying me with a closeness that was far from comfortable.

"Emma," she said, a dawning horror descending on her features like a masque in a Greek tragedy. "Is it—?"

"I'm sorry," I said, rising. "I have forgotten another appointment."

When I returned home, Lucy was there in the foyer, dusting the hall bench. She moved a little more stiffly than earlier in the day, her eyes still red, but now a fragile smile graced her pretty lips.

"Has something happened?" I asked.

"Oh yes!" she said, her relief evident even as her eyes cast about to see that no one was near to listen. "Right after you went out." She leaned in closer to whisper. "I lost it. I lost the baby."

"Oh, Lucy." I placed my hand on her arm, unable to keep the thought from forming that the loss of this child was a most fortunate escape.

"Everything is all right again," she said brightly, if a bit strained. "I will not have to go now, will I? There is no need to tell anybody?"

I thought about it. I thought about my husband, whom I would no longer look at the same way again. But, I also thought, whatever had happened between them, I could not bring myself to blame Lucy. I could not bring myself to believe any of it had been her fault.

"Of course you can stay," I said, "if that is what you really and truly want. I will tell no one. I am sure you will be more...*careful* in the future."

FORTY-SEVEN

Feeling more bereft than before, I returned to my bed, returned to my ruminations on the subject of someone I could confide in. Surely, I could not tell Lady Collins about Chance. I had seen how she reacted, suspecting John might be the father of my maid's child. If she would condemn him for an infidelity, despite her seeming independence and modernness of thought, would she not equally condemn me?

But what of other friends—was there not one person I could trust?

There was no one.

"Emma?" Constance spoke to me as if one of us might be dying. I had not heard her knock. "John said it would be all right if I came in."

When we had run into Constance that day in Sommers Tea Room, stunned, I had not introduced her to Chance; and, oddly enough, she had not asked. I suppose, perhaps, having a mind as confused as Constance's purportedly was now, it was conceivable she was incapable of grasping everything that was going on around her.

"May I ...?" she asked, indicating the chair at my vanity, which she pulled over to the side of the bed before I could answer.

Even this close, I could not see her very clearly. Although John had opened the drapes that morning, perhaps hoping some light might serve to elevate my mood, I had ordered Lucy to shut them again as soon as he was gone, closing my mind to the picture of the two of them together.

"Ever since I have been back, Charles has been ...*worse*," she said, a mere shadow, in so many ways, beside me.

I struggled to a more upright position against the pillows. "Worse? How so?"

She proceeded to explain that while Charles had always been a gambling man, he had lost quite a considerable sum in the time she was away. And now, even though she had returned, he showed no signs of stopping. In fact, she suspected one of the reasons he sent her away in the first place was that he wanted to be free to do as he liked, to lose everything if it suited him.

"I know you and I are not ...*close*," she said, "but I have always felt a certain kinship with you. In fact, I should have liked to write to you when I was ...*away*, but Charles would not permit it."

I thought of the awfulness of a husband who would not even allow his wife to write to whom she chose. What isolation Constance's life must be.

"It is all right," I soothed. "You do not need to explain to me the need to talk with another person. Please, tell me what is wrong."

Constance had always been a hesitant speaker, with a tic here, a stutter there, but her time away, meant to be a rest cure, had only served to make these tendencies more pronounced. In fact, I would not have been surprised to learn she carried a double scent bottle on her person: one of those cylindrical vessels of colored cut glass the more delicate ladies carried, pairing a perfume bottle with a smelling-salts container for dizziness spells.

"And all of his losses, that is not the worst," she tic-stuttered now.

"What could possibly be worse than a husband who loses piles of money and then sends his wife away so he'll be free to lose the rest?"

"This," she said, rolling up, with effort, the stiff sleeves of her gown.

In the dim light, she edged up, moving close to me, so close she was just a mere hand's breadth away. In irregular rows up and down her arms were bruises, so ugly and so many they could not all be accidents.

"And this," she said, using one hand to pull down the high collar of her dress.

Now she moved her head so it was directly above mine and I was confronted with the prospect of her neck, like a lover preparing for a kiss. But this was not about a kiss. Rather, what I saw revealed to me now were more bruises, in the shape of fingers, at her throat.

I felt my breath catch. "Oh, Connie..." I had not ever called her that before, could think to call her nothing else now.

I wondered if there had ever been a time when I might have done something, said something that would have kept this horror from visiting her. It is not that I was accustomed to thinking of myself as being so very powerful, but it did seem as though there must have been, should have been, a single moment when a word said differently, an action taken differently, would have altered everything that followed.

She readjusted her clothes. "It is all right," she said. "It does not hurt so very much, after one gets used to it. Sometimes, though, I do not think I will be much longer for this world. I suppose I only sought to tell you because"—and here she shrugged her embarrassment— "you know—a burden shared is a burden halved. I suppose I also thought it would make it more real somehow, as though I'm not just some insane woman like my husband and the rest of the world think I am. There are times when I wish I were a braver sort of woman. If I were, then perhaps I would be able to kill Charles before he one day kills me."

"Oh, Connie," I said again, not completely taking in her last sentence, preferring to focus on what had come immediately before; but, inside, I was also thinking, *Oh, Emma—a kindred spirit!*

And so, I told her, of course. I told her everything.

FORTY-EIGHT

Emma is sleeping with another man."

"Could you repeat that again, please? I am certain I could not have heard you wholly right the first time."

The original speaker had been Constance, her voice all atremble; the second, John.

They were in his library and I was standing just outside. I was still in my white nightgown, the lace-trimmed sleeve exposing my hand, still raised to knock on the door that was an inch ajar. I had been planning on asking John a question concerning Cook's question to me about dinner: Chicken or fish? It seemed I could no longer make even such simple decisions on my own. I lowered my hand. What mattered that now? I ask you. *Chicken or fish?*

"Emma is sleeping with another man."

There were the same damning words again. Had it come so quickly to this?

"I see," said John, "I did indeed hear you right the first time. Can you tell me, please, what exactly it is you are talking about, Constance?"

I heard her tell him then, in a voice that gained in strength as though to speak the words made the speaker stronger by the second, heard her tell him everything exactly as I had told it to her.

When she finished, John was silent for a very long time.

I waited, barely breathing, to hear the reply. When it finally came, the tone was severe.

"What you are telling me is most interesting and very serious, indeed. Can you tell me what you are hoping to gain?"

Constance told John about Charles's increased gambling.

"I do not want to betray Emma," she stuttered, "but I feel I have no other choice. I need to get away, but I need money. If you would give me enough, just enough to move away to some small town somewhere, where nobody knows me, where I may have a chance to start over again…"

"Yes?" John spoke insistently into the silence in which her words had trailed off. "If I provide you with the funds to start this new life you claim to need, you will do *what* exactly?"

Her words came out in a rush. "Then I will go away and I will not make your family the laughingstock of all of London."

"Which you *will* do if I do *not* do as you ask?"

She said nothing in reply. Perhaps what she had done already had required all the bravery left in her possession.

John's next words surprised me with their gentleness. I could almost see him taking her softly by the elbow, steering her with delicacy toward the door.

"Let us speak no further of this right now. You have said so much today, I am sure you will understand my need to digest it all before proceeding. How about if we agree on this?" It was as if he were making a suggestion to Weston that if he would only finish his meat, there might be ice-skating in his future. "I will think carefully on all you have told me and get back to you in a week with my response. Can you bear, do you think,"—and here I thought I heard his words take on a slight sarcastic edge—"to remain for just one more week with this tyrannical husband who you claim treats you so ill?"

She stuttered that she supposed she could live out just a week. "But once the week is up…" she stutter-warned.

"Oh, yes," he soothed. "Within a week, you will have the answer you need."

As they came out of his library, moving toward the entryway, I flattened myself against the wall behind the library door.

I was making my way back to my bedroom, the question of chicken or fish left still undecided, when John's voice stopped me.

"Were you looking for me just now, Emma?"

I must have murmured at least something in reply, but I cannot now remember what.

"Very well, then, my love. Do you have a moment for me now?" He held open the door of his library, his posture a demand rather than an invitation. "There is something I wish to discuss with you."

I could not refuse.

Meekly, uncharacteristically so, I sat in the chair before his desk. It felt strange, vulnerable, to sit there in my white gown, nothing even covering my feet as I waited for the blow to fall.

He looked at me with a deeply puzzled expression, as though seeing me for the very first time.

Oh no, I thought. *Here it comes.*

"Why are you dressed like that?" he asked. "You should have at least put on a dressing gown. After all, what would the servants think if they saw you walking around in that thin gown, with nothing to cover it?"

What could I say—that I had been too depressed that lifetime ago that had in reality been a mere half hour, when the most important thing on my mind had been *chicken or fish,* to bother with proper clothing or what anyone might think?

But he shrugged his own question off, not waiting for my answer as I tucked my naked feet under my body for protection as I listened to him talk, as he repeated to me everything Constance had just related to him, everything I had related to her.

I waited…and waited…and waited…

And then I heard the most astonishing sound: John laughed.

He *laughed*! "Is not that"—he clapped his hands together, his mirth such that he could barely get the words out—"is not that the most *absurd* story you have ever heard?!"

I would guess my facial expression in reaction to this outburst was more wincing grimace than smile, but John, apparently, chose to take it for rueful assent.

"It was all I could do," he said, "not to laugh in her face!"

"And the absurdity is...?" I led him now, feeling more brave myself now the immediate crisis had passed.

"Why, of course, you as well as I can easily see what the absurdity is here. No sane person would ever release your prisoner." He still called him that. "His crime was too vile." He paused briefly, considering. "Well, if he committed it, of course."

I was almost too afraid to ask, but ask I must. "What will you do?"

"Do? Well, I suppose first, I will need to talk to Governor Croft."

He must have seen the look of horror on my face, for he immediately moved to my side, taking my hands in his. Unbidden, I had a picture of him and Lucy together, flinched, but he only held on to my hands tighter.

"Oh, no, Emma, no! Please do not believe for even a second that I give any credence at all to Constance's absurd story. But, to tell you the truth, it is *so* bizarre, I feel the need to make certain the prisoner is still where he is supposed to be. On reflection, I am sure you must have merely told her of your correspondence with him and she has decided to use that to her advantage by rewriting the story large. But what if he *is* loose? He knows your name, knows where you live, knows you are a sympathetic ear—what if he were to seek you out? Oh, no, I could never live with myself if something were to happen to you because I had been incautious somehow. I must investigate this further."

I saw I could not dissuade him. Now all I could do was brace myself, try to come up with something against the day he learned Chance was free. The doom had not come today. But, if not today, then it must surely come tomorrow or on yet another tomorrow.

He laughed again, startling me. "But oh," he wiped at his eyes, "poor Charles!"

Poor Charles?

My expression must have said as much, even if I had not spoken the words aloud, for John replied to it: "Yes, poor Charles. Can you imagine being shackled to that madwoman? Someone should lock her away in an attic! Oh, I know, you who are always so charitable will say that is very uncharitable of me. And I suppose you are right. She does deserve our sympathy, poor misguided thing that she is."

He thought for a moment, then went on. "Naturally, I will have to speak with Charles about this."

"With Charles? But why?"

"Because she is his responsibility. And because, apparently, that last 'rest cure' of hers in the country did no good. On the contrary, I do believe she has returned much worse." John considered: "She has probably been spending too much time with one of those spiritists. Charles will probably want Gammadge's cousin to provide her with a sleep-inducing tonic until her current spate of madness subsides. Or, better yet, return her to the country until she shows herself fit to live among civilized society again."

The subject over, as far as John was concerned, he picked up a copy of the *Sphere* from his desk and continued his perusal of it. Presumably, Constance had rudely interrupted his reading.

"It says here, my dear, that Newgate Prison is to be demolished. Hmph. How long do you think it will take them to get around to doing *that*?"

I left him to it and snuck away.

Why had Connie not shown John her bruises, as she had me? They were her bodily proof something horrid had happened to her. Even, if by some perverse stretch, John proved reluctant to believe his friend Charles had caused them, he would have been forced to acknowledge Connie had not manufactured the physical harm she claimed had come to her.

But Connie, of course, would never have done such a thing before John. She would have been too timid, too scared of fighting against the overwhelming tide of propriety, as she would have needed to in order to expose to a man, not her husband and not her doctor, parts of her body that were covered by clothes. She could never have rolled up her sleeves, pulled down her collar for John as she had done for me.

I could, of course, have proved to John she *was* in her right mind. I could have simply told him about the bruises I had seen. He might think I was joking at first, but eventually he would believe me. But I could not tell him that now, not after what she had told him, not after what she had tried to do.

Did I blame Connie?

No, I did not blame her.

But I could not save her now, either. Perhaps there had once been a time, long ago, to help her and I had not seen it. Now I could see where help could be given and I chose not to give it. She would be sent away to the country again, and I would be safe from her accusations. In a sense, she had brought this on herself. If I was to save one person here, it had to be me. And, so, I said nothing.

She should have shown him the bruises.

FORTY-NINE

It was a dry rain.

I do know how silly that sounds, how silly it looks now on the page, but it was. It was the kind of rain that was so fine—more than a mist, really, but so fine that the sparseness of drops, when combined with the quality of the air, led you to believe no matter how long you stayed out in it, it could not possibly get you wet.

I had left John asleep in bed, moving on cat's feet through a house that was dark, asleep. Before stepping out the door, I had grabbed my cloak, wrapping it tight around me.

There were only a handful of other people out so late, whom I passed as I made my way through the rows of gaslights, past the last light from a public house and toward the park where we normally brought Weston to play. Those few I did pass all looked as though they could be up to no possible earthly good, but I moved with such sureness, speed, and determination, all glanced away from me, rather than do anything to stop the path of my progress.

Away from the lights of the street, the park was shrouded, the heaviness of the clouds blocking out almost all evening light, so only the occasional shimmer could be seen sparkling on the lake as I leaned back against a tree.

Of course, I had a reason for coming there.

"Emma?"

I had not seen him in so long, it seemed, the moon had gone out, and he had taken the stars with him.

Now, he moved around from the other side of the tree, coming to stand before me. He reached out one hand, undid the tie at my throat, slipped the cloak back over my shoulders.

I wore only my white nightgown underneath.

Not waiting for him this time, I lifted it up over my head myself. Then I slowly removed every article of clothing he was wearing, taking my time, torturing us both.

On the ground beneath him, feeling his kisses in the hollows around my throat, I moved to open my legs for him. But he stopped me. Instead, he straddled me, knees on either side of my hips, rather than insinuating himself between me as I was used to. Then he walked on knees toward my head until his stiffness was hanging directly over my face. I reached to touch him with my hand, to touch that which I had never touched before, but he brushed my hand aside with his, placed one hand behind my neck and gently lifted me upward until I was forced to support myself on my elbows beneath him. At first, I did not know what he wanted.

"Your mouth, Emma. I wish to make love to your mouth."

Then he caressed my lips with the head of it, the moisture from its tip dampening my lips as he circled around until it became almost an involuntary reflex, an imperative, for me to open my mouth to accommodate its insistence.

It was a taste I had not known before.

Tentative at first, I began to move more surely under his guiding hand—mouth, lips, tongue, the occasional grazing of teeth; circling, stroking, sucking, licking—all as he advanced and retreated, pumping with more intensity as it became one swift uninterrupted motion of moisture and skin. At the last, he pumped harder, holding my head hard against him, so that I could not even think to stop had I but wanted to.

But I did not mind.

I *liked* it. I loved having Chance in this way, *owning* him in a way I had never owned any man before.

And I swallowed it, everything—the same stuff that, when John pumped it into me, ran out down my leg—I swallowed it all.

Afterward, I moved to wipe my mouth with the back of my hand, but Chance brushed it away again, grabbed on to a few strands of my hair, and pulled my face to his. He kissed me, kissed the taste of himself still on me, pressed his forehead against mine, and spoke:

"If you could live more than one life simultaneously, would you live one of them with me?"

I smiled in the darkness, knowing what he was talking about without my words for it having ever passed between us. He was talking about what I had come to think of as "parallel lives." I thought about how the mere *idea* of him had invaded every corner of my existence. He was no longer part of a parallel life; he *was* my life.

Still smiling, I answered, "I already live all of them with you."

Apparently, though, my answer was not enough.

"Do you not wish we could be together like this all the time?" he asked.

His words were as insinuating, as insistent, as he had been when in my mouth earlier, but I did not answer.

Instead, I lay in his arms, my hair spread out across his smooth chest, and told him what had happened with Constance, what had happened with John and Constance both.

After a thoughtful pause, Chance spoke. "It does not matter that he did not believe her. In time, he may begin to doubt you, may begin to wonder if there is not some small kernel of truth in her mad ramblings, even if the details are not correct. Not to mention: What will happen when he seeks me out at the prison and finds I am no longer there?"

Again, I did not speak, and into my silence he asked again: "Do you not wish that we could be together like this all the time?"

This time, I answered, at last giving in to the futility. "But that is impossible."

"I am not asking you about that. I am not asking you about

possible, impossible." And now his voice became almost angry. "I am *asking* you: *Do—you—wish—it—were—so?*"

"Of course."

He relaxed backward, a smile playing on his lips. "Then it should be."

———————

I sat on the stoop, cloak loose around me now, more than a little damp as I reviewed the night.

"Emma?"

It was John.

"Emma, what in the world are you doing sitting out here this time of night? And in the rain, for God's sake! You are shivering." He took me by the hand, pulled me to my feet. "Come to bed."

I allowed him to lead me back in, back through the dark and sleepy house, but my mind was still back by the lake.

I loved it, I thought. I loved it and I wanted to do it again and again:

I wanted Chance to make love to my mouth.

FIFTY

A flurry of letters followed.

Obligations at home—dreaded obligations!—now kept me from him for a time. It seemed as though John's sisters had one disaster after another, almost as though they were inventing them. No matter how many disasters his sisters might have, however, the one disaster they never spoke of, and that the greatest disaster of all, was Katherine. It was as though, powerless to do anything about her loss, the wound of that loss perhaps too great, they smoothed over the hole she left, pretending she had never existed at all. Surely, though, they must have thought of her? I know I did. In the moments when my mind was not filled with Chance, or perhaps because of Chance, I obsessively imagined her new existence. Recalling the words of her letter, the talk of the cold and the damp, I would think how awful it must be for her in so many ways. But then I would think of her freedom, freedom to love as she wanted, where she wanted, and I could not help but envy her with a bitter fervor that made my mouth go wet with hunger. And still John's sisters said nothing of her. As for John...

John's novel of prison life had been at last published. Having spent so long in the birthing, one would think John would be cheerful about how well the book was doing. And yet he was uneasy, as though he had uncharacteristically been expecting some kind of failure and was now disturbed that what he found in its place was success. Our circle of friends having been awed by that latest success, this one greater than any before, meant our presence was required at a seemingly endless series of parties in John's honor.

And, so, while the social aspect of life was whirling us all around, where Chance was concerned, all there was to do was write, write, *write*—a flurry of letters, some containing no more than a halfformed thought.

I wrote first: of how I loved the thing we had done by the lake, of how I now wanted to do that very thing with him, again and again.

Him: *What you did to me, I could do to you.*
Me: *What?*
Him: *I said, What you did to me, I could do to you.*
Me: *But how...?*

And he described it to me in full, how he would lay me down on the edge of a bed, how he would get down on his knees in front of me, how he would insert his fingers, one and then two, how he would use his tongue and lips to lick, suck on, and tease that part of myself that throbbed for him.

Me: *It is difficult for me to picture you on your knees to anybody, least of all me.*
Him: *Try.*

His words, his images, stole my breath.

Me: *Oh my!*
Him: *You see? Do you see now, Emma? That is how it is for me when you say the things you do.*

There was no bed, but we did meet, by the lake again, and he did everything he had said he was going to do. I watched that dark head moving between my legs, doing things that when I had read them in his letters seemed like mere words. I could not believe a man was doing these things to me. It was like something from a dream.

More talk of being together always like that, more *words*...but no resolutions, no single answer, in sight.

Then, one last letter, from him:

Perhaps if your husband were no longer in the picture...

FIFTY-ONE

Emma, darling," John said at breakfast, taking his time as he carefully wiped his mouth, laid his napkin down beside his plate, "I spoke with Governor Croft last evening. I would have discussed it with you when I got home, but you were already asleep."

And so, the moment I had been dreading for a while, knowing it must inevitably come, was now upon me.

I scanned the table, taking in but not really seeing the common objects of normal family life: jam, toast, yellow remnants of egg on Weston's plate that he had left, asking to be excused.

Of course, I had never told John about Chance's impending release at the time I had written my letter impersonating him to the queen, that impending release which was now complete. And John, no longer going to the prison, had no previous reason to learn of it. But now . . .

And yet, it was galling to think he was about to sit in judgment on me, after what he had done with Lucy.

"Are you listening to me even a little bit, Emma?"

"I'm sorry. You were saying..."

"I *said,* dear, I went to the prison last night and was assured by Governor Croft that your prisoner is still there."

"What?"

In my shock, I jerked my arm abruptly, knocking over the silver serving bowl with the dark purple jam in it. It was as though someone had poured a pitcher of ice-cold water over my head, drenching me out of my distracted thoughts.

He called for Lucy to clean up the mess I had made; it struck me as odd, when I saw them so close together, that neither gave any evidence of what had passed between them. It was difficult for me to understand how she could bear to remain under his roof. Was there nowhere else for her to go?

After Lucy had finished and left, John sighed, clearly put out, as though I were a child who was simply too difficult to teach. "Need I repeat the same words *a third time*?"

"No, of course not. It's just that..."

"'Just that' *what,* Emma? I don't understand you. You seem so surprised—almost shocked, really. One would think you would be relieved by the news, relieved that whatever strangeness was going on in Constance's troubled mind, at least the idea she had of your prisoner now being free, was a false one."

He was right: I *was* shocked. How could I not be? *I* knew that Chance was free; *I* had been the one to set him free. How, then, was it possible Governor Croft should now say he was still at Hollowgate?

I caught John staring at me, a strange, questioning look on his face. Smiling, I sought to cover my protracted silence.

"Well, of course, I *am* relieved." I forced a glittery tone into my voice. "I am amazingly relieved! You are right: It would have been most frightening for me to think *my* prisoner was free!" That last "my" I threw in for his sake, laughing a laugh almost close to genuine, as if to prove I had returned to being my amiable self.

It seemed to work, for John settled back with his tea, smiling playfully at me over the rim. "Yes, dear," he said, "now that we know where he is—and Governor Croft assures me he will never be released—you could even resume writing to him again, if you should so desire. You are as safe from him as you have ever been."

How I would have liked, at that moment, to wipe that smug smile from his face. His words, sarcastically spoken, cut with mockery at the very thing I held most dear.

But his next words were even worse.

"I have been thinking," he said, "of using Constance's tall tale of you and your prisoner for the book I have been writing."

"Excuse me?"

"My book. Surely, you do remember me telling you about my new book. The one about gossip? This, I think, will make a most charming anecdote to add to it."

I was horrified at the notion. What did he think I was—one of the pretty insects he collected, pinning the prized ones in an open book for show?

Oh, God. Could it really be possible? John thought he was going to put Chance and I *in a book*?

FIFTY-TWO

Lucy?" I summoned her, violently drawing
the drapes myself on a new day.
Since the day when she had, in rapid
succession, told me about and then lost the baby,
we had not said another word about it. She had
always been polite enough and agreeable enough
with me in the past, as dictated by both her position and disposition, but there was a gentle tenderness in her mien whenever she was around
me now. It was as though she were eternally
grateful, not only for not being judged harshly,
but also for not being judged at all.

"Yes, madam?"

"I need you to pick out a suitable dress for
me. Mmm...best make it the violet one. Then, I
need your help with my dress and my hair. I'm
afraid I have not eaten as I should recently and I
am not as strong as I would like."

"Yes, madam."

"Then, when we're done here, you can
summon a cab for me."

"Not the carriage, madam?"

"No. If John returns early from his stroll, he might want it. I should not want him inconvenienced in any way."

I felt the mud squelch beneath the toe of one booted foot as I was handed down from the cab, and I wondered I had not thought of this sooner.

Of course, he could not come to me in my home; had in fact only been there that one first time. Our couplings were so rare, stolen in the most peculiar of places, too rare for me to stand the tension without causing a state of near madness. And I did know where he lived. Why, then, could I not go to him?

The air in the street was filled with odors I was unaccustomed to: food that smelled like nothing I would ever want to eat, human waste, the leavings of too many animals—all of it stale. The sound itself was a shock as well: the sheer loudness, noises from pain and anger and drunken joy, the whole discordant din a mock symphony of life as I knew it. And, as I looked out from the cab, I saw too many reminders of the Boer War: cripples, whose lives would never be the same, some driven mad by what they'd seen in a land too far from home.

"Damn Liberal busybodies!" I heard one cripple scream. "They all ought to lose their legs."

"What are you talking about?" another man demanded. "Stupid fool. It was Labour and the Liberals what wanted to save your legs."

"You don't know…"

As I stepped to the ground, a woman brushed against me, and it was all I could do not to reel back from her in revulsion. She could have been my age, but looked much older, a hard life bending her back, most of her teeth gone, the stench from her mouth giving me to believe she was not long for this world. Her twisted smile at me seemed to carry the knowledge that only fortune had separated her life from mine and the further knowledge that, in time, who knew whose fortune would prove greater?

I shook off the uneasy feeling she had given me, turned back to the cab. Asking the driver to wait, I paid him in advance for two hours' time.

Later, I would recall the neighborhood where Chance resided in cringing detail. How could civilized people live like that? Surely, no one would if there were any other choice. But standing in front of the door, hand raised to knock—finally here!—I no longer registered the filth of the street, the door finish that was more peel than paint.

"You surprise me, Emma."

I had not heard him ascend the steps behind me.

Reaching past me, he opened the door. "Did you want to come in?"

Hand yet raised, hoping to still the sudden racing of my heart, I entered ahead of him.

I am sure that, had I imagined the reality of it at all beforehand, I would have conjured up the meanness of his daily surroundings. The floor had no coverings with which to supply warmth to the coldness of the bare wood. Walls that I supposed might once have been some shade of white were stained with the residue of coal smoke that had not sufficient ventilation, and in one corner was the scorched evidence of a small fire; although, how long ago such a fire might have occurred, one really couldn't say.

There was a plain wooden table that could have held four chairs, but only had one; a single plate, a single spoon, a single fork, and a single knife were placed in front of it. There was a narrow bed shoved up against the wall with sheets that looked none too clean. At the head of the bed, a little up and to the right, was a window, covered by a lace curtain—remnant of some previous occupant, perhaps?—that was so threadbare as to offer only a token protection against either the late-day early-winter sun or the outsiders' inclination to stare in.

True, it had to be a sight better than a prison cell. But by how much?

Still, it did not matter.

I turned to him. The look on his face indicated he had been closely watching me as I registered my temporary surroundings, his daily ones.

"Forgive me," I said, feeling a sudden odd formality as though I were visiting a near stranger, not the man I had done so many things to and with. But it did feel strange being here, for the very first time on territory wholly his and not at all my own. "I have never thought to ask before: What are your plans for employment now?"

It may seem odd this had never come up before; indeed it felt strange to me to be asking him such a question. But in the relatively few times we had been able to meet, we had not been much for talking of practicalities, nor even in our frequent letters. In fact, the only *business* we ever spoke of was what to do about my husband and how to meet and meet again.

His smile was somewhat wolfish as he made a step toward me. In those small quarters, a step was all it took for him to loom over me.

"Is that what you came all this way down here for, Emma, to inquire as to my future prospects?" He reached out a hand, moved the hair back from my neck. "That is not something with which you need concern yourself. I am more resourceful than perhaps my past record might indicate. You should have no doubt: I *will* land on my feet."

"Actually," I said, steeling myself, "that is not what I came for."

I told him then about how John had checked to make sure he was still in Hollowgate, how John said Governor Croft had informed him Chance was still there and would be for life.

"How is that possible?" I demanded. The question had been gnawing at me.

When I first began to speak, Chance looked stunned, but now his features settled into a confident smile.

"It is obvious," he said, "is it not?"

"It *is*?"

"Yes," he said, "of course. You told me before about Constance telling John everything and about how John intended to learn more from the governor. Naturally, I wanted to protect you from exposure, so I did what any man in my position would do."

"And that was?"

"I went to the prison and bribed the governor. As I'm sure John can tell you, what with all his research, it is amazing how easily corruptible prison officials are, more so even than those in their care."

Now it was my turn to look stunned. Where had he got the money?

"Surely, you must realize by now, Emma," he said, as though answering my unasked question without really answering it, "there is nothing a man wouldn't do for a woman he truly loves."

He lowered his head to my neck, lowered my body to his bed.

Clothing was rapidly removed. I felt as though I were riding the wave even before we'd had the chance to properly begin.

The bed was softly lumpy in some parts, hard as marbles in others. The sheets were of the overused variety such that no amount of effort, and it did smell as though some effort had been recently made, could redeem them. Recollecting the afternoon later on, as I lived every moment over and over and over again, I could have sworn I remembered feeling something crawling on parts of my skin that belonged to neither of us.

It did not matter.

I arched my back to better meet him, felt myself squeezing and releasing for the first time in a controlled pattern that was uncontrolled as well, in that it seemed as though my body had become a thing of itself, possessing its own designs, wrapping my naked legs around his hips as though I might keep him there forever. I felt the nerves beneath the surface shatter apart in the fragments I now knew so well, wholly satisfied yet in the next instant regretting it bitterly as the fragments reintegrated into the whole.

It did not matter.

He did not stop. Pushing both of us forward, onward, I felt the wave start again, moved to turn away, felt his hand, his real hand, forcing my face to stay open to his.

Sweat in winter; what a peculiar thing.

And on and on.

Flinching only when he turned me over, filling a new hollow, charting a territory where no explorer had ever gone before.

And on and on.

His hair was disheveled. The light was disappearing from the day. He pressed his forehead to mine. "I do love you, Emma."

Leaning across me, he parted the near-useless curtains on the dying sun, the bustle of the street. Several hours had passed; the cab was no longer there.

It did not matter.

———————

I wanted one thing that was my choice—not society's, not my parents', my husband's, my son's, but mine—something I could claim for myself.

But how could I ever have that something?

After all, people would forgive a woman for leaving a drunken husband, they would forgive her for leaving a beating or a cheating husband. But no one would understand if she left a good husband.

Previously, I had not told Chance about what I had learned concerning John and Lucy. Perhaps I thought that, somehow, hearing that another man had chosen another woman over me would somehow make me seem less attractive, less desirable, less like a thing worth winning. But I steeled my courage and told him now.

His response surprised me. "Are you sure"—he smiled as he located papers and tobacco—"it was John?"

I shook my head, not in denial, but in incomprehension. "Who else could it be?"

What other men had been in my house in recent months besides Timmins? Chance himself had been there, but that had been long ago.

"No, of course," he said, "you are right." Anger settled on his features. "John should not have misused you in that way."

His anger warmed me, swept away any fears he would think me a woman a man could easily be unfaithful to.

Then I told Chance about John's intention to use our story as part of his new book about gossip. I told him how strongly I felt about that.

And Chance told me that there was only one choice left that still remained to us:

My husband must die.

FIFTY-THREE

How many of us choose our own lives? Still fewer, I'll wager, than those among us who choose their own deaths.

———

CUT!

I could never think of any other word to describe the sound my skates made as they sliced against new ice, the sharp cut as I turned my ankles into a slanted halt. I was always good, alone on the ice.

"I have something for you."

Chance's words brought me up short. Catching glimpses of my moving reflection in the mirror of the ice, I had been so preoccupied with that, as well as with the frozen world around me—the blackness, the blueness, the whiteness, and the transparencies—I had not noticed his approach. How had he found me here?

Cold had taken us all by surprise, as it sometimes does in early winter. Where it seemed just days ago mud had squelched beneath my feet, a drop of just a few degrees had transformed the rain that created the mud into a more solid precipitation and that same mud was now hardened, edged with rime.

The ponds had frozen suddenly, quickly, and I had taken the opportunity to lace up skates, donning a fur-lined coat and hat. The sable was warm against my body, warm against the outlines of my face, but my face itself was yet cold, and when I spoke, my words emerged surrounded by grayish-white puffs of air that carried them out into the world.

"You surprise me, sir," I said, as if I didn't know him well, as if I had not lain with him just a few short days ago.

Often and often I thought of him, so much so that it was as if he were with me at all times now in my head, rendering his sudden physical manifestation a true shock.

"Put out your hand," he said, and I listened. "Here."

He produced a bracelet, gold with garnet-colored gems that were a match to the startling color in the purplish-blue dress I had worn on that first night when he appeared in my room. The blood of the stones made a shocking statement of life in a landscaped world that was predominated now by deadly whites and blues and blacks.

His own hands were bare, despite the frigidness of the air. Pushing back the lined glove of the same hand on which I yet wore my wedding ring—mocking me with its three stones, John's gift of immortal life, affection, and success in love—he attached the gold clasp.

"But how did you . . . ?" I began, thinking to ask from where he had obtained the funds to purchase what was obviously an expensive piece.

"Shh." He placed his finger against my lips. Surprisingly, his finger did not feel cold. "It does not matter."

He had said nothing of getting a job and there was nothing about his character that had ever spoken of a thief. After all, he had been in my bedroom, had left while I was asleep. If money had ever been his objective, he could have robbed me that very night. Furthermore, as far as I knew, he had no mother, no sisters, from whom he might have at one point obtained such an item. Could it be possible, then, I wondered, that the bracelet had been something that had belonged to his dead wife?

But that is not the sort of question one can ask a lover.

I shuddered at the very thought of wearing something of a material nature that had belonged to her.

"I merely wanted you to have something of me," he said, seeing my shudder, perhaps misperceiving it as a shiver from the cold, placing his hand over mine.

I could only smile acceptance in return, push back the thought of any previous wife.

"We so rarely get to talk," he said. "We have talked our hearts out in letters, yet when we are together, though we talk through our bodies, there are so few words." He reached out a hand, palm upward as if we were in a gilded ballroom. "Skate with me, Emma?"

Other skaters had taken advantage of the new ice, not yet seasoned enough to have become pitted and scarred by too many blades scraping against the surface, as it would surely do as the season wore on. But those other skaters remained on the safer peripheries, promenading along the tree-lined, snow-dusted edges where one could be more certain the water had indeed frozen through.

Heedless to the increasing recklessness of my actions, ignoring the possible threat posed by others—surely, they were all too far away to see?—I took his hands, and we moved out toward the precarious center.

As we skated, side by side—one of his hands circling behind my waist with my hand covering it, the other holding my other hand in front of him—we spoke one heart to another. We talked at last of everything that had been said in the letters, acknowledging the depths we had sounded in each other. We talked, immodestly perhaps, of all the pleasures we had discovered in each other's bodies. We talked, finally, of love.

"Do you love me, Emma? Do you still love me?"

I had not thought to ever hear him ask such a question. I could not imagine where such doubt could come from.

"You should not have to ask that," I said, cutting to a stop. "Surely, you must know."

He held me to him; indiscreet to do so, perhaps, in public, but the other skaters were so far away now. I was fairly certain no one could know that as he held me to him, his desire was a hard and living thing between us.

"But I am asking," he insisted.

"Then the answer is yes," I said clearly. "It will always be yes."

The only thing we did not talk about was the future. He, perhaps sensing I could not be pushed on the matter we had discussed the other day—the complete removal of my husband from the picture—said nothing more about it. Perhaps he sensed what I already knew: that such an act would be too monstrous, no matter how much we desired to be together. Perhaps, I told myself, he had merely been testing me in some way. For, surely, he could not possibly think it could ever be right for us to do that.

He was apparently satisfied with my answer, for the time being at least, and we resumed our skate.

I arced my back fully into the skating dance, felt the slightest supporting pressure of his hand low down against the base of my spine as I twirled, head tilted back, eyes closed, pirouetting on the fragility of the temporary hardness beneath me. That hand seemed like very little to be standing as the only thing between me and the pain of unbalance, and yet I did not doubt him. He would not let me fall out here, spinning on the ice.

He was my safety. He was the net that was going to catch me.

And yet I was lost; out here, I was finally lost.

But just as abruptly as he had first come to me, the dance ended.

"I am sorry, Emma," he said. "I must go."

I should have liked to have stopped him, but one must know when a moment, no matter how perfect, has ended.

"I do love you," he said, giving my hands one last squeeze as we exchanged a speaking glance, clearly embedded in which was his undeniable desire to kiss me.

If only I could keep him with me. If only he did not ever have to go. But how would I be able to bring myself to do the one thing that would make it so he would never have to leave me again? I wondered if I would ever have the strength. And yet, in the very same moment, I felt as though, were the glass to appear before me right that instant, I would drink from it.

I looked around, shivered, still feeling the spin. The snow-covered trees bore witness to our passing there, trees that would still remain long after we both of us were gone.

I watched him skate away, knew it would be useless at this moment to call him back.

"Mummy?"

Weston's voice, coming as it did from behind me, startled me so much I raised a hand to my suddenly pounding chest. I had been so caught up in the world of my skating dance, I had forgotten I had brought my son with me, had left him skating alone on the peripheries with the far-distant others.

"Mummy, who were you talking to?"

FIFTY-FOUR

Before you know it," said John, "it will be another New Year and this strange one, with its double aughts, will have passed off into the stuff of memory."

His words brought me up short. It was hard to believe Chance had been free for nearly a whole year now, and yet, because of my other obligations, my other demands, we had spent so painfully little time together.

Deciding we had not yet done anything sufficient to record the passing year for posterity, John proposed we should have a photograph taken.

And so Weston and I found ourselves one chilly Saturday morning, waiting in the long corridor as the photographer set up his equipment on the black-and-white tiles. It was indeed very cold out and John said he did not want us all bundled up against the elements, he wanted us to appear as ourselves. He said despite the ice rimming the edges on the outsides of the window-panes, even the thin sun, passing through the glass, would keep us warm enough. As with anything scientific, as always, John was right.

"The hall will be perfect," he added, with a smile that said we might still need convincing. "You will see. With the light from the long windows illuminating us, we will appear as royalty upon a chessboard."

It was not easy to dissuade him when he was in such a mood.

"Wear your favorite dress," he suggested. "It will make the portrait that much more precious to me."

My favorite dress?

I selected the one dress that was not a lie: the one I had worn on the night *he* had first come to me.

Did I dare to put the garnet bracelet on?

I did dare.

In fact, I had worn it every day since Chance had given it to me on the ice. I must confess that when, over breakfast, I saw it peep out from beneath the lace-edged sleeve of my dressing gown, I did wonder that neither John nor Weston remarked upon it. As for the former, I attributed his lack of comment to an unwillingness to stir me up. I had taken to my bed for so long, earlier in the year, he must have at one point begun to despair he might have another Constance on his hands. As for the latter, Weston, I thought perhaps he was too preoccupied with the business of being a child to take note of a piece of jewelry that had never been there before.

And if John did ask?

I supposed I could always tell him I had found it in the street... in the track marks of the wheels of a carriage that had too quickly pulled away.

Next to my moody purple, my twining blue and green, my startling dark red, John and Weston's matching black suits and pristine white shirts, topped off by their fair features, were a counterpoint in light, refinement, and restraint. Their eyes were even the same eyes, save that one pair was wholly innocent with excitement, the other marred by an all too analytical inquisitiveness.

We jockeyed to achieve the proper pose, myself growing increasingly testy all the while. Even though the world outside had been frozen, the heat of the sun through the windows was enough to make it feel like summer. Could we not do this some other time? Must this be done today?

Finally, we did settle on a pose. By then, however, the brightness, the heat, and the memories of the dress as they burned into my very skin caused my mind to pull loose from that space. Thoughts, images of Chance were everywhere, harrowing me until I could have sworn he was somewhere in there with us. I attempted, mostly in vain, to rein in the pictures. At last, at least, I was able to confine him into one small corner of the room.

That is how the photographer shot us.

I can still see that photograph now, though if it were before me, I would turn it facedown against the table or smash it against the wall. John seated with Weston on his knee, both staring up at me; I with my hands only reluctantly resting upon John's shoulder, looking off into the corner at something no one else could see or was interested in at the time.

Later on, John asked me what in this world I had been looking at so intently.

But, of course, I could not tell him.

FIFTY-FIVE

I retreated yet further into the box, taking to my bed for days at a time whenever I could no longer bring myself to face the lack of choices with which I was presented.

Or to put it more properly, there were indeed choices, but I didn't like them. They were all flawed. There was no choice where I could reach for what I wanted without having to pay a great cost.

Sometimes, visitors came: John's family; my friends; Father; even Louisa.

Louisa was something of a shock. I could not recall any bedside visits from her during any of the ailments that all children are subject to during my youth. Indeed, it was always my father whom I remembered, sitting at my bedside, always in sickness, sometimes in health. So why, then, should Louisa be so suddenly determined to be my mother now?

Well, she had herself nursed a weak heart for years. She had claimed one when I was very young, saying it was brought on by the experience of birthing me. I had doubted this at the time, thinking it a thing invented as an excuse to escape whatever activity she didn't want to be part of. But as the years wore on her condition appeared to worsen. Sometimes, I would catch her straining for breath, hand to chest on occasions when she did not even know she was being observed. Perhaps, then, her visit to my bedside was a result merely of the empathy one invalid feels for another.

But Louisa? Empathetic?

"You cannot stay in bed forever," she said.

False. Actually, I thought, we were wealthy enough; unless John chose to have me removed, I probably *could* stay there forever.

"Weston needs you."

Well, that was true enough. But I did know that.

"People miss you."

I raised an eyebrow, the most energy I'd felt in three days.

"Well, your father appears to, at any rate."

That, at least, was something.

———

My earliest memory of Louisa's weak heart was from the summer I turned twelve. Although she had been claiming one for years, this was the first attack I can recall having witnessed. I cannot say I remember what even it was that precipitated it, but I do know we were in the country. It is my recollection that, at the time, we were visiting distant relatives, relatives I do not remember us ever going to visit after that summer again, and that John was with us. My father having practically adopted John as the son he'd never had, John was always with us in those days.

The relatives' house was white-painted stone with diamond-shaped double-glazed windows that had a slight warp when you looked through them. On one corner of their property was a pond stocked with trout, and I was encouraged to fish with my own pole—no matter that it made a mess of my skirts. The man of the house had laugh lines that were more pronounced on one side of his face than the other, the lady was always arrayed in some shade of blue, they had three daughters, none of whom had ever read any of the books I was interested in, the stewed tomatoes and bacon at breakfast were excellent but the kippers were not, it rained three of the five days we were there, they had an old pony named Sam, and there was a water stain in the small but unmistakable shape of Wales on the ceiling over the bed I was given to sleep in.

As I say, I do not remember what event it was that precipitated Louisa's feeling so poorly, yet I know there must have been one, for afterward when she had these attacks—and she had them fairly frequently after this—there was always some precipitating event.

And this is the odd thing, really, my lack of a clear recollection, for I have a remarkably good memory. Biased? Perhaps. But I can quote whole significant conversations verbatim going back to my earliest memories. If ever called to the witness-box at a trial, I would give perfect testimony. Odd, then, that I should only remember my mother getting sick, the doctor being summoned, and my father spiriting us back to the city.

They say that memory plays strange tricks sometimes.

I still wonder about that.

FIFTY-SIX

As one rose, the other fell.

As love for one grew, hatred grew for the other.

It was as though they were two ideas that could not live in my mind at the same time, could not go on existing in the world around me.

———————

I began the long, slow process of convincing myself that what I wanted was perfectly all right.

Chance promised this was the only way.

We had already ruled out divorce. People needed money to live. *We* would need money to live. If we ran away to be together, as my foolishly brave Katherine had done with her beloved, we would be going with nothing but the clothes on our backs. It would be a hard life compared to the one I had known. It might even be a hard life compared to the life Chance had known.

Chance said I was accustomed to more.

Chance said I *deserved* more.

And he was right. Especially, if we were somehow able to manage to spirit Weston away with us—and, oh, how I *wanted* to keep him!—we would need money, at least enough to start. Since between us we had *no* money, there was no possible start in that direction. That might have been a good enough new beginning for Katherine, but, foolishly brave though my grandniece might be, I yet knew myself well enough to know I had never been capable of being both foolish and brave at the same time.

True, Chance had somehow found money with which to bribe the governor, but I had never asked how he had done so, did not want to know. And he had gifted me with that bracelet, the provenance of which I did not wish to know either. But whatever his source for those things had been, they were trifles in comparison to the amount of money we would need to live and live well.

Chance said that, with John gone, we would be together all the time.

Chance said that, in time, we could even be together in public, like normal people, rather than stealing a wary moment here and there as we had done when he surprised me while skating.

Chance said that he would get a job, save enough money to buy just the right suit, so that when he came calling for me formally, after an appropriate amount of time had passed, he would be accepted into my world. People would believe he had his own money, had come from money, and no one would be any the wiser that in reality we were living on what John had made during his lifetime. We could remain in London.

He would reinvent himself.

He would marry me.

He would love me until the day one of us died.

And, still, a part of me hesitated.

———

Starting late in the third quarter of Weston's first year, my son and I had embarked on a series of what I would come to think of as "baby races." He, having just discovered that his new limbs could actually be employed to convey himself toward some desired object—as opposed to merely pumping them in progressless delight, like a beetle caught on its back, when something particularly thrilled him—was beginning to make cautious crawling forays into the wider world around him. Propped on his elbows, he would inch himself along, proud of every inch, not yet strong enough or perhaps not aware of the greater movement possibilities to be had in raising himself up on straight arms.

One day, as I entered the nursery, I saw him playing on the floor on the far side of the room. Seeing me enter, and seeing the look of gleeful anticipation come over his face when he saw me, Hannah moved to lift him in order to bring him directly to me. I held up a hand to stop her.

"Leave him," I said, removing my traveling scarf. Then, lifting my skirts a few inches so they would not get in the way, I lowered myself to all fours on the nursery floor and faced off against my gurgling son.

Seeing my attempt at keeping a sternly competitive look, and being a natural mimic, as all babies are, he attempted a serious look of his own, watching me closely to see what I might do next. Propped on my own elbows, I took one elbow step toward him, moving the knee on that side of my body in concert with it as my skirts made rustling noises behind me. Having observed what I was doing, Weston caught the rules of the game.

Weston matched my movement, then stopped.

I moved again; he moved again.

Now I waited and gave him time to take over. Smiling a baby triumph, he seized the lead role. It did not take him long to discover the charm inherent in being in charge. Setting the pace, he squealed as, immediately upon his moving another and then another elbow step toward me, I each time answered his challenge.

I do not know what Hannah made of this, her mistress on the floor with her posterior in the air in a most unladylike fashion, nor did I particularly care. If she told the other servants I had taken leave of my senses, what matter that? It was enough to see the look on my son's face as we moved faster and faster toward each other in our baby race until at last we met in the middle. Like two foals meeting, when we were finally face-to-face we studied each other; then we commenced to a nuzzling, his nose against my cheek, mine resting against the comfort of his.

In all my life, up to that point, I had never known such joy, such a moment of complete peace.

Naturally, I told no one of my newly conceived idea—*Chance's* idea—that my husband must die.

Does that bold statement look as shrill in print as I fear it must? Of course it does.

What I wanted, however, did not seem bold to me at all; but, rather, basic: I wanted to survive. And, the way I saw it, there was only one choice: Either my husband must die in body, or I, in turning my back on Chance, must abandon my own spirit.

But, returning to the main point, who was there for me to tell? Surely, anyone but we two would think me a monster.

I looked at Weston. He had changed so much since being that baby I had once raced against. That baby had been pure innocent joy. But he was growing up now, with glimmerings of the man he might one day become.

I studied him with an almost clinical eye:

Could I really take his father from him?

I knew then why a part of me still hesitated: My anger was not yet big enough; I did not yet hate his father enough. Nor could I see that I ever would.

FIFTY-SEVEN

There are some things that happen in a person's life that are so unspeakable, we never talk about them to anybody, not even to ourselves.

———

Winter was spring was summer was fall was winter, and I had taken to my bed again, the one safe harbor from a world that ever wanted in, in, in. I tried to keep out everyone I could keep out, but some would not be denied.

Louisa had already left the room, although she had lingered long enough that I had nearly risen from my bed in order to push her out.

Then, once she was gone, Father bent to kiss my cheek, his brown eyes meeting mine. At the same moment, John, who had been standing sentry at the draperies as family members came and departed, drew the drapes partially open.

Back still to me, I heard his voice: "Is this what you like, Emma?"

My mind instantly reeled with it. What a strange way for him to ask that question! Not "Is this the way you like the drapes, Emma?" But, rather, "Is this what you like, Emma?" His words held the echo of something from my childhood in them. I had heard those words, and exactly in that strange configuration, before. And, in a flash so instantaneous it could not have moved through me faster if someone had leapt out and jammed a knife through my heart, I remembered something. It was a horrible something, a something I had buried so very far deep down inside myself I had not taken it out to look at in over twenty years, had never taken it out before.

I do think that, in that moment of Father's brown eyes meeting mine, he saw I did indeed remember, saw I was now seeing everything very clearly for the first time in a very long time, maybe even ever. Yet, I do not know how he did so, but he had the strength of purpose to continue with the downward motion, as if doing whatever he wanted to do had always been an inevitability for him, finishing off the kiss on my cheek before departing after my mother.

How could he leave so easily, knowing what I now knew? Was it that he believed himself to be safe from my reach, as he had undoubtedly always been certain he must be? Was his masculine sense of protection so strong?

And was what I remembered, visiting those distant relatives when I was twelve, the man of that house having laugh lines that were more pronounced on one side of his face than the other, that man stealing into my room at night, the room with the water stain in the small but unmistakable shape of Wales on the ceiling over the bed I was given to sleep in, stealing the warmth and yet more from my child's body? How much that man had stolen, my memory was unclear, yet surely not everything, for I would have suspected as much the first time I lay with John, surely one of us would have suspected. Finally, after all this time, was this the source of my reluctance to be around my parents, that my parents had turned their heads away from what had happened to me, somehow allowed it to happen, the reason why Louisa always treated me more like a rival than like her daughter . . . *that a male relative had lain with her own daughter, me, and she could think of nothing else to do save compete?*

No wonder I had never been willing to leave Weston alone with them.

Had such a thing ever happened to any other woman?

If it had, no one had told me.

A long time ago, when I had felt myself to be abandoned out on the limb by Chance, I had thought myself the angriest I had ever been before. But this anger was now greater than that anger. My rage, directed at nearly my entire world, was far greater than anything I had felt up to this point.

And I had nowhere to go with it.

I saw John standing still at the half-opened draperies, wholly unwitting of the painful recollections his words had caused, and I had nowhere to go with that raging anger.

FIFTY-EIGHT

Once upon a time, two years ago, I had thought myself happy. I had prepared for the annual celebration at the Collinses' thinking myself happy: happy in my husband, happy in my friends, happy in my life among society.

But I saw now I had not been happy. I saw now, with contempt, that all I had ever been was a pale form of content.

———————

New Year's Eve 1900 was less eventful than the one that had gone before. Now that the world knew, had known for just one day short of a full year, that it would not stop with its turning to those strange double aughts, things had gone back to what was considered to be normal.

The world might change, and had, but it would not stop.

Our own New Year's Eve came and went without celebration or resolutions. After all, what was there that yet remained to be resolved?

Still, it did seem a recounting of the past year's events was in order.

As John would be quick to point out, on the literary front things had been hectic. Sigmund Freud published his *The Interpretation of Dreams* (which undoubtedly was not literature but which did, also undoubtedly, shake everyone in sight including the literary world), Stephen Crane died, Oscar Wilde died.

Apparently, it did not matter how earnest one was. Everyone needed to die.

People were dying in other fields as well. Still, painters kept painting, composers kept composing, and a little newspaper called the *Daily Express* appeared for the first time on the streets of London.

But I ask you: Who really cared?

FIFTY-NINE

Queen Victoria's death on 22 January 1901 should have bothered me more, since her life had always impressed me a great deal. After all, it was she who had been the architect behind the release that had released me.

The shopwindows were now all filled with black, and John commented on an advertisement in the newspaper: Apparently, the Parisian Diamond Company of New Bond Street was recommending diamonds and pearls for mourning accessories.

My beloved Katherine, despite her lack of interest in fashion, had always loved pretty jewels and glass objects and it occurred to me that, morbid as the purpose of these items for sale were, she would yet find them attractive. How I missed Katherine: her sheer energy, her hopefulness.

Still, despite the public display of mourning that surrounded me, I hardly marked the event at all. If the nation wished to put on black, so be it. I would join them. Black suited my current mood; black suited the clouds gathering all around me.

Winter had come for good now. I could not imagine it leaving again.

————————

He parted my lips from behind, an echo of the mirror fantasy.

And so it went, on and on.

My life had become a fever dream.

————————

Weston said, "Mummy, you have great big gray bags under your eyes. Are you unwell?"

I did not feel as though I were lying. "No, darling." I hugged him. "Mummy just hasn't had the chance to put on a face to confront the world with yet."

Then Weston did one of those utterly surprising things children do sometimes, the kind of thing you could not get them to do by merely entreating them, not in a million years. Rather than seeking out my body's ability to comfort him, he placed his fingers gently against my face; a touch like a benediction.

I felt somehow certain it was the last moment of real peace I would ever know.

SIXTY

John had never been much of one for the hunt, so it did surprise me somewhat when he insisted we join a weekend party made up of the Collinses, the Larwoods, the Gammadges, and Captain Brimley at Brimley's mother's country estate.

Though it was still eternal February, though the nation still mourned, Maeve Collins was determined to get away. And, for once, Joshua was inclined to indulge her. All of the husbands had seen what had happened to Constance, who was once again in the country. None wanted his own wife to go the same way.

Captain Brimley's mother was herself away, and so, Lady Collins had been pressed into service to make up our numbers. It had been some time since I had last seen her—I had not wanted her to ask any more probing questions about the maid I had told her was in trouble, nor did I want her to see the changes being with Chance had wrought in me—and yet she had added very few wrinkles, was still pretty. It was as though she had made some unholy deal with someone; or maybe it was simply she was that good a person, even Time wished her no harm.

"You are changed, my dear," were the first words she spoke to me.

I had never been, to the best of my recollections, anything but happy to see her in the past. Now, however, "happy" did not at all describe what I felt, my own cold hand restless within the remnant warmth that was still alive in hers, despite their gnarled tapers, her hands the one part of her that fully reflected her years.

Perhaps she sensed my unease.

"We must talk later." Her eyes attempted a sparkle that wouldn't ignite. "I see where you might have all manner of new things to tell me."

I did my best to ensure Lady Collins's "later" did not come.

At dinner the first night, I let the conversation wash around me as the others discussed the immediate future of England. Lady Collins endeavored repeatedly to draw me out, but I remained impervious, smiling benignly. It was as though I myself were inside the funnel of the tornado, while all around me swirled debris that couldn't touch me.

After dinner, while the men performed their tedious routine and the ladies retired to wait for them, I was forced to redouble my efforts at evasion. Seating myself between Maeve and Hettie on one of Captain Brimley's horsehair sofas—black, slippery, scratchy, buttoned, and tufted, they were revolting things—before a cheery fire that did not cheer, I spoke just as Lady Collins was opening her mouth to address me.

"Do you know what John does that I positively detest?" I asked impishly, turning my attention to Maeve.

Out of the corner of my eye, I saw Lady Collins turn her face from me.

I did not sleep that night.

I was not used to spending an entire night in an unfamiliar room. I'd never been comfortable being an overnight guest, never liked indulging comfort that felt as though it were on loan. Naturally, I would have loved to spend an entire night in an unfamiliar room with Chance, even if it was that mean room where he currently resided. Was it possible we had never spent even one full night together anywhere?

I tossed, I turned, but sleep would not come. Finally, around two in the morning, I gave up. Perhaps, if I had a good book to read—or, better still, a boring one—it would help.

But I had brought nothing with me.

So I began going through John's travel valise. Surely, he would have brought something to read.

It was then I came upon the manuscript pages for *Gossip*.

Unlike his previous books, he had shown me nothing of this one, had not read to me one word of it.

I began flipping pages.

"The Royal Family"?

Yawn. There could be nothing new to excite me there.

"Whispers Among the Elite"?

Double yawn. I knew all of that.

"The Prisoner."

I began to read:

> ...She was a lonely woman, trapped within a life that had somehow built itself up around her, with neither her will nor her design...

Good God, I thought, he was writing my life!

> ...When, on top of being lonely, a woman is permitted too much time for self-reflection, she may begin to manufacture imaginary suitors, knights in shining armor—or, for that matter, prisoners who have been wrongly imprisoned themselves—to satisfy her need for company and romance. If further left to her own devices, she may begin to even believe her imaginary suitor is real. But, that is the thing: He is *not* real.
>
> I can give, as an example, a woman I knew all too well...

John had told me he was going to put in what he referred to as the "charming anecdote" of Constance's tall tale of me and my prisoner, and I had even told Chance, but I suppose a part of me had not really believed my husband would betray me, use me so. And I had never imagined it being so personal, so contemptuous. It was awful, demeaning.

In John's overzealousness to beat Harry Baldwin at what he perceived as being the other man's game, he was writing my life, and he was laughing at Chance and I in the process.

I read further, saw he had included letters, purportedly written by this woman he "knew all too well" to her prisoner, but there were no letters written by the prisoner in return. The woman gushed; her letters were tawdry and sentimental, the kinds of things *I* would never write.

> ..."*if you will but come to me, I will be your slave*"...

It was devastating.

I was a human being. I was not one of his characters, to be manipulated around the story as he played God. I was not material for his book!

So what if he had not used my letters, because he did not have access to them?

I felt as though, in writing my life, he had killed Chance, killed *me*.

But he hadn't. I was still here.

———

I could not imagine, when I looked out the window the next morning, spare blanket wrapped around my shoulders, that the hunting would be very promising. The sky was the color of a gun that had somehow been caused to fade over time, losing some of its depth of hue while retaining all of its dull threat. As for the cold, it had become a nearly visible thing.

"Wake up, John," I called behind me. "It looks like a perfect day for a hunt."

Breakfast, as far as I was concerned, was no more than a dismal con-
tinuation of the night before. Food upon food—the repetitive need
was tiresome. Breakfast; dinner—one meal leading into the next. I
had no interest in it, no patience for it. I was ready to be gone.

"I am not at all sure this is the best idea any of us has ever had,"
observed Captain Brimley, slathering butter on his toast.

"You may be right at that," said Winston Gammadge. "What
say we spend the morning around the fire? It is never too early in the
day to play charades."

"Do not be ridiculous." My words forestalled any further de-
murrals. "It is a perfectly perfect day for a hunt."

Time had begun to move like waves at the seaside as the tide comes
in: rolling forward, retreating back, moving just a little bit farther forward each time.

The discussion had taken place between John and I the night before, after we had retired to our room, but before my bout with sleep-
lessness.

"Are you quite certain this is something you wish to do?" he
asked.

He was referring to the statement I had just made about wishing
to accompany the men on the following day.

"I have never known you to care for hunting," he continued, removing his dinner jacket. "For that matter, I have never cared for it
myself."

Seated before the mirror, feeling it strange to be seeing myself in
someone else's mirror, I kept my eyes on the eyes of my own reflection
as I brushed out my hair.

"Both of your statements are undoubtedly true," I agreed. *"But,"*
I appended, "when the choice is between accompanying the gentlemen and remaining behind with the ladies *for nine hours,* just biding
our time until it is suitable for us to commence dressing ourselves for
dinner with the gentlemen at eight, well, then, give me a gun."

"Very well, my dear." He placed one hand on my shoulder. "If that is what you wish."

John now lay flat on the ground where the horse had thrown him. As I moved toward him, I was conscious of the rifle in my hand, pointed downward but with my finger gently poised against the trigger. In no time, it seemed, I was standing over him; felt my own features looking down upon him, unsmiling; took it in when one of his knees raised up, almost defensively; saw him raise hand to brow, in a vain attempt at blocking out the orange ball of sun that had made a sudden and startling show in the sky, blazing behind me.

"Emma?" His single word was yet even more of a question than it appeared. Did he not know that it was I, or was it that he no longer knew who *I* was?

Without giving thought to what I was doing, the gun was rising in my arm, the end no longer pointed toward the ground, instead raising up, and farther up...

"Emma?" he asked again.

Odd, but his lips did not move. It was then I realized the voice had come from behind me, not in front.

"Emma?" The same voice.

Turning, I saw Captain Brimley. I do not know how long he had been standing there.

It turned out Winston Gammadge had been paying some small attention when his cousin studied medicine. He knew enough, at any rate, to judge John had received a mild sprain to the ankle. It was not an injury that should stop a man of his good health for very long, but it would make it slightly difficult to get around in the immediate future and was sufficient to halt all sport for the remainder of the weekend.

SIXTY-ONE

I was beginning to think, contrary to my long-held belief, that the devil did indeed exist after all; and, if my suspicions were correct, I was going to have to make some kind of deal with him.

"Can I get you anything else?" I asked my husband.

We were back home again. He was ensconced behind his writing desk, underneath which I had fitted a stool so he could keep his ankle elevated. I wondered what he worked on. Was he writing more about me, perhaps?

How I hated to think what he might be writing. How angry it made me.

"Another pillow, perhaps?" was what I suggested aloud. "More tea?"

He smiled. "I am truly fine. There is no need to hover around me."

"I was only trying—"

"Yes, and I appreciate that. But nothing will make me feel better quicker than getting back to work." He looked pointedly at the library door. My, but he was in a hurry to see me gone.

"Very well..."

I shut the door gently behind me.

Naturally, Weston was curious about John's injury, having never seen his father wounded in any way or even ill before. He wanted to touch John's swollen ankle, seemed to think the perfect cure for his father would be if his father were to indulge in more games with him. But John had little patience for this. All he claimed to want was his work.

John's sisters also sought to help him. Perhaps they saw his invalid status as an opportunity to at last restore order to their universe, returning him to a state of dependency upon them. In Ruth's case, perhaps she saw it as a chance to replace the granddaughter she'd lost by returning her own brother to a childlike state.

But John was having none of that either.

He would only allow me to wait on him, and that grudgingly.

During this period of John's convalescence I saw little of Chance. I was too busy playing nursemaid, even despite John's irritable objections; it was my duty.

And then there was this too: For the first time, I did not want Chance to see into my heart. I wanted him beyond all reason; would have done anything, given anything, I thought, to be with him.

Had I known the price tag, would I have still felt that way?

I still believed Chance was testing me about the...removal of my husband. Could he still love me once he saw how black that heart of mine had become? I was willing to entirely wipe one slate clean— *somehow*—so I might begin writing my own story anew. What, I tried to tell myself, was so awful about that?

And, I told myself, these were mere thoughts I had from time to time, mere fantasies, and thoughts and deeds are not the same thing. The vicar might say thoughts and deeds are one. But I knew that wasn't true. If thinking were the same as acting, at least half the world would be dead from someone wishing it so.

But, even as I told myself that, another part of me knew the deeper truth.

I now knew without doubt I was going to burn for all of this. The only question that remained was:

When?

SIXTY-TWO

It goes without saying the window should never have been left open in the first place.

But as with so many other things in life that go without saying, it changes nothing about the facts of what happened.

———

I fired Hannah, of course.

Even if I did not believe it to be her fault—and in my grief I had to blame someone—not only was there no longer any reason for her to be there, under my roof, but also, I could no longer stand the sight of her. If I died myself without seeing her again, it would suit me.

The story as it came out, as it was told and repeated again and again until I thought I might go mad with the swirling vortex of it, was too simply common to be anything but the awful truth it was.

Hannah and Weston had been playing in the nursery, something to do with her pretending to be the late Queen Victoria's favorite horse and he pretending to be John Brown. Weston had grown warm with the play and had asked that Nanny open the window for him.

Nanny had insisted it was still too cold out for open windows.

Weston had laughingly insisted back that, no matter it was late October, it felt to him just like the middle of July! Besides, did she not know yet who worked for whom around here?

At that, Nanny, ever good-natured where Weston was concerned, laughed right back. Another servant might have taken grave offense at such a young child speaking so. But Nanny adored Weston, always had. What's more, she had long been concerned he was too timid for a boy of his station in life. And so, lately, when he had taken it into his little head to see if he could get away with playing lord of the manor, she was happy to let him. Rather than correcting his insolence, then, she congratulated him on his most excellent use of "who" and "whom," picked her equine self up off the floor, and moved to do his bidding.

No sooner had she done so, however, throwing the heavy window wide to the bracing air, than she imagined she heard someone call her name.

Later on, she could not say for certain if it had been Lucy or Timmins, neither of whom, in turn, could remember calling for her. When this could not be resolved, she wondered if perhaps it had been John or I who had called to her. But John had been working in his library when Lucy had come running in, distraught, having glimpsed Weston broken in the street, and the library was on the far side of our home. Surely, John could never have shouted loud enough from there for her to hear him, as he had not heard her shouts of anguish when she returned to find the nursery empty. That left only me as a possibility for the caller and I was, I had been . . .

. . . not at home.

No, it was none of us, nor had anyone left a calling card that day, an unseen, unidentifiable, boisterous caller who had shouted for the nanny by name and then failed to stay.

It must have been a phantom; there was no other logical explanation, either that or the overworked imagination of a lonely servant always expecting to be summoned by somebody, somewhere.

Regardless of the ascertainableness of the unfortunate circumstances, a few things were undeniably true: that when Hannah went to answer her summons, she turned back at the last moment and, curtseying low, excused herself with a smile to her "lord and master." He, in turn, bowed benevolently, and only tried to look stern, yet wholly failed to conceal the open affection behind his "Hurry back, then, Nanny. I have another game scheduled that you must participate in."

I know this loving exchange to have factually taken place because: one, Hannah told me so; and, two, I had observed the love that lay between them often enough not to doubt the veracity.

The other undeniable truth was that after Hannah had exited the room, Weston had somehow fallen to his death out of the window. This final undeniable truth I knew to be so because I had discovered his crumpled body myself, coming upon it in the street on my return home, having escaped my nursemaid duties for one day to see Chance.

The nursery was on the third floor, the ceilings of each being very high; three stories was an awfully long way for such a small body to fall.

My screams were so loud and went on for so long, finding him like that, in such a position and so lifeless, that for a long time afterward it seemed all I could hear was the bell-tower clanging of my own grief, tolling over and over again in a world grown mute around me.

They had to tear me away from him.

In a perverse echo of his birth, it was like having him ripped from my body a second time.

I gave Hannah one month's wages and requested she be gone from my sight, turning my back to her even before she moved for the door.

It is possible that the specter of guilt drove my hand where she was concerned.

Did I blame myself for what happened? Did I leave the window open myself, order someone else to open it, seduce Hannah from the room for a moment, just a long enough moment for my only son to fall to his death?

No. No to everything.

Surely, on the surface of things, then, my child's death could in no way be divined as being my fault. Yet I had allowed myself to want something for myself, to want something so much, beyond all reason, I was willing to pay a great price, to allow everyone around me to pay a great price in order to achieve it.

That night, as John sat alone in his library, I can only assume crying, I stole into Weston's room by myself, looked at the nursery rhymes and fairy tales of youth on his walls for the last time, and sobbed bitterly over the loss of fiction.

SIXTY-THREE

The staff was provided with white mourning garments and black armbands, as was the custom. Blinds were drawn; clocks stopped, as well they should be; mirrors covered to prevent Weston's spirit from getting trapped within. This last presented a particular problem for me. It was difficult now to live in a world without mirrors. Without that reflection, that reflection that somehow revealed to me what Chance saw, who was I?

I cannot say I was happy with the idea of a public funeral. Happy? What was "happy" now? But the rest of the family seemed to want it, to need it so, that all of a sudden I realized it made little difference to me. If my parents, my wretched parents, if John's sisters, if our friends and Lucy and Timmins all felt the need to say good-bye to Weston, I had no fight in me to stop them now. I was too numb to everything to care if there were two hundred people around me there on the hard earth of the church graveyard.

I think John did hold my hand the whole time, standing stiffly beside me, his ankle not yet fully healed, making him stand yet stiffer, but when I try to remember the day—and I can honestly say this is the only time I have braved this—I think I must believe he did so only because it would have been like him and not because I have an actual picture of it in my mind.

His grief, after all, must have been as great as mine. His only son, bearing the stamp of his features, had been his single bid that even beyond death, he might somehow extend his life on earth. And, of course, he had loved him. To think that at such a moment he would have been capable of offering comfort to another seems too much to ask from a mere human being.

He was there at the graveyard, of course. I know, because I saw him hovering in the background. And even then, seeing him so suddenly and unexpectedly, I wanted him. God help me, even then, I wanted him.

———

With Weston gone, it was no longer possible, do what I might, to get warm enough.

In the middle of the sleepless night, I felt John turn to me, felt him reach for me.

But it did not matter.

He was another human being, so I suppose his warmth should have tempted me.

But it did not matter.

I should have felt one way or the other about it. We had done it a thousand times. I had thought we were through with this.

But it did not matter.

In the end, what did one more time matter?

I looked at John coolly, even as I allowed him to enter me:

There was no longer anything left to tie me to him.

SIXTY-FOUR

Due to the conventions of society—how I now *hated* that word!—I had been forced to spend the better part of the year in confinement due to my household's state of mourning. Had I gone about my business as I once had, even if John in his own preoccupation and grief had not noticed it, it would surely have been called to his attention by Timmins. And it was not as though I wanted to do anything frivolous now that Weston was gone, it was not as though I wanted to go out *shopping*. I merely wanted... all I wanted...

Having stolen out of the house for once—finally!—we were walking in the streets outside his room, the labyrinth laced with the scent of dung.

Everything I wore was black. I had my hat pulled low and my wrap pulled high, protection against anyone I knew recognizing me, but it was unlikely anyone I knew would be in this part of the city. Oddly enough, I was no longer bothered by the smells, the sights, the sounds of where he lived. Indeed, because he was there, it now had the peculiar feel of home. Could I learn to live like that?

I pulled the wrap tighter against the cold. November had grown to be the month I most detested. It seemed to me sometimes, now, that I had spent my entire allotment for living inside the month of November.

"Please forget I said anything," I said, as we passed a pawnbroker's shop, a tobacco and snuff shop, the shafts of a rather shabby tradesman's cart. "It was a foolish thought, best left unvoiced."

At last, he spoke. "I did not say I do not understand."

He placed his hand under my elbow, assisting me at the curb. Afterward, he did not remove his hand.

"It is just," he went on, "that I was marveling at the originality of your mind. My words were not a judgment on its workings, nor was there in them any attempt to either persuade or dissuade you from your set course. I was merely admiring the fact of how differently that mind works from anyone else's I have known."

I let out a breath I had not known I was holding.

An early snowflake landed on my cheek, melting to a pinpoint of water on contact. As we stood there, looking at each other, more came, faster. I saw them land in his hair. As they did so, it was like a foreshadowing of what he would look like when he went gray. I was never more happy than at that moment that I had been instrumental in releasing him from his own life sentence.

He put a hand under my chin, determined not to let me look away. For a moment, however, I kept my eyes downcast, keeping a partial view of that scar on the back of his hand, the deep scar that no amount of time would ever heal.

"How did it—" I began, but he would not let me finish.

"Were you, by some chance, Emma," he asked with a sardonic grin, "asking for my help with your problem?"

I could not look at him; I could not look away. *Let the enigma of that scar be my hideaway,* I thought. *Let him draw me out again if he can. Better still, let me remain lost here.*

"But if you do want it," he said, this time forcing me to look at him with a use of strength that did cause pain, "then you are going to have to ask me outright yourself. Well, Emma. Do you want my help?"

I looked at the street around me: the noise; the squalor; worst of all, the smell. I had been lying to myself when I had entertained the thought that I could live like this. I had been trying to tell myself that now, with Weston gone and no longer there to hold me to my former life, I might have had the bravery of Katherine, might have been able to leave home with nothing. I would have gone; John would have stayed. I would have left; John would have lived. But I could not do that. I could not live like this.

Still...

"No." I shook my head. "No. I think you must have misunderstood me. That is not what I want. If we are to go on at all, we must merely go on as we have done."

He was silent.

Then we talked of unimportant things for another half hour as we moved out of his neighborhood, walked around the city. At one point, I was fairly certain I saw Hettie Larwood coming out of a milliner's. Thankfully, I did not believe she saw me.

After we were done speaking, we returned to his room. The meager fire could not heat even that small space sufficiently, and even his touch failed to feel warm against my skin.

Not that any of that stopped me.

Later, I would wonder, briefly, why he had not turned me away then. I no longer represented any kind of growing future for him, if I ever had. And now, just because I saw no other way out for me, that was not necessarily reason to conclude he would not see any other way out for himself. Could he not start a new life, *have* a new life without me?

But no answer came easily. Further, I was not of a mind myself to press for one.

SIXTY-FIVE

And then the strangest thing of all happened: My husband turned into the man I had always dreamed he would become.

It started, at first, with small things: inquiries into how my day had been, what it had involved, as opposed to merely going on about whatever news in the daily papers interested him most.

I was, I must confess, puzzled at the change and said as much.

He approached the lady's chair in which I was seated, gently took my hands.

"We have lost so much together," he said quietly, "losing Weston. Does it not make sense I would now want to cling to you as being the only person of import left in my world?"

He looked so sad. There had been times when I had fantasized about his death. And now he looked so sad. Could I not find in me some sympathy for him?

"I have not been as good a husband to you as I might have been," he confessed, appearing more humble than I had ever seen him. "There have even been times when I have...when I have...*exploited* situations for something as frivolous as my own artistic ambitions."

I suspected he was referring to his novel, *Gossip,* and how he had used me in it.

But I said nothing.

"I have even," he went on, "divided my attention between you and...and...*others* in ways I ought not."

Now I was certain he was referring to his affair with Lucy.

But again I said nothing.

"No," he said, "I have not been as good a husband to you as I might have been. But if you will help me to learn how, I should like to try to become that man now."

But how, I thought, *how is that possible? Even if I could forgive the novel, even if I could forgive him Lucy. I love Chance. I do not love John.*

And yet, as I was to come to learn as the next several days piled up, such a thing *was* possible. John became so helpful, so solicitous, so willing to learn *through my teaching* how to be better, it suddenly seemed possible, if only remotely, that I could love my husband once more.

He approached me, tentatively, as I lay in bed one night, placed one hand gently on the top sheet.

"May I?" he asked.

We had not had relations since the night of Weston's funeral. I would not have thought it was in me to consent again and yet, he had been so tender of late, in everything, I found I could not deny him.

Almost imperceptibly, I nodded, watched as though he were a stranger climbing into bed beside me.

"Perhaps," he said, "perhaps if you were to show me what you like..."

And I did.

Oh, it was not the way it was with Chance—nothing could ever be like that!—but I showed him with words and without how to do one thing and another that pleased me. If not the greatest passion a person could feel, it was sufficient.

As I watched him sleeping afterward, that ever-changing face I had known for over a quarter of a century, I saw John was right: We were the two people in the world who had loved Weston best. Without him, we could only survive together.

SIXTY-SIX

"Emma, have you gone mad?"

The speaker was Chance, of course. I had come to tell him good-bye.

For the last few weeks, I had done something previously unimaginable: I avoided him. His letters to me, one after the other, went unanswered.

But of course I read them, read all of his love, all of his confusion, and, finally, all of his pain.

At last I had decided that, having been through all we had been through together, I at least owed him an explanation. I at least owed it to him to say good-bye.

"Emma!" He put his hands roughly on my shoulders, physically shook me. "What can you be thinking of?"

I thought of the first night I had seen him, when he had come to me in the bedroom I shared with my husband, when he had shoved me so violently against the wall, preparatory to taking me, it had raised a lump.

"You do not *love* John, Emma! You love *me*!"

I did not want to think about that.

"And John does not love you!"

I looked at him sharply.

"What do you mean by that?" I asked. "John has loved me forever."

"What are you talking about?" He almost laughed, but there was a desperate cry in it. "John does not *know* how to love. He certainly does not know how to love *you*. Only I know that."

I did not want to think about that either.

"I'm sorry," I said, turning my face away from his. "I do not wish to hurt you."

He put his hand under my chin, forced me to face him: "Then *don't*."

He lowered his face to kiss me, but when his lips were just a breath from mine I pulled away, turned from him.

His voice when he spoke was puzzled, almost like Weston used to sound, whenever he could not get some toy to work properly.

"Emma?" he said. "You are turning away from me?"

I put my hand on the doorknob, my back to him.

"I must go," I said.

"But when will you be coming back?"

I could not answer. I could not speak aloud the words, telling him I would never be coming back. Instead, I watched my hand turn the knob, watched my feet walk out the door, down the stairs.

"What about John's book? What about Lucy?"

I kept walking.

"EMMA!"

SIXTY-SEVEN

I walked, taking the long way home.

And, with each step, I felt myself getting stronger, felt my resolve growing stronger. I had married John, for life.

What about the book? What about Lucy?

Those things no longer mattered. John's acknowledgment of his errors wiped the slate clean. I was doing the right thing.

Along the way, I even bought flowers. So what if they were *Amaranthus,* known in some circles as love-lies-bleeding? No one else would think about the flowers that way while looking at them but me.

I was doing the right thing.

I smiled and walked on.

I placed my things on the hall bench, including the flowers. My first thought was to go to John right away. After all, if we were to be closer now, then my place was with him.

But, turning to shut the door, which a sudden draft told me had not closed properly, I saw I had picked up far too much debris on my boots during the course of my overlong walk and was trailing it behind me on the parquet. I sought to clean the boots off on the ornamental boot-scraper, situated conveniently by the front door. But they were too dirty and I finally took them off, proceeding to John's library on stocking feet.

The library door was not quite shut and as I raised my hand to knock, I heard someone speaking.

"Yes," John said, triumph mixing with the wonder in his voice, "it is truly the most remarkable thing. I had thought her lost, but now she has come back to me."

Who was he talking to? Who was he talking *about*?

"But, please, sir,"—I heard, with shock, Timmins speak—"can't you give me some small details of how you brought this about?"

John laughed, a hard, self-confident laugh. "It was no more difficult, really, than it was getting her to submit on our wedding night. I always knew it was just a matter of time. And, this time, I did not have to wait ten years to get what I wanted. It really is amazing how much a man can accomplish in this world when he knows how to exercise and maintain total control."

My first instinct, upon hearing how John had manipulated me, hearing how coldly he discussed it, was to run from that house. I raced back across the floor on stocking feet, heard John's desperate shout—*"EMMA!"*—behind me. I grabbed my boots, not even stopping to put them on, thinking to take them with me.

I had the door open, was about to cross the threshold, when I felt John grab my shoulder tight with one hand while with the other, he punched the door shut. He spun me around.

"What did you hear," he said, an edge, a nervousness, in his voice I had never heard before, "that you shouldn't have?"

"Nothing," I said, eyes on the floor.

He put his fingers under my chin, forced me to look at him.

"You are lying," he said.

"I'm not!" I insisted.

"Then why were you running out? Hmm? Can you answer me

that? You just came home from being out. Why would you leave so suddenly again?"

"I remembered something I wanted to get when I was out."

"And what was that?"

"Flowers," I said.

His eyes immediately shot to the *Amaranthus* on the hall bench.

"You are lying again," he said, smiling now.

And that smile, so out of place with what was going on, chilled me.

"Come," he said, grabbing on to my shoulder again, even harder this time, yanking so hard he nearly sent me tumbling as he pulled me across the floor behind him.

"What...? John, what are you doing? Stop! I can walk myself!"

But he didn't stop. He dragged me past the library door, past Timmins, who was standing smirking in the doorway, dragged me through the long corridor and beyond to our bedroom. He shoved me into the room, slammed the door behind us, clicked over the lock.

"Take your clothes off," he ordered.

"*What?* No!"

"If you do not take them off yourself," he said coolly, "I will rip them from your body."

He took a threatening step toward me and I held up one hand to stop him. With the other hand trembling, I commenced doing what he commanded.

When I was naked, he approached until there was no space between us, his clothed body pressing against my naked one. Then he forced my legs apart with his hand, shoving his fingers inside me, a thing he had never done before. I was bone dry down there, but that did not stop him.

I felt his breath against my ear as he spoke. "Is this what you like, Emma, what that male relative of yours, the one with the peculiar laugh lines all on one side of his face, did to you that summer?"

My eyes shot to his. How did he...?

"I used to follow you everywhere, at least when we were younger. Don't you remember? I had thought to visit you myself that night. Of course, I was just coming to chat. But then I discovered someone else had beaten me to it and was doing much more than chat. At first, I wanted to kill him. He was where I should have been.

But then I found myself overtaken with an overwhelming sense of curiosity and all I could do was listen at the door, to the sounds he made, the sounds you made, the words he spoke to you so clearly." He shoved his fingers deeper. "Is this what you like, Emma?"

And in his words I heard a memory-echo: his voice speaking those same words the last time my father had visited me, the same words the man with the peculiar laugh lines had spoken to me when I was a child.

Then, pulling his fingers out, John commenced removing his own clothes with great speed—how I hated the sight of him naked now!—as he had done on our wedding night.

Again, he forced me down on the bed. Again, he forced his way into my dryness.

As he thrust into me, over and over again, he became one in my mind with the male relative with the peculiar laugh lines from my childhood, and I began doing what I had done that night as a little girl: counting thrusts, as if that simple mathematical task could remove my mind from what was happening to my body.

One...two...three...

With one last great thrust, he collapsed on top of me.

I was still dry as the desert and now I ached too.

He looked down at me, sweat beading his forehead, with something akin to fear.

"Don't you understand?" He caressed the side of my face and now it was his hand that was trembling. "I will not lose you, Emma."

He studied me closely, continued to caress my cheek. If anything, that soft touch was worse than anything he had done before.

My instinct was to flinch from him, to shout at him, but I remembered words Katherine had spoken when I counseled her long ago: *Sometimes it is better to let the other side believe they have won the battle. Then, while they are resting confident in their glory, you sneak in and win the war.*

Hearing those words in my head, I gave the performance of my life.

I reached up my own hand to John's face, caressed *his* cheek.

"You are so right, John," I said, looking deep into his eyes so that he would not doubt my sincerity. "You are always right. How did you know that this was exactly what I needed?"

"Do you mean that?" he asked.

"Of course I mean it," I said, lying through my teeth. "I love you."

With many more such words, I eased the fears in him. And, before long, my husband was doing what he always did after...*lovemaking*: My husband fell asleep beside me and slept the sleep of the dead.

SIXTY-EIGHT

I had not dreamt it would get as ugly as it did.

Poison would have been my first choice. Curare, to be specific. Back in 1812, while in South America, one of my fellow countrymen, a Mr. Charles Waterton, had discovered the poison. John, partly for research for one of his books and partly from characteristic curiosity, had always been interested in the sciences. It was he, just as it was he who had told me about the recent experiments involving Pavlov's dogs, who told me about Waterton's discovery. Apparently, curare acts on the nervous system. It had been used for a while as an anesthetic during surgery, but I thought a large dose of it might be enough to solve my problem. I had been wondering aloud about where I might procure it without raising suspicions, when Chance pointed out my folly to me.

I had returned to Chance, of course, while my husband slept on in our marriage bed, the mud still caked on my boots from my previous trip home, and Chance had taken me back, forgiven me everything.

Earlier, I had used all the strength in my mind to deceive my husband into believing he had not lost me, would not lose me. By the time I got to Chance, I was an empty shell, like one of the walking wounded from the Boer War one sometimes saw in the streets.

"What happened?" he said, concern etching his face as he took in my disheveled appearance.

I said nothing, remained silent as he slowly removed my clothes with the tenderness one might show to a baby.

"Who did this?" he said, a gentle urgency in his voice when he saw the bruises on my arm from where John had grabbed me, dragged me.

"John," I said finally, touching the bruise with my own hand. Then I took my hand and pressed it between my legs. "And here," I said. "John."

"He should not have done that." Chance shook his head. "He should not have used you so." Then he laid me down on his narrow bed, washed my body as best he could with an old cloth he dampened with water from a basin.

But it was not enough. It did not make me clean.

"Erase it," I said, pulling him toward me. "Make it as though it never happened."

And he made love to me then with such exquisite tenderness, I cried. There were tears in his eyes as well.

"Everyone knows," he said, kissing my temple as I lay nestled in the crook of his arm afterward, hair splayed across his naked chest, "poison is a woman's weapon. The surest way to draw immediate attention to yourself, then, would be to employ it now. Women," he added, speaking softly, nose in my hair, "do not typically like to get their pretty hands dirty. They do not like to be too close to the nastier deeds they sometimes feel compelled to do."

Lower lip held between my teeth, I traced whorls among the smattering of hairs between his navel and his groin.

"What do you suggest as an alternative then?" I asked.

What he suggested involved the committal of a crime more close and personal than any I had ever imagined.

"Make it look like a robbery," he said. "Or better yet, make it look like the work of a madman."

I would not have believed there was so much blood in one human being.

It seemed to me as though the streets ran with it, having dribbled first and then poured down from the steps leading up to our front door.

We surprised him coming home from his editor's. It was I who had suggested he go there in the first place. I told him now that things were perfect between the two of us, and always would be, he must take better care of himself for a time. I said it might be a diversion from all that weighed on his mind, that talking to Connor about the book on gossip would give him something else to focus his energies upon, as if there ever could be a diversion now, now that the specter of the loss of Weston was an omnipresent part of both our lives.

It was a struggle for me to contain and continue to disguise the massive anger I felt toward him—for all of his betrayals, for what he had done to me in our bedroom, for merely being still *alive*—but I knew this was one struggle I must overcome.

"It will be good for you to finally get out," I said, thinking of my own recent trip to see Chance, adding with a sigh, "and it will be good for me to have you get out. Do not be offended, but sometimes it is easier to heal when one is alone. And do not worry either: I will be here, waiting for you, when you return."

It was also I who summoned him back early. Having suggested he spend the entire night at his editor's, having made sure the servants heard of this plan, I snuck out myself several hours later. Under cover of darkness, I gave money along with a written message to a cabdriver, beseeching John to return home at once, informing him I was mistaken; that "alone" was the last thing I needed.

The waiting after I saw the letter on its way with the cabdriver, written on the black-bordered mourning paper I had been using since Weston's death, was hard. Indeed, it took a few hours before we saw John's own carriage pull up in front of our home as we waited among the shadows on the other side of the street. The foggy mist created gray swirling wisps against the blackness of a moonless, starless night, the sparsely scattered street lamps giving off the only illumination.

It was as though I were a dragonfly out of place in the night.

Outside for so long my eyes had grown accustomed to the dark, I saw John step from the carriage, saw as his foot was set down on the first step, watched until the carriage driver pulled out of sight. Our hurrying two paces matching his every one, we at last caught him up on the final step.

I can still hear the almost imperceptible squelching sound as the knife penetrated heart, penetrated skin, penetrated flesh, penetrated fat, penetrated sinew. His blood was all over me and yet, the penetration would not stop.

Did he cry out?

Odd, but I do not remember. I do know that, later on, when questioned, the servants allowed as that they had heard nothing.

Perhaps I was too busy with my counting to hear anything else.

For, as the knife went in, I counted thrusts; it was the only way to keep my mind distant from what was happening in front of me. I did not stop counting until he fell, until he finally lay still, until, bending over, willing myself to be deaf to the pounding of my own heart, I could no longer detect any beating of his at all.

———————

I do not think that he saw us.

I am almost certain he never turned around.

SIXTY-NINE

With each moment, each hour, each day, that passed after John's death, it seemed more and more as though some other person, not I, had killed him so violently. Whose hand had been on the knife? *Did I really kill my husband?* my mind screamed at times. Still, as the hours passed, the days, it was as though, with him finally gone, the anger diminished in inverse proportion to how it had been leading up to the event, like an hourglass whose dimensions were all wrong.

The high tide of anger had finally ebbed back out to sea.

With the first clarity of thought I had experienced in a long time, I wondered about possible threats. My bloodied dress: I recalled myself burying it beneath some floorboards along with Chance's bloody clothes. As for possible people who could point the finger at us, the only one I could come up with was Constance. If she were here, she would be, I saw, a constant threat. But she was not here. She was still in the country and now I found myself hoping she would stay there for good.

The police had come. No one had heard a thing. The case lay open.

Unlike the prescribed pure white of the atmosphere following the death of innocent Weston, by contrast, the servants were provided with black mourning dress in honor of their master's untimely passing. Lucy wore a simple black dress and bonnet, with collar and cuffs made of crepe, a black handkerchief tucked into one cuff for when she felt the need to spontaneously burst into tears, which was alarmingly often; while Timmins made his dourly creeping way around the house in a black suit, minus the usual shiny buttons, but with a matching black tie and armband.

Black-bordered handkerchiefs. In ten days' time, callers would begin leaving cards, with handwritten messages, on the silver tray in the entrance hall. The world had seemingly gone black.

At Harrods, I purchased mourning enough for a year: merino wool for the current winter; lightweight silk crepe de chine for the long hoped for spring and summer. I could almost hear the whispered criticisms of society, that I had not allowed a fitter to come to me but had rather ventured outside before the funeral. But I had to get out. I even went so far as to purchase some of the diamonds and pearls John had told me had been recommended for mourning following the death of Queen Victoria.

When I found Lucy in tears one too many times, I almost admonished her: After all, *she* was not the widow; I was. But I could see where she might feel that way and, in an effort to show sensitivity for her, I said so.

"What are you talking about, madam?" she asked, raising her nose up for once from her black handkerchief.

"Why, you and John, of course, and the trouble you were in a while back. You know, the two of you and . . . and the baby."

She spoke so quickly, it was obvious she had not had the chance to think, the chance to concoct anything but the truth. "That wasn't Mr. Smith what did that!" She was clearly horrified. "It was Timmins!"

Ever since Lady Collins had implied the father of Lucy's child must be someone under my roof, I had assumed it was John. Now it was my turn to be horrified, as Lucy proceeded to explain to me how, up until the crisis of her unexpected pregnancy, Timmins had repeatedly forced himself on her.

It was that last, indicating he was no longer doing so, that finally spared him his position in the household. I could not imagine how awful it must have been for Lucy, lying with such a man, but it was actually she who pled his case.

"He doesn't bother me no more." She shrugged. "Not since the scare about...you know. Plus, there is no one else here for him to bother really and he is old. Where would he go?"

Even if I didn't fire him for abusing my maid, surely I should have fired Timmins for his...overcloseness with my husband. But the house was in too much turmoil already and I thought it better to keep him where I could see him. After all, who knew what he might say of me, if he were turned loose.

I thought about my firm belief that John had been the father of Lucy's baby. Where had that come from? Surely, the mere implication of Lady Collins—that if my maid would not tell me the identity, it must be someone who could hurt me in that way—had been thin enough. Other than a few common things between them—a similarity of appearance; a love of holiday decorations—there had never been anything deeper. Certainly, I'd never seen them behave together in anything other than a professional capacity. And yet I had seized on to it so quickly, never entertaining any other possibilities. Why had I done so? The answer to that seemed clear to me now: It was convenient for me to believe thus. Having already turned against my husband in my heart, I wanted to believe his character dark in everything. And, since the night he had attacked me, I saw that I was right to judge him. Even though he had nothing to do with what happened to Lucy, I was still right.

John had lain in state, as it were, for two nights following his death, allowing friends, neighbors, and servants the opportunity to file past the coffin in order to pay their respects. Looking down at him there, as I felt called upon to do in accompaniment of each new visitor to his side, I tried to recall the companion of my youth—the boy in occasional girl's clothing, my first suitor, my oldest friend—but all I could think about now was that the last barrier to my desire had been removed and I could not bring myself to mourn his loss.

At the graveside, observing him being lowered into the ground as Timmins and Lucy tossed offerings of remembrance upon the descending coffin lid, it was all I could do to hold back what could only be described as an open smile that I was finally free at last.

SEVENTY

Yes, I was free of the constraints of a husband now, but I was not free of the constraints of the society surrounding me, the society that wanted to keep me with my husband even once he was safely in the ground.

Would the world I lived in allow Chance and I the opportunity to be together openly, without waiting for a suitable length of time to pass?

Hah!

I had a greater likelihood of gaining a seat for myself in Parliament.

In truth, then, I was no better off now than when John had been alive; worse, in fact, since now I had the nightmares of his end to devil my attempts at sleep. *Whose hand had been on the knife? Had I really killed my husband?* There were times when I could almost hear that bloodied dress talking to me, pulsing out its violent story from beneath the floorboards.

Still, during the moments when I was able

to convince myself that what had occurred had been inevitable, I was more content than I had been in I cannot say how long. I was free now to indulge my thoughts of Chance and, even though any kind of public meeting and all but the most clandestinely arranged private meetings were too risky, it was bliss to no longer be nettled by the distractions of obligation.

If only Weston were still here. I only allowed myself the thought at moments when I felt strong enough to endure it, crying bitterly when no one else was near to hear me. He was a distraction I should not have minded having again.

Indeed, if I could undo everything, if that was what it would take to bring him back, I would undo it all.

SEVENTY-ONE

But I was wrong.

Society was only content to keep me a widow for just so long. They might not have wanted me to go out on New Year's Eve, they might have resented my putting a new luster in the dining room—a great big chandelier decorated with massive cut-glass prisms—not to mention the fairy lamps I'd installed in both parlors, but they did not want to keep me alone forever. Apparently, the idea of me being paired with someone other than John was more palatable to those in my orbit than the idea of having an uneven number of people sit down to dinner. Further, not only was my single status numerically inconvenient, but, given my relatively young age for widowhood, my solitary presence served as a bothersome reminder that what had happened to me could befall any one of the others. Oh, not the gruesome murder of a spouse, perhaps; but rather, the accidental death or death due to untimely illness, leaving one to be a social question mark.

It was thus then that, after a suitable length of time, my friends began gently prodding me toward becoming one half of an even whole again. To my great surprise, even John's sisters became most interested in seeing me paired off with someone new.

Victoria: "You are still so frightfully *young,* Emma."

Elizabeth: "John would not want you to be alone forever."

Ruth (most surprising of all): "I know a man who…"

It was all I could do *not* to allow them to persuade me to spend time with the plethora of unattached men they all suddenly seemed to know.

Honestly, you would think they would be more interested in preserving their brother's memory!

"'I know a man who…'" Chance mimicked a high falsetto as I lay in his arms in his mean little room.

Enough time had passed that I felt safe visiting him. I reached out now, swatting his shoulder playfully with the back of my hand. "It is not funny," I said, trying hard not to laugh. "You should see some of these men they bring to me as so many leftovers after everyone else has eaten the best of the feast: a baker who smells of yeast; a butcher who smells of raw meat; why, the other day they even brought me a would-be writer who says he never reads!"

"These are the men John's sisters propose for a woman of your station?" Chance queried.

"Perhaps I exaggerate," I said.

"Or perhaps"—he smiled wryly—"they fear your situation is more desperate than they let on. Next, they may come at you with the fishmonger."

"The *fish*—"

He silenced my lips with his finger. "Your greatest mistakes, Emma, are always the ones you make when you do not take me at my word."

"Pardon me?"

"I meant what I said: 'I know a man who…'"

"Would you care to rephrase whatever you are saying in terms that I can understand?"

"It is just that: I know a man who…*me.*"

This time, I merely raised my eyebrows at him, waiting for him to elucidate.

"If your friends and even John's family deem it time you find a man to replace the one you've . . . *lost,* then it means they are also quite ready for *me*."

———————

Of course, it was not quite that easy, despite Chance's insistence it should be so.

First off, my behavior had to appear natural. I could not very well introduce him into my world abruptly, nor would it be seemly, when I did introduce him, to present him as someone I had developed a great and sudden passion for, despite that being the truth.

Addressing the latter clause first, I thought it best to actually talk to some of the stray men my friends and relatives kept showing up with, if only so that later on it could not be said I had acted impulsively. As can be imagined, Chance did not love this idea, but he could be persuaded to see the wisdom behind it.

"Very well, Emma," he said, "entertain these others, if you must. But do not let any of them inside your skirts." He reached a possessive hand toward my face. "Or your mouth."

It was a piece of advice he needn't have stressed so. I was no more interested in the company of the available-men parade than he was interested in having me be in their company. Listening to each for the bare minimum amount of time politeness demanded, I saw them back to the door so quickly that Penelope, keeping faith for Odysseus, would have been proud.

The second problem was the appearance of Chance himself. Handsome enough—sometimes too handsome, if my reactions were anything to go by—his attire was still wrong. Well, that was easily enough mended. John's money was now my money and if I wanted to use it to re-outfit Chance from hat to boots, there was no longer anyone to say I couldn't.

Clad in his new attire, no one would ever question his right to appear in any drawing room. We did consider working out some of the rougher edges of his personality, but then, we thought: Why? After all, it was in part those rougher edges that had so greatly charmed me. Surely, they might have the same effect on others as well? It was enough he kept up with the newspapers, was able to converse with authority on any subjects that might arise.

"A job, Emma," he prompted. "I still need a job so your friends will think me respectable."

"Hmm..." That was a puzzle.

"It should be something no one can trace."

"Hmm..."

"I know!" He spoke as if the idea had just come to him. "I could be in publishing! That editor of John's,"—he snapped his fingers impatiently—"what was his name again?"

"Connor?"

"That's right: *Connor*!"

"What about him?"

"Well, you did once say none in your circle had ever met him, despite the efforts of some of your would-be-author friends to persuade John to do so. Could I not be some associate of his you had been introduced to?"

"I suppose..."

He was excited now. "That's right. I could be some associate who had made his own rags-to-riches fortune in publishing in some other country—oh, say, *Italy*—and had now returned to London a wealthy man—"

"—who had been so successful, he now no longer had any need to work!" I finished for him, caught up in the wave of his enthusiasm.

He grabbed my hands. "It could work," he said.

"It could," I agreed.

"If only we can be smart enough not to rush things."

———

It occurred to me I was on the edge of happy then, in a way I could not recall ever having been before, save at times with Weston. But this was a different kind of happy. It was a dizzy, giddy, almost scary happy. Despite everything that had happened, despite everything I had lost and everything I had done, it was a sheer joy to physically be in a room with a mind that so delighted my own, with a person I had wholly chosen for myself.

SEVENTY-TWO

Not rushing things was against my nature, but I did recognize Chance was right: To make the thing work at all, we would need to proceed with caution.

Apparently, though, what Chance and I deemed to be necessary was not viewed so by the rest of my circle. So taken with him, so tickled with his rough personality, so relieved to have even numbers at dinner once again, it was all they could do not to *throw* me at him. Once more, it was John's sisters who most surprised me.

Victoria: "He is so handsome!"

Elizabeth: "He is so daring!"

Ruth (if grudgingly): "You could do worse."

Even my parents liked him!

Well, Louisa did, at any rate.

With my recollection of what had transpired the summer I was twelve and my family visited distant relatives, my feeling toward my parents had altered. I had since tried to avoid them as much as possible, but while I could hate them for what I believed to be their complicity in the matter, I yet felt sorry for them as parents. Was it possible that, even for them, the situation was too horrific to do anything other than push what had happened completely out of memory? Perhaps they felt guilty over their lack of ability to protect me? Perhaps—despite the guilty look on my father's face when John uttered the words "Is this what you like, Emma?"—perhaps they had never been sure at all? And it was impossible, was it not, I could be so involved with a man whom John's sisters had even met and endorsed and yet avoid a meeting between him and my parents? And so...

"You are so...*refreshing*," Louisa gushed in a girlish tone I had never known her to use before, gazing up at Chance as though he were a new star in the sky, the brightest to be seen.

Now that I was enjoying the opportunity of seeing Chance with other people for the first time, I became aware of this startling effect he had on others and on women in particular: They all looked, very quickly upon meeting him, as though they might be falling in love!

It was as though he were the embodiment of the work of Franz Mesmer. True, he was handsome enough, the most masculine man in any room, giving off an air of raw power that was intoxicating; there was none of the weakness of a Charles Biltmore, a George Larwood, or even a John Smith in him. But that was not all. It was that, in the moment he was speaking to you, you felt as though you were the only person in the world. There was that air of sunlight, of being found by the sun, that I remembered from the first time he visited me in my home after his release from prison. And now I saw that sun widening its orbit, shining its light on others.

The first time I saw it, I thought to be jealous. My instinct was certainly to move in that direction. But then I saw the way he looked at the woman to whom he was speaking—Diana, I believe it was— with an amused tolerance, and saw the way he looked at me with an intimacy and an almost publicly naked desire that said, "Can't we leave and go make love *right now*?" And I knew it didn't matter how many women he met. I knew it didn't matter how those women felt about him. It was only me he wanted.

My father was, of course, a different story. Scared to death of what Chance might think of me, I had yet forced myself to tell him about the thing I had remembered from the summer I was twelve, told him how guilty my father looked when John spoke those words that were so awful to my hearing, told him how John had used it against me that time when he abused me himself. It was not easy, but there was such an openness between us now, I did not feel right keeping such a thing to myself, not when I was so used to sharing everything with him.

And it was all right.

I should say it was all right for me. I do not think it was all right for my father.

Turning from my mother, whose hand he had just kissed, prompting that *"refreshing"* gush of hers, Chance took my father's hand, hard, met his eyes. Chance's lips looked to be smiling, but it was such a hard smile, so very hard, I wondered if my father saw what I was seeing. I saw Chance's smile, saw his eyes shining, saw the tightness of his grip, and I saw the sum total of it saying, "I know exactly who you are, Edward Crane. I know exactly in what ways you have failed your daughter. And if your daughter ever asked me to do so, I would gladly kill you."

I saw it all and saw my father see it too, falling back a pace, reacting as though there had been a physical impact.

"Is this what you like, Edward?" Chance asked, gripping my father's hand yet more firmly, as though his peculiar question referred to the firmness of that shake.

I knew where those words came from. I cannot help but believe my father knew where they came from as well.

Yes, except for my father, they were all charmed by him, right down to a man and woman. What matter that, when out of their hearing, he ridiculed them to me, cocking one sardonic eyebrow as he aped what he clearly perceived to be their affected forms of speech?

"'Do you really think potatoes are a necessary thing for you to eat?'" He mimicked Hettie Larwood addressing just about anybody weighing more than a small child.

"'If Chance has met John's old editor—oh, all *right,* so they were in business together—I do not see why I cannot one day do the same.'" He mimicked Paul Jamison's outrage over Chance's having met a man whom he, with his long-held writing aspirations, would kill to meet.

"'Do you think another pregnancy will ruin my figure?'" He did an admirable Maeve Collins.

"Stop it!" I laughed loudly, pelting him with pillows. I loved being naked with him, had never been so much myself before as I was when I was with him like this. "Stop it!"

"No," he said. Then he appeared to pause, considering. "Why should I stop it?"

"Be-*cause,*" I said, rolling over on top of him and putting on my most menacing face, "if you continue, I shall never be able to face any of them."

He considered that for a moment as well. "No, sorry, that is not sufficient reason."

But then he used his superior strength to roll us both over so he was back on top, grasping both my wrists within his hand and pinning them over my head. His mouth moved toward mine. "Very well," he murmured.

I can honestly say I had never been happier with any man.

———————

Did I ever feel guilt about what had been done to John, even despite what John had done to me?

Of course I did. But I tamped it down, down, down, hiding it away as I had done the bloodstained clothes from that fateful night. Chance never brought it up, and if he didn't, then I certainly wasn't about to. What—talk about all that ugliness and risk losing this fragile shard of peace I had finally achieved? I would have to be mad.

As for the memory of Weston, I had shut up his room; no matter how much healing laughter I now shared with Chance, it was a country I could no longer go to.

SEVENTY-THREE

I had been **wrong about** another thing as well—in addition to society's views on me as a widow—wrong to believe winter had come back into my life with a force that would never leave. Winter was *not* here to stay; spring *could* come again, and with it a riot of color, joy upon joy, a vivid happiness like none I had ever imagined. Previously, I had only danced on the edge of happy. Now I *was* it. And it was as though God, or some other divine creator, had taken big splashes of oil paint, resmearing a previously drab canvas of beiges, blacks, and grays with every color of the rainbow, with passionate reds, stimulating purples, and, best of all, greens: the color of life.

Yes, to steal a line from Brontë: Reader, I married him.

At the shocking insistence of nearly everyone we knew, positively *encouraging* us, Chance and I were married in a very public ceremony in June of the year following John's death; the lone dissenter was my father, who was still missing my first husband, the son of his heart. The bride even wore white, a wreath of flowers replacing a veil. A sumptuous feast followed, plus a quantity of fine wine: I do not believe we either of us stopped laughing or smiling for more than a single moment that day; we were that giddy.

As I looked around me at all of my family, all of our friends, I thought that if only my beloved Katherine could be with us, if only my dearest Weston were still alive, the day would be complete.

There was only one moment that gave me pause. It was when I saw Charles Biltmore, standing there alone. Unbidden, a picture came to my mind of Constance, standing beside him, pointing an accusing finger at us. As quickly as the picture came at me, I shoved it back down.

When the last guest had gone, Chance and I retired as man and wife for the first time to the bedroom I had previously shared with John. Before, he had always had to sneak in; now he was the legitimate master of the house.

I had changed much in the bedroom in preparation of his moving in. The heavy furniture had been replaced with lighter pieces, the dark draperies with something filmy in white. I had even chosen mirrors that were less ornate, the gold trimming the glass untouched by any black.

White: I wanted the color of innocence to surround me now as much as possible.

My escritoire I kept just as it had always been.

I had also ordered a new bed for us. Even though we had slept a few times in the one that had been there before, it seemed it would be wrong somehow, an ill omen, to begin my new marriage by sleeping in the same bed I had primarily shared with the old husband. And so, in place of the four-poster bed that had been there before, there was now a great big brass bed with massive posts and sheer white drapes, their sashes tied to the posts on all sides. Entering that bed, untying the sashes so the drapes surrounded us, I felt as though I were entering a sultan's harem in which I was the only woman who might please.

Making love with Chance that night was like a new experience for both of us. Even though we had now lain together such a quantity of times I could no longer count them—any chance we could get, really—there was a freshness in the air as we slowly undressed each other, a confidence with each other's bodies that stood in marked contrast to what I had had with John, but also an awe-filled tender newness as though we had never done anything quite like what we were now doing. I wondered, as he slowly entered me, as I wrapped my legs around his hips the better to hold him closer: How many other women ever get to be a virgin a second time?

"I love you, Emma." He looked into my eyes, pushing deeper. "I believe I will always love you."

"I love you." I opened myself wider still to him. "You are my entire life."

In contrast to the dank honeymoon I had spent with John in Scotland, Chance and I chose to tour the Continent instead: France, Spain, even Italy, where we got to see the country where Chance had supposedly made his fortune.

After the noise of Rome, the splendor of Florence, I asked Chance if we mightn't proceed to Venice, there to seek out news of Katherine, who was weighing on my mind. He proved in that, as in all things, agreeable.

And so we found ourselves in the city of canals, which were equal parts pretty and smelly. Venice seemed such a small place, when taken in comparison with London, that I commenced my search at the center of the Venetian world: St. Mark's Square. But the pigeon droppings there gave no more answers than could Josephine Bonaparte's long-deceased fortune-tellers. Growing increasingly anxious to find Katherine, I took to haunting the shops surrounding the square. It was finally there, in a place specializing in pretty stationery and writing instruments made out of Murano glass, that I at last achieved success. Despite her indifference to fashion while growing up, Katherine had always loved to look at pretty things. "Ah, yes," said the shopkeeper, his thick moustache twitching. "She always looks but almost never buys." Then he gave me directions, involving a number of narrow canal alleys, to where I might find "the young

Englishwoman with the flame of hair." He also said something about a "bambino."

It turned out Katherine was living in a rather mean pensione, with noisy neighbors above and below, but that did not matter: My darling Katherine was alive!

As was the "bambino," a boy, clinging to her skirts.

"Aunt Emma!" she exclaimed in shock, upon opening the door, as though I were the ghost risen from a grave, not she.

She was still beautiful, if a little faded, her clothes not as grand as they once had been. And she was older, only by a few years on the calendar, but really in so many ways, than the last time I had seen her, a few early lines of struggle added to her face.

She introduced me to the boy, Antonio. "Hugh insisted we call him that," she said. "Hugh said if we are to live here, then our son should have a name like the children he will be growing up with. Plus," she added, "if I ever see my father again, hopefully he will be pleased I sort of named his grandson after him."

Hugh was not at home, would not be back for hours. Katherine seemed to be grateful for this, as was I, although I suspect for different sides of the same reason. She, I would guess, did not want me to judge him harshly as the man who had brought her down so low in the world; for the circumstances of her day-to-day life were clearly far removed from the opportunities I would have chosen for her. And I did not want to judge him harshly, because she obviously still loved him so well.

She asked after John and I realized how little she knew of what had gone on since her disappearance. Determined not to let her see the crying I still experienced every day on the inside, I told her about the loss of Weston. Then, clearing my throat, I told her of John's murder. And, of course, I told her of my remarriage to Chance, whom I had not brought with me to see her; perhaps I, for my own part, had not wanted him to be judged by her and found wanting in any way.

"This...*life*," I could not stop myself from asking, thinking on how little I would like to live where she lived, unless of course I had the money to buy my comfort, "do you like it? Are you happy here?"

"No," she said with a strained smile, "I do not like much about my life here." And then her smile grew both more serene and vehement, all at the same time. "But I *am* happy. As long as Hugh and Antonio are here, I shall always be happy."

I looked at Antonio playing and thought of Weston. I was sure Antonio would grow up to be smart, like his mother.

"And what of you?" Her chin jutted out. "Are you happy, with your new Chance?"

"Yes," I said, feeling the truth of it, "I am."

And so there we were. It appeared we both had what we wanted; that we were indeed happy with the worlds we had chosen for ourselves.

I opened my reticule, gave her everything but my return fare back to Chance. She resisted, but I pressed it upon her. It was the least I could do.

As I was leaving an hour later, longing to return to Chance, Katherine stopped me at the door. "Please," she said, "when you get back home, don't tell any of the family about seeing me or what it is like here." She glanced at the meanness of the room around her, sniffed the bad air. "I do not think any of them would understand."

———————

Through it all, through the entire extended trip, Chance and I never once argued, were always of one mind in everything.

It seemed there was nothing missing to make our lives together complete.

SEVENTY-FOUR

Well, perhaps one thing was missing.

Home once more, I began to wonder if it might be possible Chance and I could have a child together. Perhaps seeing Katherine's Antonio was what put it in my mind.

No, of course Weston could not, could never, be replaced. But why could I not have another child? I had always assumed the fault in my inability to have more than one with John to be my own. But perhaps it had been his? Surely, Chance, on his most tepid days, was a more virile man than John had ever been. And, in spite of my advancing years, I did still bleed every month, so there was that hope.

I thought Chance might laugh at my idea; thought that, worse, he might not like it.

But he surprised me.

"You surprise me," he said, gently grazing the back of his hand down the contours of my face. "I would not have thought you had an interest any longer..."

"I have an interest in having *our* child," I said. "But I cannot have one alone. What is it that you want?"

"I'm touched," he said, and he so obviously was. "But this is so different from the design we had previously made."

"Can we not change the design?" I asked. "Must we complete things in the same way in which they have been started?"

I was thinking, but did not say, that everything we had now had been built on events others would deem horrible. That having been the base, did that then mean we could not now write a perfectly normal future?

And a part of me also still worried about what he really thought of my idea. Would he be jealous of a new person being added to our equation? I could see where he might have that in him.

But no.

He said, taking my face in both his hands, "Of course we can change the design. It is indeed a wonderful idea."

Then he told me how he had been missing the traditional idea of family, how absent it had been from his previous life.

Odd, but we had never talked before about any family he might have left, about any friends he might have made before or after his release. He said now that he had no family left anywhere in the world—just me. He did not say anything about any friends.

"A family." He spoke softly, his words touching me deeply. "I think that I should like that."

Now we made love with new purpose, as if our nearly unconquerable desire for each other had not been purpose enough.

A new life—and I now believed I could attain it, have it—would wipe clean the slate of the past, erasing all sins, and healing the world.

SEVENTY-FIVE

Of course, spring could not go on forever. Why had I ever imagined it could?

When the threat came, it came from a quarter I had once anticipated but then dismissed: It came in the stuttering, innocuous form of Constance Biltmore.

———

The first year I had known Chance, when he had still been in prison, had passed slowly. But each succeeding year had seemed shorter, had passed more quickly, as though with each year lived, time had sped up, as though life were getting compressed as one grew older. Indeed, sometimes it flew so swiftly, it seemed as though an entire year might pass without marking the change in the calendar.

New Year's at the Collinses' was a staid affair that year.

Maeve was still recuperating from yet another pregnancy and childbirth, but Joshua would have his party. In acknowledgment of the burdens on her, however, he had reluctantly agreed to halve the usual party down to the bare essentials: the Jamisons, the Larwoods, the Biltmores, Captain Brimley, Lady Collins, and, of course, the Woods.

Sometimes, even I still had trouble getting used to my new name.

The Biltmores were late in arriving. The clock was moving on toward nine, and still they were not there.

"…You are really quite pragmatic, aren't you, in your views on the current publishing climate," Joshua was observing to Chance as the two shared drinks before the roaring fire.

Chance, as a former publishing success story, was a pump that Joshua repeatedly liked to prime. In fairness, though, he wasn't the only one who liked to be close to Chance. It seemed my husband was just as attractive to men as he was to women, and all the men liked to be near him, near his energy, even if they did instinctively tend to hold their wives in closer view whenever he was around.

"'Pragmatic'?" Smiling, Chance raised one inquisitive eyebrow. "I'm not sure that's a word I am familiar with."

"Not familiar with 'pragmatic'? And you a man of books?"

Chance colored slightly, shrugged his shoulders, but before he could say anything, Joshua let him off the hook.

"Oh, right!" Joshua laughed. "You were in publishing in *Italy,* weren't you? You probably know all kinds of words in Italiano, while missing their own counterparts in your own tongue!"

"Grazie," Chance said, using one of the few Italian words he had picked up during our travels. Indeed, I had teased him mercilessly: If he was going to choose a foreign country where he supposedly made his fortune, why choose one where he did not know the language? Why not pick Spain or France, having picked up some of both languages while in prison? "Thank you, Joshua, for letting my ignorance off so graciously."

"Not at all," Joshua spoke expansively. "At any rate, here is as good a definition as you will find for 'pragmatic': being practical as opposed to being idealistic."

"'Being practical as opposed to being idealistic.'" Chance

repeated the words slowly, as though he were trying on a new verbal coat, and then he smiled. "Pragmatic: Yes, I suppose I am."

I had not seen Constance since she had been sent to recuperate once more in the country, oh so very long ago. Indeed, her protracted stay had been so long this time, I had assumed that, her having been sent away twice already, no one would ever take anything she said seriously again. But her words, just an hour after arriving, were enough to teach me I had left off worrying about the threat she represented at my own peril.

From the moment of her first sighting of Chance, she had been unable to keep her eyes from him. A jealous woman, especially a woman married to such a husband as mine, might have deduced this to be due to her husband's nearly universal desirability. But I had learned not to be a jealous woman where Chance was concerned, and I had good reason not to suspect an attraction for Chance as being the cause of Constance's intense interest. For I knew exactly what she was doing: She was eyeing him in the way one eyes someone when she is certain she has seen him before, but cannot for the life of her place where or when the meeting occurred. And she had seen him, of course, seen him in Sommers Tea Room with me; and later, she had heard me speak of him at length.

She kept circling around him, observing, at first remaining safely on the perimeters of the room, but drawing ever nearer to her target as curiosity began to get the better of her.

Chance, for his part, eyed her occasionally in return as he continued his conversation with Joshua, aware—as how could he not be?—of her interest in him without guessing the cause. Well, why should he have recognized her? He had only seen her briefly the one time and she had changed much since then. She was so thin now she could meet with even Hettie Larwood's approval; I should not have recognized her myself had I not seen her enter on Charles's arm.

Now she was right at Chance's elbow and could no longer be ignored.

"I'm sorry," said Joshua, raising his fist to his forehead in self-admonition. "Where are my manners? Constance, this is Chance Wood, Emma's new husband. I forgot that you were...*away* when they wed."

It was obvious, from her lack of comprehension upon being introduced to him now, that she could not place the name. Well, at least that was something: Perhaps I had been wise enough to hold that one thing back when I made my confession to her.

Chance's face registered surprise, now that he realized who his close observer was, but he covered quickly. "I have been in Charles's company often these past few months," he said, taking her hand as though he meant to kiss it, "and it is nice to see he does indeed have a better half."

"I know you," Constance said, seeking to withdraw her hand from his, as though she sensed that rather than she being a danger to him—which she was—he posed some sort of threat to her.

"I can understand your saying that," Chance spoke reassuringly. "Indeed, all of Emma's friends have made me feel so at home, I feel sometimes as though I have known all of you all of my life."

"That is not what I mean," Constance stuttered. "I mean that you look so familiar. I am sure we have met somewhere before. If only I could—"

"Now, Constance, there, there. Where could you have possibly met Emma's husband? He used to be in Italy. And since he has returned from there and come among us, you have not been...*around*." Charles had snuck up behind her and was patting her hand placatingly, but with an unnecessary force that led me to believe, were we none of us around, he should like very much to strike her.

"Constance still imagines things sometimes," he addressed the room at large. "I am quite sure she does not know what she is talking about."

The dinner that followed was strained, to say the least.

one she had offered John. The difference was, I had much more to lose.

"I should not, of course, *like* to tell people that you and your new husband met while you were still married to your old husband, should not *like* to cause you public embarrassment in that way. I, above all people, understand what it is to find oneself married to the wrong man, understand what it is to be perceived as a public embarrassment."

I could not stand to hear her go on. "What is it you want from me, Constance?" I asked, perversely needing to hear her speak the words aloud. She was no longer Connie to me, could never be so again.

She would not be rushed, though. "I know I should not have betrayed your trust with John. But then, you had the knowledge within you to convince him of the truth behind my allegations against Charles and yet, to save yourself, you chose to remain silent, didn't you? Please do not think I am angry," she hastily added, still wary of causing offense, despite the sword she was holding over my head. Then, cannily, "I know how desperate a person can get to save herself. Shall we say we are even on that score—my betrayal and yours—and let it go?"

For someone so otherwise timid, she was a good chess player in her own way. And she was persistent too—God, she was persistent!—a paradoxical resoluteness of character I had reluctantly to admire even as it worked to my disadvantage.

Arms crossed, I nodded my grudging consent.

"But now the slate is clear, I find I must assume the role of wrongdoer again if I am to save myself. I find—"

This time I would not let her finish. "What is it that you want, Constance?"

"Why, money, of course—the same thing I wanted from John— money enough to get away and start a new life for myself just as you have managed to do here. I am not *greedy,* Emma." She spoke in the most persuasive of tones, a wheedling Siren trying to convince all who heard her, including herself, that what she was doing was all right. "I am not looking to *bleed* you dry—"

"Give me time to talk to Chance about this. I'm quite sure you"—and here I stressed her own signature phrase—"*of all people* understand that a wife cannot make any financial moves without the consent of her husband."

SEVENTY-SIX

I knew it would be only a matter of time before Constance remembered where she had seen Chance before, only a matter of time before she put one and one together and came up with we two. From there—her remembrance of us together in Sommers Tea Room, her remembrance of my confession to her that Chance was a murdering prisoner and I was in love with him—how much of a leap would it take for her to make the connection that we were somehow involved in John's death?

As for the first part, it took her even less time than I had suspected:

The day after the Collinses' party, she was on my doorstep.

The proposal she had for me, delivered in stuttering speech, was remarkably similar to the

SEVENTY-SEVEN

I did not even give him the chance to remove his coat.

"We must talk," I said, meeting him at the door, leading him to the room that had formerly been John's library, shutting the door firmly behind us.

"You are always eager enough to suit me, but I have never known you to be *this* eager." He kissed my neck—how I longed to give in, to lose myself within the seduction of that kiss!—and moved to put his arms around me, on his face an expression of sheer delight that I knew instinctively I should not see again for a very long time, if ever. "Hadn't we better at least remove your skirts first?"

"No!" I pushed him away.

"Emma?" Now his expression was puzzled. "What has happened?" Not "What is the matter?" but "What has happened?" It was as though he, in turn, instinctively knew that for me to ever physically turn from him, the cause had to have come from outside myself.

"Constance has been here today," I said.

I saw him look at me with the open expression of love I had come to expect as my right from him, followed by a thoughtful look as though he were weighing two similarly weighted things in his mind. But then that passed too and his face hardened slightly into a look of caution. "And?"

"And she wants money." I wrung my hands, ran them through my hair. My gestures were very un-Emma-like, but I no longer felt like Emma, not when my world might be on the verge of collapsing. "Well, of course, she wants money. Surely, we had to have seen this coming. She has remembered where she saw you before and now she wants money in exchange for her silence. Otherwise, she will tell everybody we knew each other *before* John's death, she will tell them we were lovers!"

"And?" There it was again.

"Surely, you must realize how disastrous that would be!"

"To your reputation, of course." He shrugged. "To mine as well, I suppose. But people have survived worse scandals than having affairs of their hearts exposed." He shrugged again. "We will undoubtedly survive. If need be, we can always move."

I knew my voice was growing strident, did all I could to lower at least the volume, so the desperate screech that lay within my words would not reach the servants' ears. I stood up close to him, unflinching, whispering the shrieking words that had never been spoken between us before. *"But what if people figure out that you and I killed John?"*

As I spoke, his features hardened completely. Now his expression of full-blown shock and outrage—finally!—matched my own.

"I didn't kill John!" Unlike me, he did nothing to modulate the volume of his voice.

It was as though the world had begun spinning around me, as though I were standing in the middle of a hurricane that had come up with no warning, engulfing me in sound and fury.

"What?" I nearly shouted back at him, as though I needed to shout to be heard above the pounding in my own ears.

He put his hands up in a gesture I had not seen before, as though to ward me off.

"*You* killed John?" he shouted again.

"Please, what are you talking about?" I asked, taking another step toward him.

Once more, he retreated from me. "But *I* thought it was some sort of *highwayman,* perhaps the same one who robbed your acquaintances the Palmers before John's death. That's what the police concluded."

"But you and I—"

"—*killed John?*" he finished for me, a question where my statement of certainty would have been.

"Of course we did," I said.

Seeing the look of astonishment that yet remained on his face, my mind raced through the past.

"When we met in Sommers Tea Room, the day Constance came upon us, you said there was a simple solution to our being together."

"Of course," he said. "I assumed then it was just a matter of time before you would see the only real way for us to be together was for you to divorce John, despite the hardships that might follow."

"When we met together that night in the park, you asked if I wanted to be like that with you all the time, you said we *should* be together like that all the time."

"Of course," he said again. "Our love for each other was tremendous and I believed we *should* be together like that all the time ... once you divorced John."

"That day we walked in the street, I remember it was starting to snow, and you asked me if I wanted your help—"

"In finally divorcing your husband, not killing him."

"You said if my husband were no longer in the picture—"

"Yes."

"You said I deserved more."

"Yes, and you did. Certainly, you deserved to be with a man who loved you properly. But I never said anything about killing John."

"You told me to make it look like a robbery. You said my husband must die."

"*No!* I never said any such thing."

"But I remember—"

"And are you sure you are remembering things correctly? Do you also remember me once writing to you that there came a point when I did not know what we had said aloud to each other and what we had yet kept back for ourselves?"

"Yes, but—"

"Before John's death, his...*murder,* I remember you being increasingly distraught. I had no idea what was going on with you at the time. And then after John was...*murdered*—"

"Which we did together!"

"—you seemed to get so much better. And yet somehow it never occurred to me that it was *your hand* that had done the deed. Worse, that you had somehow built up some idea in your mind that this was what I wanted too."

"But you were there! You were with me!"

He backed to the door, reached one hand to the knob and turned it, securing his own escape, on his face a look of horror, as though he had perhaps never known me at all. "I don't know what you are talking about, Emma."

It was as though a God with a giant foot had kicked at the round toy ball of his own Earth: The world beneath my feet had dropped away.

SEVENTY-EIGHT

I cannot say it surprised me when they came for me.

The knock in the night, the insistent knock—no, I cannot say it surprised me.

It was three days and nights since I had seen Chance, three full rotations of the Earth since he'd disappeared after saying he did not know what I was talking about concerning our joint crime. As he had departed, the servants nakedly witnessing my loss, my shame, I saw him turn to me one last time before removing himself from the house. It was as though a vacuum had suddenly sucked all the air out, leaving behind a vapor where he had been. A moment later, it was as if he had never been there at all.

Already, even his memory seemed little more than a shade. In the interim, I had taken to wandering the cold halls of my home in my dressing gown. There was no longer any appeal in going out, if I had not him to go with, and there was no longer anyone I wished to see in.

As I wandered the house, I think I sometimes spoke aloud, arguing to myself. Certainly, I muttered. The servants must have thought me mad.

How is such a thing possible, my mind screamed, relentlessly, *that he should appear to have no awareness of what we have done? Can I have somehow* imagined *his complicity, his encouragement, the fact it was really* all his idea?

I began to review events in my mind, over and over again.

I thought of him saying, when I said he and I had killed John, that he didn't know what I was talking about; that I had killed John alone.

But that was not my recollection of events on that fateful night. And yet, when he said he knew nothing about it, I was so shocked by his words, the earnestness in his expression, all I could do was react defensively.

My recollection was that there had been but one knife. We had been two, and I could not deny my complicity in being there, but it was only one knife I remembered plunging in over and over again. Surely, it must have been he who wielded it?

And yet his memory of events, clearly, was different from mine.

It just is not possible! How could I have acted as I have done without *his hand to guide me?*

Then I began to think about my marriage to John, what it had become in my mind over time, my feelings of betrayal, how I had even convinced myself that he was the father of Lucy's baby because it was convenient for me to believe so, how much I had wanted him gone, how much I had wanted Chance to take his place.

I thought of Chance's look of total incomprehension at my words, reviewed more conversations in my mind, and began to wonder.

Is it possible, that I somehow *manufactured* Chance's words and deeds in my own mind, because to admit my own desires and responsibility for them would have made me too much of a monster even to my own self?

I reviewed the time since I had first written to Chance, reviewed my whole life. For years, for decades, I had refused to allow my mind to remember the thing that had been done to me the summer I was twelve.

Does a normal woman do such a thing?

I remembered our letters to each other when he was in prison, how much, even then, I had been given to manufacturing in my mind things that were not on the printed page, things I wanted to be there.

Was that normal?

I remembered how depressed I had become when I could not figure out how to have him, taking to my bed for days at a time.

Was that normal?

I remembered the things I had been totally wrong about, things like believing John was the one who had caused Lucy to be with child. I remembered standing over my husband with a gun, not knowing how I had got there. I remembered how confused my mind had become after John's violent taking of my body. Surely, I had wanted to kill him then. I had made up so many things over the years, repressed so many things—*Why not this too?*

I thought about the increasing red haze in the months before John's death and the ebbing out to sea of that anger afterward. I thought of how increasingly obsessed I'd been with the idea of removing my husband from my life, recalled—or *thought* I recalled—words passing between Chance and I on how that might be achieved. And yet, since John's death, I could not recall either Chance or I saying one word about it. Chance had spoken to me after John's death of my husband being lost; he never once referred to him as being murdered. Was it possible we could act together in such a thing and then, afterward, never speak one word, not one single word of it?

I thought of Chance's look, thought of how much and for how long I had wanted him beyond reason, and suddenly it indeed seemed possible I alone would have done anything to have him.

Could I have been that insane?

Yes, I supposed, finally, *I could.*

The letter! my mind screamed at me. *The letter in which he implied something should be done about John!* He had set it all out in writing. Surely that would bear out his involvement in the crime.

But when I looked in the places where I kept all of his letters hidden, my hands moving frantically as I pulled the drawers open, felt the undersides with my fingers for what I expected to feel attached underneath, the one I sought for wasn't there. The ones I had originally received from him from prison were, but not the one that said, "Perhaps, if your husband were no longer in the picture..." Was it possible it had never existed at all? It was hard to believe. And yet I knew *I* would never have willingly disposed of a single one of his words to me. Had my mind then made up, once again, what it was convenient for me to believe?

I had trusted Chance so much, invested so much in him. And he had been worthy of that, I was sure of that. Why, he had even taken care of me with such tenderness after John hurt me so. After all I had lost, all I had staked, I had to go on trusting him. It was like the Arabian gentleman's words about his religion when Hettie Larwood brought him to dinner so long ago: Chance *was* my religion. If I let that die in me now, it would be as if my whole life were for nothing.

And yet, I now wondered, how much that had passed between us had been real? How much had I manufactured?

I sat on the black-and-white-diamond tiles of the long corridor, my back against the solid midnight wall, the bank of windows in front of me, not caring who saw my exposure any longer. In my hands, I held what had been my favorite letter from him, the one he had written in response to the letter where I had asked him if he knew that the real definition of vertigo was the fear of wanting to fall and he had written:

Fall, Emma.
Fall.
I will catch you.

I watched the black-and-white tiles spin dizzily around me.

And, I began to worry—and I'll grant you, given my circumstances, I probably should have been worrying about other things—*if my mind can turn itself into such twisted knots to imagine him telling me to, helping me to kill my husband, is it not then also possible I have similarly* manufactured *some of the memories of us together I hold dearest? For, if those memories are all true, then how could he leave me now like this?*

I pictured us that day as we had been, out together on the ice:
It is a wonder I did not fall.

And then, in one final burst of energy, I raised myself from the floor as I remembered something: *the bloody clothes!* Despite my reluctance to admit so much between Chance and I had been the stuff of

imagination and fabrication, despite my refusal to renounce what had
become my only religion, Chance, I raced to John's library, leaving the
letter behind me on the cool tile.

Once in John's library, I commenced prying up the floorboards.
But they were stuck and so I attacked the edges with a poker from the
fireplace.

*The bloody clothes, Chance's and mine, that I buried away here after
the murder of John!*

I pulled up the floorboards at last with one great yank and
looked down into the space below.

There were my clothes. Only my clothes. There was nothing else.

I had killed my husband. I had acted alone.

SEVENTY-NINE

When the knock came, it should have been Timmins who answered it, or at least Lucy, but I could hear the increased volume of the knocks from my bedroom, far from the front door as it was. As it became obvious no one else was going to respond, and further obvious that the persistent knocker would not cease, I moved to answer it myself.

Well, the one detective was polite, at any rate.

Behind him, I could see the police wagon waiting, the mares stamping their impatience.

"Mrs. Chance Wood, we are here to arrest you in the murder of John Smith. I'm afraid you're going to have to come with us."

What—even in this, was I not to have my own name, my own self?

I stared the two of them down, but they did not budge, did not seem to understand what was troubling me.

"I am Emma," I said finally, opening the

door wider. "Please come in." I indicated my dressing gown. "Can you wait while I change?"

It was not until they were leading me out that I saw Timmins, watching from the shadows.

Apparently, the last time Chance had been here, his raised voice had carried far enough that Timmins had heard.

"*You* killed John?" Chance had shouted at me.

How satisfying that must have been for Timmins to hear. If his master had to die, then why shouldn't the woman he had always hated be the one to pay for it?

Wily as ever, Timmins did not go directly to the police. After all, what sort of evidence did he have—words shouted in the heat of anger? He obviously suspected—rightly, I think—such would not be enough.

No, he had been cautious. Rather than saying anything immediately, he proceeded to methodically search the entire house from top to bottom.

In John's library, where I had failed to adequately reposition the floorboards after my discovery, he found the dress, of course, the cursed bloodstained dress.

Like the heart in that dreadful tale by Mr. Poe, it had lain there all this time beneath the loose floorboards, telling its silent tale and beating, beating louder and louder all the time, waiting with patience to point the finger of guilt finally at me.

EIGHTY

Perhaps it should not have surprised me when Louisa died. The shock of my arrest, my husband leaving me, must have been too much for her.

It was Father who came to tell me, visiting me in the women's section at Hollowgate as I awaited my turn at trial.

His first words to me since my arrest: "You have killed your mother."

Another father might have asked his daughter how she was. Another father might, at the very least, have asked if his daughter had indeed committed the crime for which she now stood accused.

"John Smith was the finest man I ever knew," my father said. "John Smith was like a son to me. And now you have killed him."

After that, there was nothing for either of us to say.

EIGHTY-ONE

Having once wondered what it was like for Chance to live in prison, I now knew what it was like firsthand. I now lived in a space a mere thirteen by seven by nine feet high. I now lived in a space where the guards wore padded shoes so as not to disturb the silence. I now lived in a place where the female subwarders were known for "tampering" with female inmates; a practice that could most politely be called "growing overfond." I now lived in a place where women were known to "breakout," a term for a very particular form of temporary insanity, wherein the woman would smash everything in her cell, rending clothes, rending hair, until someone came and punished her by putting her in a place referred to as "in the dark."

A couple of women down the row, in prison for violently protesting for a woman's right to vote, actually believing one day such a thing might be attained, were inclined to rend things. Sometimes they liked to starve themselves and were then force-fed, unimaginably long tubes shoved down their throats, in a most disturbing fashion.

Thank God the treadwheel had been abandoned, and the oakum-picking, which I had read about in John's research notes on prisons, was now a thing of the past. I could handle shirt-making, hemming, stitching, even doing laundry for seven hours a day.

Besides my father, I had only one other visitor at Hollowgate in the entire time I awaited trial. It was, of all people, Hettie Larwood.

She told me after my arrest, Chance had moved back into the house. She told me all of my friends had rallied around him. She told me he would not be coming to visit me, could not bring himself to do so.

"That poor man," she said. "What he has been through. He feels, and he is not the only one, I might add, *betrayed* by you. He thought he *knew* you better."

I said nothing.

"I have never seen a man more broken up by anything. Really, I do not know how he will survive this."

I had nothing to say to that either.

Then she told me a surprising thing: "Constance Biltmore is dead."

"Constance? But how?"

"They say she was murdered; poisoned, to be exact."

I sat, stunned, wondering who would ever kill Constance, and why. Of course, there had been a time when I would have had a very good motive: to ensure her silence. But I had been in here when she died and could not be held accountable for her death.

"Do they have any idea...?"

"Oh, yes," Hettie replied, with what could only be called a satisfied smile. "They have arrested Charles."

For the briefest of moments, I was shocked. Despite what she had tried to do to me, I could not picture anyone being evil enough to snuff out Constance's life. And then I realized I had been paying too much attention to the *what* of what Hettie told me and not enough to the *how*. She had said Constance had been poisoned. And Chance had once told me, as I well recalled—or had I imagined that too? had I merely learned it from John?—poison was a woman's weapon.

"Charles did not kill her," I said with a pleased certainty.

"How can you know such a thing?" Hettie was shocked.

"Because Charles would not do it in that way. Charles Biltmore is many things, but he is not a woman. Constance must have grown desperate, taken her own life."

The horrified expression Hettie turned on me showed, clearly, she thought me mad. And in that moment I saw that anyone else I might tell my theory to would have the same reaction. People are, after all, ready quickest to blame the spouse.

Well, what matter that?

If Charles Biltmore was in this prison with me, if he was to hang for the death of his wife, then I could only think it justice.

If I was the only person in London to know the truth, that Constance, in desperation over a life trap she could no longer find a way to escape, had taken her own life, what matter that?

The last time I had seen Constance, I had thought her resolute to persist in trying to blackmail me. Was this the act of a resolute woman, now, taking her own life? Reading Flaubert, as I had once done to see what my fictional fraternal twin was like, I had not approved of his heroine's final decision. It had seemed cowardly to me and, perhaps worse, unnecessary. But I thought now of Constance, who, with my incarceration, must surely have grown convinced there were no longer any exits out of the box. After all, no one but I had ever believed her that her husband was a danger to her and even I had been unable to help her. Society had never helped her, would never help her, not in this year, not in our times. Where, then, had she to turn for help? Perhaps it was a strength that, rather than waiting for Charles to eventually kill her, she had taken the matter into her own hands.

It gave me a cold pleasure to think, even though I did not believe for a second Charles had poisoned Constance, he would die for a death he was responsible for nonetheless.

EIGHTY-TWO

The dock where I stood was set up at a slight angle to the examining magistrate's bench.

For three long days of testimony I stood like that, in front of a courtroom crowded with family and friends—no longer my family; no longer my friends. For three long days I stood like that.

The servants gave the bulk of the testimony.

Timmins was so earnest in his demeanor, so self-righteous in his delivery, none who saw him doubted he had been a witness to all my shame, all my crime. And he had, after all, been the one to find the dress.

Lucy came next and that was, in some ways, even worse. For it was obvious to all that, unlike Timmins, she did not want to be there. She liked me, despite everything she had heard and seen, still liked me, felt gratitude toward me—her reluctance to speak said so—and yet the law, not to mention her conscience, required she do so now. If it were only up to her...

Nanny, as others still thought of Hannah, and whom I myself had blamed for Weston's death, gave testimony such that one could see the dawning of disbelief on the faces of those assembled: They were obviously caught up in sharing with her the version she laid out concerning Weston's death. A version in which I suddenly appeared culpable! She claimed he must have looked out the window for my coming, that I must have called up to him to gain his attention, like Circe calling him to disaster, even though there had never been any evidence of such a thing. If I did not know my own innocence, why, to hear her speak, I might have believed me guilty too.

Why did she do it? I wondered. Was it perhaps that, even at this late date, she hoped to exonerate herself of any lingering responsibility in her own mind? I could not say.

Everyone else was surprised—save me, of course—when my own father banged the final nail in.

"It is true," he said, "although I am sorry to have to say it, Emma has always had the most violent temper when crossed. Even as a child, if she did not have her own way, there was the devil to pay."

Since my mother was no longer alive to deny it, and since John's sisters—the only others who might have testified on behalf of the fact that I had not been as my father described me; that I had, in fact, been the most even-tempered of children—were disinclined to do so, his words were taken as hanging proof of my bad character. As for himself, now he no longer need fear I should ever come unhinged and come at him with accusation of his own inability to protect me as a child; more to the point, should I attempt to do so now, no one would ever believe me. My father had loved my husband so much, he could not but hate me for removing him from this world.

The only thing remaining was for me to speak my piece. My solicitor had refused to allow me to testify, but I would at least be permitted to make a statement at the verdict.

"I dispute my father's words," my voice rang out with a bell tone harsh even to my own ears, "although I know you cannot believe me. And I wholeheartedly dispute Hannah's attempts to push blame for my child's death upon me. I loved Weston beyond any measure. Even in my maddest moments—and, I will grant you, I have had them—I would never have done anything to purposely harm him and would do anything in my power to bring him back to life. If you believe nothing else good about me, you must believe this. His death was an accident, regardless of what Hannah may say to you now or in her own mind in an attempt to ease her own guilt at having left a small child unattended with the window wide open. If I am to blame at all, it is merely in that had I but been at home that day, and not away, I might have somehow prevented it. As for the rest, however, it is pretty much, in the main, the truth of what has happened here. For the few departures between evidence and fact, I have no wish to pick quarrel."

It would be easy for an outsider to wonder at why I did not resist more, why I did not fight the charges against me. But to what purpose? I was guilty. I knew that, had always known that. And I knew now I alone was guilty. Having lost Chance, what was there in the world for me to fight for any longer? Freedom does not matter when the only thing one desires is no longer attainable.

For three long days I stood like that, waiting to learn my fate. For three long days I searched the crowd desperately, hoping to see one single face.

But, search as I might, Chance was nowhere to be seen, Chance was nowhere to be found.

EIGHTY-THREE

Who knew what season it was outside? There had been a time when I would have wanted to know if it was cold or if it was hot, so I might know how to dress. But where I was now, it was always cold, always dark, always damp.

For all I knew, in the outside world the sun might be shining brightly every day. Certainly, the world outside still kept turning.

———————

Having been convicted of what was considered to be high and petty treason—the murder of a husband—my hair was cut short, my clothes exchanged for a loose, claret-brown robe with a blue apron and neckerchief and a white muslin cap. The prison system did not believe in originality and I now looked just like everybody else.

Sometimes, I daydreamed about what still lay ahead of me: the rope.

At 8:00 A.M. on the first day after the intervention of three Sundays from the day on which sentence had been passed, I would be taken to a place, the portable gallows with its collapsible floor erected within prison walls, and hung by the neck until dead. A prison bell from a nearby church would toll for fifteen minutes before and after my execution. A black flag would be flown over the prison for one hour after my death.

On the Sunday before my Monday hanging, a funeral service would be held in the drafty chapel on the third floor and I would have the privilege of sitting by an empty coffin while the chaplain denounced my wickedness. Would any members of society try to bribe their way in to the spectacle so they could enjoy the honor of looking down on the condemned? Would my family? As awful as it would be to have Katherine see me brought so low, it would be some comfort to have her as witness, the one member in my family I felt would never turn her back on me, regardless of what I had done. And yet I knew such a thing was impossible. We each, she and I, would have to content ourself with memories of each other in simpler times.

I thought of the notes I'd once stolen into John's library to read: his scribblings on prison research. Unlike the Swiss valet François Courvoisier, over sixty years before me, there would be no Dickens or Thackeray to watch me swing. Nor did I think the ancient and long-forgotten practice of Benefit of Clergy would save me now.

Dreaming of the rope around my neck, the executioner pulling it tighter—well, it would at least be an escape from the tedium of prison. And yet, nowhere I was now, physically, could be any worse than some of the places I'd gone to in my mind.

Somehow, the religious books the chaplain had given me so I could prepare myself for the world to come, including *Prayers for Prisoners Under Sentence of Death,* were not helping.

The prison of the self versus the prison of the mind. Lord Byron ended his "The Prisoner of Chillon" with:

> *My very chains and I grew friends,*
> *So much a long communication tends*
> *To make us what we are:—even I*
> *Regain'd my freedom with a sigh.*

Well, *my* chains and I were not becoming friends. True, any attempt at physical escape would undoubtedly fail, as had those of the legendary Jack Sheppard. Unlike Sheppard, however, if I was so fortunate as to one day find myself again outside prison walls, I would not stop at an alehouse, practically begging to be recaptured.

The prison of the self versus the prison of the mind: Ah, what did any of it matter now?

Just when I had given up hope of ever seeing him again, *he* was there.

"You're looking very well, Emma," his voice came to me from the gloom on the other side of the bars; then he added, "considering your present circumstances."

Was that a sardonic tone in his voice? I had seen the look that matched that tone often enough when he was referring to others, but it had never been leveled at me.

I shook off my misgivings and rushed to the bars. Perhaps he had forgiven me.

"You came!" I cried.

He was still so very handsome, the only imperfection being that slight gap in his front teeth.

"Oh, yes," he said, "I came."

There it was again: that tone.

"But Hettie Larwood said—"

"Yes, I do know what she said." That tone would not go away. It was a taunting thing, like discovering tin where one expected silver. "Hettie can be a most"—pause—"*annoying* woman." Pause again. "But she can be a useful one at times as well."

"Useful? How so?"

"Because she can be depended upon to carry a message when one has expressly asked her not to do so."

"You sent her to me?"

"No, I did not *send* her. I asked her *not* to come, knowing full well she would be unable to resist doing so."

I felt tired by all of this. "What does that matter now? You sent her before trial to tell me not to expect you, and yet now you are here. What has changed?"

"Your conviction."

"Pardon me?"

"Knowing the matter of John's murderer has been successfully settled, at least from the public's standpoint, I felt it safe you should receive an honest accounting of what really happened. Indeed, it feels as though you are almost entitled to it."

"Why do I suddenly feel as though I should be sitting down?"

"Because you should be, Emma. You have always been good at guessing what a given situation required. Please, do sit."

I suppose I should have taken the chair from the table, but, un-thinking in my pleasure at seeing him, I contented myself with sitting on the cold floor, skirts around me on the dirty surface. As for Chance, he produced a chair from out of the dark recesses behind him. Looking up at him, I felt at a disadvantage. But I had yearned to see his face for so long now—had believed I never would again—I was willing to accept any disadvantage, even the strange air he now carried about him, if it meant I could look upon him once again, the face I loved like no other, if only for a little while.

"I suppose it would make sense for me to start at the beginning," he said, "and yet I find I must begin at the middle."

What could I possibly do but agree? He, after all, had all the power here.

"Very well," I said.

He lowered his voice now to a whisper. "You did not act alone, Emma."

"What?"

"I was there with you all the time, the night you killed John, the night *we* killed John together."

"But you said—"

"I know what I said. And I am, believe it or not, sorry for any confusion my previous statements—that you acted alone—may have caused you. Indeed, you must have believed you had gone mad." He held up a hand as if to forestall any further questions from me on this particular subject. "All will come clear in due time. I merely wanted you to know, before I begin my story, you were not crazy. There may have been times when you have acted in what others might deem a crazy fashion, but you were not crazy to believe we acted together in bringing about your husband's death. Well, in truth, I killed John; you merely watched. As I said, though, this is the middle of the story and it would be best now if I began at the beginning."

He paused as if, having decided to start, he was not sure how to do so. With a deep breath, he at last began to speak:

"It was no accident I was chosen to be the prisoner with whom you corresponded. John and I had met during his visits to Hollowgate to do research for his novel. I suspect he must have found me to be a more"—here he paused for a moment, considering—"*literate* prisoner than the others, for when it came time for him to choose a prisoner through whom you would become a better person, he chose me."

EIGHTY-FOUR

Each sentence Chance spoke, each sentence he subsequently spoke, presented a new shock to me, wave upon wave of shocks, sweeping me ever backward. To respond with verbal outrage at each new sentence would have been somehow impossible; to do so now would impede the progress of his tale. And so I will present it here as I first heard it: as a block of horrific information, with few stops.

"I would not go so far as to say John and I were ever *friends*. But I would say a healthy respect grew up between us. He felt, oddly enough, I could be trusted to do my part in an experiment he had thought up. An experiment concerning *you*."

To continue looking upon him was too much of a distraction. I rose from the cold floor, unable to sit still any longer, unable to stop myself from pacing occasionally as I listened to his incredible story. It was as though he were a fireside storyteller, spinning a tale of people I had never known.

"When you originally made your New Year's resolution to become 'a better person,' I suspect you provided him with an opportunity for which he had long been waiting: the opportunity to test you. So, when he came to me, he already had the structure of the experiment pretty much well mapped out in his mind."

He kept using the word "experiment" and I suddenly recalled the notebook I had found in the drawer of John's desk in his library when I'd gone looking for his research notes on Hollowgate. The notebook had *The Experiment* on the cover and opened with the words: *A person can wait years for an opportunity—look for it, hope for it, work for it—and then, suddenly, serendipity drops just the perfect opportunity in one's lap....*

Apparently, I should have been paying more attention to those words when I first came across them, but I had been too busy thinking of Chance to bother. Now I kept those words foremost in my mind as I listened to Chance talk on.

"'I want to see if my wife is as virtuous a woman as she has always appeared to be,' John said. He then told me you would be writing to me soon. He even told me what to say in my replies. 'Do not make it too easy on her,' he instructed. 'You will have a greater chance of winning her confidence if she feels she must first work hard to earn yours.' What was in it for me to cooperate with him? you may well ask. And yet, the answer is all around you now: prison. Prison is, finally, a boring place. I thought this would offer me some, however minor, diversion. And money, of course. John said he would deposit a small amount into an account for me. It seemed a useless gesture to both of us at the time, but 'Who knows?' he said. 'You may one day find yourself free again. Stranger things have happened. If you do, then you will at least have something to start with.' As it turned out, he was right about that.

"And so it began. You wrote to me twice, I replied in abominably rude fashion twice. Everything was proceeding according to John's plan.

"But then a strange thing happened. I began to develop...*feelings* for you, feelings I had not looked for. I found I no longer wanted John to be a party to what passed between us. And so, I told him I had developed scruples; that it felt wrong to me for him to see what you wrote to me believing your words were for my eyes only.

"Naturally, he balked at this, which was not good, since I did not want the letters between us to end, which they would most certainly do if he became too angry with me. All he had to do was tell the governor not to post my letters to you, nor deliver yours to me, and the association would be ended. Of course, he could have opened your letters at any time, but you proved so adept at haunting the postal slot and I'm sure he realized that, if you believed your letters were being read, you would never write honestly, never respond honestly. Then, too, he could have had the governor show him mine, but I threatened him that at the first sign of censorship, I would cease all cooperation. But, angry as John was with me, he did want the game to go on.

"Timmins was in on everything from the start, of course. Imagine how shocked he must have been later, when I turned up as your new husband, living in John's house. But he would not expose me. To do so, he would have had to expose John's own darker side in the game he was playing with you, and that he would not do. His loyalty to John, and maintaining John's good name, ran that deep. Timmins even knew I came to you on that first night. Indeed, John set that up. I told John later you had seen me, that your own curiosity to meet the man behind the letters was too great for you *not* to see me. But I also did what I had always done in this, since it began: I told John exactly what he wanted to hear. So, I told him, while you had of course seen me, even seen me in your bedroom, you had behaved in a wholly virtuous fashion. Timmins, as we know, had reason to doubt this. But he was given to doing what I was doing: He liked to tell John what John liked to hear. He said I came, stayed awhile, and left.

"But then there was also this: Rather than being relieved nothing had happened between us when I came to visit you at home, John appeared to be *frustrated* by the information, as though he were disappointed in the outcome. In the beginning, I believed John that what he wanted to do was test the virtue of his wife. If he wanted to go about it in a rather unconventional way, who was I to object, so long as I was kept entertained and well paid? I could easily understand a husband wanting to test his wife's goodness. But as time wore on, and I grew to know John better and saw his reactions to what passed between us, I began to suspect a darker motive in his game. I began to believe there was something sick, almost evil, behind it. He did not want to see his wife succeed in his test—he wanted her to fail! He wanted to take the goodness that he had somehow become bored with and smash it. Perhaps he had grown tired of loving everything about you. Perhaps he had discovered loving a woman who is perfect is not nearly as satisfying as loving a woman who has lived.

"But, getting back to the letters. To keep John from ending what I had now developed a need for, I told him this: I said I would gladly tell him what was in the letters, but I would no longer show them to him; it made me too uncomfortable. Of course, he did not *like* this. But if he wanted the game to continue—and he did; very much so— he would need to begin assenting to some of *my* rules. And so he contented himself with the purest form of the game he had himself set up: With no concrete knowledge of what passed between us, he would observe you, his favorite pet, to see how you were changing, how the association altered you.

"Of course, when your good friend Constance attempted to blackmail John with her knowledge of our relationship, we were all brought up short. When John asked me about it, I said *yes,* we had met, but *no,* there was nothing going on between us. 'Emma merely likes to talk to me in person from time to time,' was what I told him. Again, John appeared to be frustrated with this news, confirming my sense that what he wanted most was to see you fall.

"I know how surprised you must have been when John came back and told you I was still in prison. But that was John: He couldn't resist the temptation to make the game he was playing with you that much more complex. He even encouraged me to begin writing to you again. He wanted to get farther inside your head, so to speak.

"How did he imagine things between you and I would end? I cannot say. Maybe the new psychologists, maybe Sigmund Freud, could tell you what goes on in a man like John's head. I certainly cannot. I never did fully understand him. All I know is he never grew tired of the game, never grew tired of testing you to see if you were really a virtuous woman. Did he hope one day you would fail? I believe that is exactly what he wanted. As you and I both know, you did fail, but far more spectacularly than the writer in him had ever imagined.

"Well, perhaps I made you fail, made you fail when I fell in love with you and realized I wanted you for my own, wanted John to no longer have you.

"That doesn't matter now, though. You did fail, but I don't believe John ever knew of it, not even at the end. As I have said, again and again already, I only ever told him the things I wanted him to hear."

I noted Chance had changed his story. He had begun by saying he had always told John what John wanted to hear and ended by saying he had always told John what *he* wanted him to hear.

But it did not matter.

I could no longer remain silent. It was, finally, too much.

"Yes, you are very good at that, aren't you, picking and choosing, telling people what you want them to hear?" I was shocked, angry, and, as what he was saying began to sink in, far more angry than shocked. "You are like Mr. Stoker's Dracula. Once let into the house, you are impossible to remove. The sin is in having invited you in the first place. I suppose I must take full responsibility for that."

"As I said before, Emma, we are both responsible. Anyway, none of that matters now." He looked tired all of a sudden. As if it were an afterthought, he said, "John's dead, you will soon be dead, and then all of the money will be mine."

Money? my mind screamed. "Had this been your plan all along?"

"*Plan?* I don't know about *plan.* No, in the beginning, it was merely the diversion of the experiment John had set it up to be."

"But I am about to be hanged before too many more days have passed! Have you forgotten about that small fact?"

"It is nothing *personal,* Emma, nothing against you *personally.* I simply couldn't stand the idea of going to prison again."

There it was: He had killed John with me. He would have killed my father or anyone else *for* me. But he would not die for me.

Chance had once said he would love me until the day one of us died. Apparently, that *one* was going to be me.

It was my turn to look at him wryly. "Then you took a great risk, didn't you, committing murder?"

"Perhaps, but sometimes one must take great risks to make great gains. And, after all, it is not as though that were a risk I had not willingly taken before."

"Ah, yes," I said, "your first wife. But then, you lost on your risk that time, didn't you?"

"No, my dear. That time, I won."

"Won? But you went to prison for it. And you just said—"

"But I won my freedom *from her.* Believe me, had you but known her, you would have agreed, along with just about everyone else who ever met her, she was a woman badly in need of killing."

"I have always wondered about her and your ... *killing* of her."

"Yes, and I have always known you wondered about that."

"And yet you never said ..."

"Somehow, Emma, it seemed bad form to tell the woman one hopes to court about how, when the previous woman grew intolerable to be around, it became necessary to remove her."

"Could you not have just left?"

"No. She made me too angry for that."

"Didn't you *ever* love me? Would you have killed me too?"

"Of course I loved you. I was even obsessed with you for a time," he answered abruptly, as though my question were an annoyance he did not like to think about overmuch; not anymore. "Did I not say earlier I had been in love with you, developed a need for you such that I wanted you for my own? Do you not remember how desperate I grew, that one time you left me briefly to return to John?"

I had wondered about that, his omission of it during his confession of his joint history with John. It must have been hugely frustrating for him: having gained so much control himself, to then have John wrest it, however briefly, away.

"Do you not remember," he spoke the words strongly, as though reluctant to admit that strength of feeling and yet powerless to keep it from creeping in, "how I cried with you when we made love, after you came back to me that day?"

It was true. He had cried.

"Did it never occur to you," he said, "that I could have left London at any time after my release from Hollowgate? That I could have gone somewhere and found a woman less complicated to take up with? That I could have even found such a woman here?"

Of course those things had occurred to me.

"But I chose to stay here," he said, "with you. And why do you think I stayed?"

"For the money," I spoke the words with venom. "You stayed for John's money."

He laughed, a harsh sound. "Sometimes, Emma," he said, "I really do wonder if you *might* be crazy."

"Why do you say that?"

"Because John's *money* would not have been sufficient motivation to go through what I have gone through with and for you. If money were my objective, I could have found a rich widow or a wealthy spinster. Surely, you saw the effect I had upon your female friends and relatives—and they were all of them married! Imagine, then, how easy it would be for me to find a freer woman with money? No, Emma, there was only one reason I stayed with you for so long: Because I loved you."

I let out a breath I had not known I was holding, a sigh of relief. At least, with everything else I had been wrong about, I had not been wrong about that.

But then:

"Why should I believe you now?" I demanded.

"Because," he spoke plainly, "think about it: There is no reason left for me to lie, not about anything. You are in there; I am out here." He pressed his suit. "Do you not remember how willingly I took you back when you returned to me? How I took care of you then? That all came from love," Chance continued. "So, no, to answer your earlier question, I would only have killed you if I absolutely had to."

I stepped backward as though he'd physically struck me.

"Oh, do not wear that wounded look, Emma." Now he appeared mildly exasperated. "You know, it is not so very different from the situation between yourself and Constance Biltmore."

"How so? Constance is dead."

"Yes, I know that. It is unfortunate how things ended for her. I'm sure she must have committed suicide. But, no," he said, "that wasn't what I was referring to. When things became desperate, even though you felt sorry for her and would have liked to help her if you could, you left her to hang alone. When it came right down to it with John—save yourself or save Constance—you chose yourself. I do not see, my dear, how that is any different from what I have done here. The choice came down to you or I. In the end, as anyone else would have done in my place, I chose my own survival."

"You are wrong about there being no difference between the situation with Constance and the situation with you and I."

"Oh?"

"It is *because* it is you and I that makes the difference."

I could have sworn he stifled a slight yawn at that. This renewed my sense of outrage. "If the roles had been reversed," I went on, "I would have chosen your survival over my own."

He appeared to start at that, as if hearing about a country he would *like* to be able to see, but that, for one reason or another, he would never be able to travel to. "Yes, I'm sure you believe you would have. And who knows for certain? Perhaps you are right. Perhaps you would have saved me over yourself." Then he shook off the strength of whatever powerful emotions he was experiencing, the sardonic expression returning once again. "To give everything is, after all, the *woman's* way."

"'*The woman's way?!*'"

"It is as Lord Byron said: 'Man's love is of man's life a thing apart; 'tis woman's whole existence.'"

How galling to have him quote Byron to me when I had been recently thinking of Byron, but in a very different way, myself. His words made me wonder if there was any love left in me for him. I could not honestly say.

I still had some questions left.

"After you told me, *lied* to me, that you were not with me on the night of John's death, I went searching for the letter you had written, the one in which you implied we should...*remove* him. When I could not find the one I wanted, it seemed proof to me you were telling the truth, that your involvement was all my own mental fabrication. Now you tell me you were there, that it was in fact you alone who wielded the knife, and so I must ask you: Did *you* take the letter?"

"Of course." He shrugged. "I could not very well leave it for you to keep, now, could I? It might have incriminated me."

"Was that your plan from the beginning," I said, "to incriminate me?"

"You keep asking about *a plan* and I keep telling you, there was no plan. I merely made sure to remove all evidence that pointed to me. Even that day I shouted loud enough for Timmins to hear me, I had no plan other than to avoid being found guilty myself. In truth, as I walked out that day, I prayed that you would somehow prove smart enough to extricate yourself so that we might go on as we had been.

But I had to be sure, no matter what, that no guilt would attach to me. I also removed my own bloody clothes from beneath the floorboards and destroyed them, although I did that long before destroying the letter." He laughed harshly. "Now *that* would have certainly incriminated me."

His mocking words now brought to the fore something else that had been vaguely whispering at the back of my brain.

"Why *were* you never incriminated?" I demanded. "Why were *you* never investigated more closely? After all, you did murder your first wife."

"Yes," he said, "and now everyone knows that, including your circle of friends. But they all feel sorry for me. Even Hettie Larwood is sorry for me."

"How is such a thing possible?"

"Because everyone feels I am the most unfortunate man alive: First I was married to a woman so awful, prosecuting me for her murder was more a matter of form than justice. And then I was released from prison, only to find myself later married to a madwoman."

"Why did you kill Felicia?" I asked the question again.

"Are you quite certain you want to know?"

"If I did not want to know the answer," I spoke with steel, "I would never have asked the question."

"Very well." He sighed. "Are you familiar with the novel *Jane Eyre?*"

"Of course."

"It was one of the books I read while in prison. Rochester's first wife, Bertha, reminded me greatly of my own first wife: the promiscuity, the insanity..."

"Why ever did you marry her in the first place, then?"

"Because she was beautiful. And I was young. And stupid."

"You could not tell in the beginning, then, what she was really like?"

"No, I could not. I was blinded by her beauty." And here he laughed, as though at himself, a harsh sound. "But I found out soon enough."

Despite all that had happened, I wondered how any woman, having him, could want another man.

It was as though he read my thoughts.

"It was not that she didn't desire me, Emma," he said. "On the contrary, she could not ever seem to get enough. But she could not seem to get enough of any man, constantly needed attention to shine on her. As soon as I would turn my back, she would be after whatever man she could find. Even the fishmonger was not too poor a choice for her. And then there were her rages..."

"Her rages?"

"Oh, yes. Even though it was she who was the promiscuous one, she would constantly accuse me of the same thing, flying at my head if I so much as said good day to another woman. It was intolerable. The whole thing was intolerable."

"And when you killed her?"

"It was more of the same. I came home, having heard rumors all day long of her latest dalliance with a publican, only to have her rage at *me,* accusing *me* of being unfaithful with the woman next door. Previously, she only came at me with cooking utensils, but this time she had a knife."

"And that is why you killed her? Because she was unfaithful and insane?"

Chance laughed again, only this time his amusement was clearly directed toward me.

"Your view of the world is so simple," he said, "and everyone in your world shares your simple views."

"Meaning?"

"It is quite easy for people like Hettie Larwood and all the rest, for even Felicia's brother, to forgive me for killing an insane and promiscuous wife." He put his hand to his face in the same womanish gesture he'd used once upon a time to mock my mother. "What man should have to put up with such behavior from a woman?" He let his hand drop. "Besides," he added, "unlike Charles Biltmore, I did not have sufficient funds to banish my crazy wife to the country."

"And so you killed her instead."

"Yes, but not for the reasons everyone else believes and sympathizes with me over, although it is convenient for me to have them believe so."

"Then why did you kill her?"

"Because she bored me, Emma, pure and simple. At the end of

the day, all of that drama becomes boring and Felicia had become to me a very boring woman."

He was a monster.

"I will say one thing for you, Emma, in the time we were together, you never bored me. Not once."

Was I supposed to find comfort in this now?

"So you see," he said, "everyone who knows my story believes I was sinned against not once, but twice, in having my lot cast with the wrong women."

"Surely, everyone cannot believe that," I spoke with renewed energy. "Surely, the police do not believe that."

"Oh, but they do, Emma."

"But how? How is such a thing possible?"

"My diary, of course," he said.

"*What?*"

And here he produced a slim leather volume from his jacket pocket. Instinctively, I reached for it.

"You would like to read that, wouldn't you?" he asked. "But, no, I don't think that's wise. Perhaps someday you might get the chance"—he paused, shook his head sadly—"but, no, probably not."

"Tell me," I said, "what is in there?"

"Everything," he said. "Well, certainly anything the police would want to know, at any rate."

"Tell me," I said again, "*what is in there?*"

"I fear," he said, "we do not have time for you to hear the whole thing, so I will just review the highlights for you."

"*Tell me.*"

"I began this shortly after my release from prison. I sensed even then that one day I might need some sort of...*insurance*. All of the dates are not filled in, of course—what sort of busy man would keep a diary every day?—but the story it spins is an interesting one. In it, of course I express regret for the killing of my first wife. I write of how I killed her to protect myself, but how the justice system, while sympathizing with my situation, deemed it excessive that a man my size should need to have stabbed a woman so much smaller than me so many times if it was purely self-defense. After all, while they felt there was good cause for me to defend myself, and that she had clearly provoked my hand—indeed, that is why I did not hang for it—they could not very well say I had a right to do so quite so...*energetically.* And so I also write how, over time, I became reformed, came to understand that justice had been purely fair in my case.

"I write about how you and I corresponded while I was in prison, with your husband's permission. I write about how John Smith sponsored my release. I write of how grateful I was to him. I write about how you and I stayed in contact afterward, engaging in a mild acquaintanceship; this, I put in, in case Constance should ever say anything about seeing us together with such persuasion that anyone might actually believe her. I say how shocked and upset I was upon hearing of the murder of John Smith. How good that man was to me! I write how, after John's death, you and I gradually grew closer, as two people who share a love for a third party often do. I write about how surprised I was to find myself in love with you and how thrilled I was to learn you returned that love and that your wonderful circle of intimate family and friends endorsed that love. I write of our perfect marriage. And then, finally, I write of my horror upon learning that my precious wife, whom I loved so well, had in fact murdered her first husband in cold blood.

"It is," he said, head tilted to one side as though considering, "a somewhat pathetic tale, when one hears it presented like that. But it is, I have found, a persuasive one too. No one can bring themselves to believe I am anything but what I appear to be: a man who has been greatly wronged by life and wife. Certainly, no one can bring themselves to believe that a man so desperately grieving over such a monstrous betrayal could possibly be calculating enough to have kept a false diary just in case."

Each word had been like a fresh blow.

I thought of my own feelings, how once I would have *killed,* how I would have *died,* to hold on to every single last one of his words to me.

"Joshua Collins had the right of you, then," I said.

"How's that?"

"When he said you were pragmatic."

"Ah, yes. You are both correct: I have always been practical as opposed to being idealistic."

He put his face to the bars, touched his fingers to his own lips and then pressed those same fingers to mine. "You may not believe this right now, Emma, but I did love you. I loved you more than I have ever loved another person in this world, more than I could have imagined myself ever loving anybody. That is the one thing you should never doubt. As I said before, at this point, what need have I to tell lies? Indeed, I love you still. I love you nearly as much as life itself. The problem is, I do not love you *more* than life. Were it but in my power...if it did not mean the loss of my own freedom..." He drew back from the bars, visibly forcing himself away from me. "I do wish you the best, Emma. I even wish for your survival, although I do not know how you can achieve that at this point, nor am I the man to save you."

And my last question:

"Why did you pick the time you did to tell me that my husband must die?"

He pulled back farther still. "You are toying with me, aren't you?"

I shook my head.

"Because he was going to put me in a book, Emma!" He laughed. "Christ! I wasn't going to let him put me in a *book*!"

What do you say to that?

"And then, later, there was another reason," he said.

I raised my eyebrows at him.

"Because of what he did to you, Emma, the violence he did to you. I loved you, wanted you with me always, and I could not let him get away with that."

I had no words with which to respond to that: that he could love me so much and still let me come to this.

EIGHTY-FIVE

This much can be said of prison:
It does give one time to think.

How quickly one becomes accustomed to the unimaginable, learns to put a brave face on it.

Bad food, when one has always been accustomed to the best?

One can stomach just about anything to survive.

Contemplating one's own death?

Well, one must surely do so sooner or later. And, in prison, where time loses its shape, sooner and later become close to one and the same.

Left with no society but oneself?

Now that is a little harder. It takes a strong mind to survive hour upon hour with no other entertainment but the meanderings, wantings, and recriminations of one's own mind. Even the sturdiest minds have been shaken under similar circumstances.

But I had been shaken too often before. It was now time to assess where I had come from, where I was going.

It occurred to me that for all of Chance's self-confidence concerning his knowledge of John, I might yet know my dead husband better than he did. His theorizing about John's motives was fine as far as it went, but I suspected there was something even further beyond what he'd seen. Perhaps John had wanted to test me. Perhaps he had wanted to see me fail. But I believed John's great deadly sin was pride. This he had in common with Chance, the man who was moved to outrageous murder at the notion of being put in a book. John's pride led him to want a wife who knew about sin, a wife who had been tested, *but who still loved him.* John had once said, "I choose Emma. I will always choose Emma." In laying his great test before me, he had gambled, and lost, that I would choose the same.

Well, I would learn from them. Pride would not be my sin.

It took me a long time to accept what Chance said with such sureness, about there being a difference between the ways in which men and women go about the business of love. Was it possible he was right, that men are able to confine it to one corner of their existence, no matter how strong their feelings might be, while women let it infect every corner until nothing else matters?

I thought that, based on my own admittedly limited experiences, there must be some truth in his words. It was depressing, in his case, to think how much truth there was. He had been able to feel great feelings and yet still remember to protect himself. I, on the other hand, had risked everything for him and I had lost.

But whose fault was it really, my descent from normal society into the place I now found myself?

True, I had been used, manipulated, by both Chance and John. But did I see myself as a victim?

No.

I had acted. It had been my decision. Even when it had been Chance's hand, it had somehow been my hand too.

True, I had been influenced, confused. But I saw this was no excuse for abdicating responsibility for what *I* had done: I had wanted the descent; I had wanted to fall.

Well, at least, I knew now I had never been crazy.

Confused?

Perhaps.

But never crazy.

There was a peculiar satisfaction to be had in that, a peculiar satisfaction in owning my responsibility.

I had passed through a crucible and I had failed the test, been found wanting. And, when everything was said and done, there was no one to blame but myself.

But, here is the thing: Just because I had failed once, no matter how miserably, no matter in how deadly a fashion, must I remain on the same seemingly predetermined course? Could I not, perhaps, act to change the future, act to achieve my own resurrection?

I knew one thing. There was no point in my trying to tell someone the truth: that Chance had acted with me; had, in fact, been the hand that held the knife. For one thing, no one would ever believe me. They would assume I was lying to save myself.

Then it occurred to me: Perhaps they would believe me! After all, he *was* a convicted murderer. Despite the diary—that blasted diary!—should not his own murderous past speak out as some sort of proof against his nature?

But then I thought, what good would that do in saving me? For it would only bring him down with me. Unless of course I was able to persuade someone *he* had acted alone, that I had somehow been forced to accompany him as witness on that fateful night. But I would do neither of those things: the former, because it was pointless, save for pure revenge; the latter because, even if I was on the path to becoming more pragmatic, I could not do that to him, even if it was what he had done to me.

I knew one other thing now for stone-cold certain and that was that Chance was right, *the men's way* was right:

There was something to be said for a modicum of pragmatism.

Pure romanticism, on the other hand, could get a person killed.

EPILOGUE

This is my story. As I await the hangman's noose, I regret nothing.

For John? I wish we had not killed him. But he bears his own share of the responsibility for his end. Had he not laid a trap for me, had he not treated me so violently, he would not ultimately have ensnared himself. Still, I suppose I am sorry for John.

But for myself? No. I am no longer sorry for myself in the slightest.

If I succeed in this...this...this new... *plan* I have thought of—if I succeed in gaining my freedom once again, gaining a new turn of fortune's wheel with my own sardonic smile—I would not make the same mistakes twice. In the past, I have always relied on others—men, specifically—for happiness, for support. Now I know there is only myself, there has only *ever* been myself. It is a hard lesson, but sometimes, just occasionally, I am a fast learner.

I do know I need to live, if I am to become a

better person, as I very much want to do now. In death, I can benefit no one. In life? Who knows what I might yet become?

I do know the governor is coming soon, very soon. *Will he find me attractive?* I wonder. *And, if he does find me attractive, would he be willing to find a way to give me my life, my freedom, in exchange for the temporary use of my body?*

I do know that he will need to at least stay my execution for a few months now, once I tell him the secret I have been keeping, the secret I imagine beating beneath my dress as I place my hand on my lower abdomen: I am carrying Chance's child.

But perhaps I will not tell the governor about the child just yet. Perhaps, I will tell him of it only afterward, hoping for an early delivery so that I may then pass off Chance's baby as the governor's own.

As yet, the fullness of the plan remains unclear.

Who knows? Maybe, through using the governor, I will find release and, when I do, this book will one day be published. It is nice to think of Chance's face, when he one day finds himself in a book, when he one day learns of this child, *his* child....

I do not know the answers to my questions as yet. I do not know what the future will bring.

I do know I need to live and that no one is responsible for how I live but me, no one is responsible for my choices but myself.

After all, we each of us make our own chances.